SACRED SPRING

DIVORAN LITES

Real Life Books & Media
379 Cheney Highway #230
Titusville, FL 32760
www.reallifebooksandmedia.com

Cover designed by LLPix
Mixed Media Painting by DiVoran Lites, Watercolor Impressions

ACKNOWLEDGMENTS

I wish I could thank everyone I've ever known, because all have contributed, in one way or another, to getting this book published

Thanks to Hercules editor, Beth Lynne, Ed. D., for grooming Sacred Spring so it can go out into the world holding its head up.

I thank my dear husband, Bill Lites, whose gifts of love and helping exceed those of anyone I've ever known.

Thank you to my family for loving support and hours of joy and humor from which my characters drew their lightness of being.

Thank you Alta and Rebekah Lyn for your help and counsel and for being such good friends for life.

Thank you Ivan and Dora Bowers for being my parents and teaching me so many good things I could never count them all.

To all my teachers from kindergarten up. To writing and painting teachers who were there to help this late bloomer along. Linda Rawls, Charlotte Griffin, B. J. Hollister, Quin Sherrer, and Mary Harwell Sayler. I must thank, as well, all the wonderful writers whose books have enthralled and taught me from the time I was a child.

Thank you Google for being there for quick fact checks.

Most of all, thank you, Lord, for giving me the desire of my heart and then fulfilling that desire. I now know that Your calling on my life has never changed, and that you will never leave me nor forsake me no matter what.

To Bill Lites, the Lovelight of my Life

"If anyone thirsts, let him come to me and drink. Rivers of living water will brim and spill out of the depths of anyone who believes in me this way."
~Jesus, John 7:38, The Message

CHAPTER 1

$\mathcal{E}$laine Donovan sat on the edge of the spring-fed pool, wearing a turquoise bathing suit and holding a mask, snorkel, and flippers. Sighing happily, she studied the watery reflection of the Old Mill and its slowly turning wheel. A deceptively smooth, shiny circle in the middle of the pool outlined the parameters of the boil. Suddenly, she heard an ominous sound in the distance. They're here, she thought. We may be next. I must figure out what to do, soon.

Lifting her heavy blond hair to let a slight breeze cool her neck, she turned her attention back to the wonderful spring that she had tried so hard to save. The flumes shot water into the broadening river, and as always, she marveled that so much--millions upon millions of gallons--could surge from caverns deep in the belly of the Earth day after day, year after year, seemingly forever. Her gaze followed the run to a bend where it coursed out of sight. On both sides, oaks, maples, pines, and palms laced themselves together with Tarzan-type vines, all struggling for space in the sun.

The Sacred Spring Campground and surrounding wilderness that she had inherited from her father now belonged to her as she belonged to it--the rustic place that was home and heart and family.

As much as she loved it, though, she had suffered pangs at having to give up her teaching job at the college and her consulting business to take over the management when her grandfather had his stroke a year ago. She liked her work and the people she had worked with and she missed them.

Elaine watched two bald eagles soar and circle above the river, scanning the water for fish with their binocular vision. Yes, there were the two eaglet's heads bobbing above the rim of an enormous mass of sticks high in a long-leaf pine. Elaine's eye caught a flash and she stared in time to see one of the eagles swoop, rise with a mullet, and flap upward with the fish in her talons. She landed on the edge of the nest and started shredding it for her young.

The increased roar of heavy construction equipment once again shattered Elaine's peace; this time it was too loud and too close to ignore. She jumped up and ran to the house where she strode down the breezeway, looking for her eight-year old brother, Scotty. She found him playing tug-of-war with his tiny Yorkshire Terrier, Rags. He loved that little dog with all his heart, and Elaine loved them both.

"Somebody's tearing up the woods," she said. "Come on. We've got to see what's going on."

"Okay, Laney." Scotty let go of the sock and the small dog tumbled into a corner, yelping in protest.

"I'm going to put something over this bathing suit. Wear your boots in case of snakes and be sure you take care of Rags if you explore the bushes. I'll meet you at the truck."

Elaine rushed into her own room to pull on an old pair of cutoffs and a red tank top that skimmed her full breasts and settled around her flat stomach. She grabbed a wooden clip from the top of the dresser and pinned up her hair. After rolling khaki socks down over scuffed hiking boots, she was ready to go. "Come on, Scotty," she yelled.

Outside the kitchen door, she paused, watching her grandfather, Ira Thompson, tinker with the engine of their small gray pickup truck. He wiped his hands on a grease-blackened rag and stuffed it into the back pocket of his overalls. The late afternoon sun glinted on his silver hair. "Always going somewhere, Laney. Where to now?"

"We've got to check on that bulldozer, Granddad. Hear it?"

"Yep." He nodded. "Maybe I'm getting long in the tooth, but I ain't lost my hearing yet."

She watched him shuffle around the truck, and a wash of remorse and compassion flooded her. He had slowed a great deal since his illness. Maybe she should get another outside job, so she could hire someone else to do his work. She reached the bottom step, still pondering. I probably couldn't get my old job back, but maybe I could go to work for the health department. No, I can't; I still have to run the Old Mill Restaurant. It's the only profitable thing we've got going; I can't afford to hire anyone else. Besides, I need to be here to look after Scotty and Granddad. Her thoughts often rode this merry-go-round, and she had to work to find a place to get off.

"I'm on my way," Scotty yelled from his window.

"The truck's fine now," Ira said when she stood at his side. "Shouldn't give you any more trouble. Sorry about the breakdown yesterday." Elaine slid behind the wheel and he slammed the door so it would latch.

"You know those people are demolishing habitat," she said, trying once more to explain her feelings about the campground. "You've seen the stacks of paper I used to bring home. Every one of them was about animals in trouble and the pollution of our springs. If people keep building the way they are, there won't be any Florida left for animals or for people, and you know if the spring gets ruined, it will cut way down on the available fresh water for the surrounding area." She darted a glance at the house. "Where is that boy, anyway?"

"Slow down, girl. Be patient," her grandfather said. "You can't save the whole world, not all in one day, anyhow."

Elaine focused on Ira's face and let her tense shoulders relax. The old man's blue eyes, now as faded as the ancient chambray shirt he wore, shone with love. His grizzled eyebrows met in a frown that told her his joints ached, and the skin of his hands resting on the window frame was the texture of well-worn deerskin. She thought about how those hands had toiled for her and Scotty with loving care for such a long time.

"It wasn't so bad," she reassured him. "We broke down right outside the gate. Scotty and I just pushed it on in--down hill all the way. You do so much for us--looking after us ever since Mother left." She touched his hand in unspoken gratitude. He had, after all, left a comfortable retirement in town to become her guardian and then Scotty's. He then spent his life savings on her education.

Moisture welled in his eyes. "Wouldn't have it any other way. I'm proud of you and of your mother. Don't be too hard on her for leaving. She had wanted to be a model, since she was a little girl." Before he could say more, the screen door banged, and Scotty came running with a large, dried Polyphemus moth held aloft like a toy airplane. Rags ran in circles around his feet, barking wildly. As the boy opened the pickup door, the dog sprang onto the seat and scrambled to lean panting against Elaine's leg.

"Make her stay over there by you. She radiates heat, and it's hot enough as it is." Elaine started the motor and drove to the dirt road that skirted the campground. She pressed the accelerator to the floor. Hunched over the steering wheel, she glanced in the rear view mirror and saw the dust boiling up behind the truck like smoke from a forest fire.

Scotty's freckles glowed as his Huck Finn energy filled the cab. "This is fun! You haven't been this mad since I put molasses in your bed."

"Somebody rips up the woods right next to us, and you laugh and make jokes!" she scolded, but even then, he didn't stop grinning.

As they approached the neighboring property, which had always been a tangled wilderness, they could hear the protesting screech of fractured saplings going down under the onslaught of the giant machine. Elaine swerved around an orange pickup truck parked beside a small camper-trailer, slammed down the brake pedal, and jumped out with Scotty and Rags close behind.

"Hey there; hey you!" she shouted at the man on the yellow behemoth, but he couldn't hear her above the roar of the engine, the beeping of the back-up signal, and the crash of young trees falling to the blade. Head bent, he kept grinding backward and forward; man and machine united in perfect rhythm like the mythical centaur, half man, and half beast. Concentrating on his work, he reversed the controls, twisted around to look behind him, and backed up. He shoved the controls forward, this time without checking, and the bulldozer roared full throttle toward Elaine and Scotty.

"Hey, mister, watch out!" Scotty yelled frantically and grabbed Rags up in his ready to run.

The man's head jerked up, and he immediately cut the engine. He swung off the bulldozer even before it chugged to a complete stop. "What's the matter with you, lady? Are you crazy? You could get your kid killed."

Rags growled as Elaine and the angry man faced off. At five-feet nine, it had been a long time since Elaine had to look up at a man in order to stare him down. He had taken off his hat and in a fleeting second, she noted the auburn hair and the green eyes that look directly at her as though he could read her whole life. In spite of herself, her gaze flicked over the muscled arms and chest displayed by a sleeveless shirt with the front unbuttoned. She wondered why he even bothered to wear a shirt.

"What do you think you're doing here, anyway?" Elaine snapped.

"Well, you see, that's a bulldozer..."

"I know what it is. It's a cussed machine that does nothing but destroy..."

"...and I'm clearing this property to build a subdivision." The man grinned a cocky grin.

Rag's staccato barking added to Elaine's fury. "Shut up, dog," she scolded.

The man made a soothing sound and clapped his hand against his thigh. Rags wiggled to get out of Scotty's arms and when he set her down she ran over to the man and he picked her up. You're a fierce one, aren't you? There's nothing to be afraid of." He scratched the pert ears.

"What are you doing?" Elaine repeated, ignoring Scotty, who was tugging on her hand.

"We haven't been properly introduced," the man said. "I'm Hank Schaefer. My sister, my partner, and I own this land." His arm swept the woods surrounding them. "All of it."

"Don't you land owners usually hire somebody else to do your dirty work?"

"Not me." He spoke amiably. "I like to operate the earth-moving machines myself. It's fun."

"Fun! How can you destroy every wild thing in the woods and call it fun?"

"Laney!" Scotty jerked hard on her arm.

"What?" she snapped.

"Look there." He pointed to half a tiny mottled eggshell lying atop a pile of dirt and twigs. Elaine snatched it up and shoved it in the man's face.

"This is a mockingbird egg you've smashed."

"You better watch it, mister, this here's my sis you're talking to, and she's good and mad." Scotty bravely stuck out his chest, but his voice was quavering.

"Sis who?"

"Sis...I mean, Miss Elaine Donovan," she snapped. "I own the campground next door."

Schaefer put the dog gently on the ground and stuck out his hand. When she refused to shake it, he plucked the eggshell from her grasp and capped the end of his little finger with it. "I'm sorry about that. If I'd seen the nest in time, I would have left the tree until the birds were through using it."

She wondered if he was making fun of her. "How can you see anything from up there on that...that...monster?"

"Well, look," he said. "Can't we talk this over calmly?"

"Go away, mister, and leave us and our woods alone," said Scotty.

"I admire your spunk, kids, but we've got to plan for all the folks who are moving to Florida. People should have comfortable homes in beautiful communities." His smile revealed even white teeth. "Do you know who owns that campground over there? We'd like to have that one." He pointed in the direction from which Elaine had come.

"Over there?" she said, her voice rising."

He laughed again, and Elaine knew she had to tone down her emotions, or the man would never take her seriously. "Yes, ma'am," he answered with an exaggerated jerk of his head, "over there."

"That's Sacred Spring Campground. It's our home. Nobody touches it, except over my dead body."

His gaze rested on her face. "Your body, dead, would be the crime of the century," he said. "Do you ever smile, Miss Elaine Donovan, or does worrying about nature take up all your time?"

"You are one person who will never see me smile." Suddenly, unaccountably, she felt like laughing. She bit her lip clamping down until it hurt. Some people might think it funny to see the two of them, strangers, standing in a clearing on a hot afternoon, shouting at each other, but she really didn't see anything funny about it.

"You'll smile at me someday," he said. "Wait and see." As he handed back the eggshell, the hairs on his arm glinted copper gold. "Even you have to admit, people need clean, quiet places to live and rest. You must think so too, or you wouldn't run a campground, of all things."

"But that's different. I know how to live with nature, not destroy it." She had to admit she loved living near the big spring surrounded by forest. "We have bald eagle nests that the birds reconstruct and use every year. Each bird needs almost a mile of undisturbed land to fly over in order to survive. You people start coming in and building, and you'll be responsible for the loss of a lot of habitat—not of just eagles, but also all kinds of birds and animals and plants. Don't you get it?"

"I won't allow my partner to build an industrial park. There's always mitigation," he said, serious now. "We'll have trees--cedar chip paths--a lake with a waterfall. We want to develop a real community here. That is if I can persuade her to change her plans," he said half under his breath.

"Gee, that sounds neat." Scotty's eyes grew big as he listened. "Maybe we could live here if we ever have to move."

"Hush!" She glared at her brother then frowned at Hank. "That's the kind of thinking that caused the dusky seaside sparrow to become extinct. The last one died in a cage in 1987, the last one the world will ever see."

"I'm sorry, but what we're doing here isn't wrong."

"You may not think so," she said. "But I..."

"I hear your place is about to be closed because it's so run down. Your electricity is bad, isn't it, and your plumbing too. I heard you might have to sell out."

"Who told you that?"

"My partner, Reva North," he said, his mouth a grim line.

"Well, you can tell *your partner*," she spat out the last two words, "that somebody has made a big mistake. We have no intention of selling."

"I heard you might have to," he persisted.

"No. The university is going to lease the property for a field study site. I can fix everything with the money I get from them."

"My partner told me the project was canceled."

"I don't believe you. How would an outsider know what I don't?"

Frowning, he thought a moment. "It's a good question." She waited for an answer. "She's on some committee or other at the college--says its good public relations," he finally said.

"Did she tell you why they canceled?" Elaine felt sick.

"Maybe they didn't want a place that was having trouble with the Department of Health. Maybe they wanted untouched wilderness, who knows?"

"I've got plenty of untouched wilderness--all they could want."

"I don't know." He shrugged. "I guess you'll have to call and find out for yourself."

She grabbed Scotty's hand. "Come on, let's go. We're wasting our breath."

"Ride, Rags?" Scotty called to the dog, who had been sniffing the edge of the clearing.

"I'll be over to see your place--and you--tomorrow." Hank Schaefer tilted his head. "I'll bring Reva if she's free."

"Stay on your own property," Elaine snapped as she stalked away, dragging Scotty along. "Get in," she ordered. She turned the key and revved the motor viciously. "That man is not going to tear up our campground. Not if I can figure out any way to stop him."

Boiling with anger and frustration, Elaine deliberately took a deep breath to steady herself. She felt the need to talk to somebody, somebody who would care. As long as she could remember, her grandfather's friend, Annie, had been a refuge, a haven when she needed one; and she definitely needed one now. She ground the gears and spun the truck out onto the highway in a run for Annie's.

CHAPTER 2

As they drove past The Crossroads Mercantile, Elaine saw Raker Slocum sitting on the porch staring morosely out at the road. He wore a black cowboy hat, black shirt and jeans, and black tooled boots. Elaine had no doubt that he picked his clothes to match his heart. She looked away with a shiver of disgust.

"Hey, Laney, there's that guy you knocked out on the school bus," Scotty said, his voice high and anxious. "We better not stop for licorice this time," he added.

"He doesn't scare me," she said, straightening her shoulders. "We'll stop on the way back." She drove on through Crossroads, Florida, past a few short blocks of small houses, and out into the country where woods lined both sides of the dusty road.

"But he always says nasty things and calls us names." Scotty stared at her as if he couldn't believe her foolishness.

"We can't let him know we're afraid."

"I am afraid." The boy hugged his dog closer. "He's mean. He could really hurt us."

She remembered Raker calling her ugly names on the playground of the school that they both attended. "Teacher's pet...Skinny Minnie."

On the bus, he often pulled her hair, laughing when she jerked away. What hurt even more was the laughter of the other children and the studied nonchalance of the driver who happened to be Raker's father--a no-good father, Ira called him. Bo Slocum didn't care what his son did or said because, as he often stated, he believed in leaving the children to settle their own differences. Raker once carried on so unmercifully that she got out of her seat, stepped across the aisle, and socked him in the jaw. To her amazement and consternation, he slid off the seat, out cold. His father had to pull the bus over and revive him.

"Daggone, Elaine," he said, "that there was a stupid thing to do. Don't you know my boy's got a glass jaw?" She didn't know what a glass jaw was, but she did know that the other children treated her with respect from then on. Over the years, she ran into Raker from time to time at the country store. Lately, he'd been commenting snidely on parts of her anatomy whenever he could get close enough to talk to her.

"Maybe he'll be gone by the time we come back," she told Scotty as they turned into Annie's lane. The Victorian house, painted white and trimmed in green, stood framed by giant oaks against a sky aflame with sunset. It had once been the home of a pioneer family, but now it doubled as Annie's home and antique shop.

As soon as they were out of the truck, Rags gave an invitational bark. "She wants to go down by the spring--can we?" The little boy's feet were dancing in the sandy drive as if he were already on his way. Living Spring was another natural water source like Sacred Spring. It was where the manatees went in cold weather to stay warm, but there would be no manatees on this hot day. They'd all be swimming and lolling in the St Johns River.

"Okay, but we aren't staying long. You know Granddad worries if we're out after dark." Elaine stepped onto the veranda with its gingerbread turnings and wicker furniture and paused to admire a basket overflowing with white and purple petunias. That same basket had held a succession of geraniums and petunias for as long as she could remember.

She shoved open the etched glass door, anticipating the merry jingle of the shop bells. Moving through the gloom of the foyer and past the stairs, she sniffed the clean, dry odor of the loblolly pine that had gone into the construction of the floors and walls over a hundred years ago. Many older houses in Florida smelled of age and decay, but not this one. Nodding with satisfaction, she remembered Granddad telling her about the house's indestructibility because of the loblolly pine's high resin content. "Termites don't chew it up," he said, "and it doesn't rot." In the front room window, rays from the low sun filtered through ruby and cobalt glass vases, turning them into rare, sparkling jewels. Over the breakfronts ranged around the room, dust motes gave flower-patterned plates a misty, impressionistic look. She quickly checked over the desks, rocking chairs, tables, and headboards that populated the room and sighed with relief. They all reminded her of history and heritage and folks who lived long ago. She was thankful that nothing had sold since her last visit. Quiet settled into her soul: everything was the same as always, the way it was supposed to be.

"Oh, it's you." Annie's voice rang out from the shadows.

"Hi," Elaine greeted the small woman coming toward her through the gloom. Annie's pure white hair was a cloud of life, framing her wrinkled face. She wore a pair of white capris and a navy blue tee shirt.

Annie plucked a pair of round spectacles from the top of a case displaying hats, fans, and jewelry. She wrapped the wires around her ears. The round lenses gave her an owlish look.

"I'm so glad to see you!" Annie said, enveloping Elaine in a hug that smelled of soap and freshly washed clothes. "Let me show you the guitar I got yesterday. It's a beauty." She led Elaine to a corner of the big room where an upright piano sat with a guitar case lying on top. She took the instrument out and laid it in her young friend's hands. "It's a vintage Gibson."

"It's beautiful," Elaine said, caressing the inlaid mother-of-pearl on the soundboard. "Has Nick seen it?"

"Nick would love to have that guitar, but on a wildlife officer's pay, he can't afford it. I told him we could barter, so he's going to restore the old piano. Remember it?" Not waiting for an answer she went on.

"I said he could take it and pay me a little at a time; but you know Nick, he's proud and such a loner since Constance died. It's a pity--a nice young man like that. Too bad he's your cousin," said Annie.

The heat of embarrassment crept up Elaine's neck. "Oh, Annie, you're always playing matchmaker."

"You obviously need one," Annie countered as she smiled fondly. "Where are Scotty and your granddad?"

"Scotty's down by the spring and Granddad stayed home. I'm sure he'll be over one morning this week."

"I hope so," Annie chuckled.

"I feel so peaceful when I come here and see all these old things. Why do you think that is?"

"I've often wondered about that. It's what keeps me in the antique business." Annie slid back the piano cover, exposing yellowed ivory keys. "Does it have anything to do with the time and skill and craftsmanship that went into the making of all these fine things?" She pressed the middle C. It responded with a sweet note that hung reverberating in the room.

"Maybe it's because the lives of people long ago were less rushed than today, and they took the time to attend to details." Elaine laid the guitar back in its case and snapped the latches. "Back then, they were content with a quiet life. That's the way I'd live right now if people would just leave me alone."

"We're all too harried, and for what?" Annie led the way toward the kitchen. Its large table was invariably loaded with bills and invoices, but the air always smelled of the home-baked muffins and spices she gave to her customers. The lilting music of Chopin came from a boom box on top of the refrigerator. "I guess I'm going to have to get a computer," Annie lifted a stack of files from a chair and put them on the floor. Sadness crept over Elaine, bringing tears to her eyes and forcing them to spill over. She wiped her cheeks with a paper napkin from the table. She hadn't been fully aware of her distress until Annie's kindness unraveled her self-control.

"What is it, dear?" Annie might look fragile, but she was practical and compassionate, as well as a good listener and adviser. She ran hot water into a teakettle. "My grandmother always said a cup of tea and a chat would solve any problem. Your granddad's all right, isn't he?" Annie dropped a peppermint into each cup, so that when the water boiled and she poured it in, the candy would crackle and sweeten the tea.

"He doesn't have the energy he used to, but he's happy." Although it tasted delicious, sipping the hot liquid made her perspire. Some days this late in March were broiling by late afternoon, and this was one of them. She wished she had thought to suggest iced tea instead, but Annie's British grandmother might not have approved of iced tea when someone needed tender loving therapy.

"You look more like your mother every day." Annie's smile crinkled the corners of her eyes, and Elaine did begin to feel better. She was sure it wasn't the tea.

"Me? Are you kidding? Monica is such a glamorous woman. Her hair's always loose and swingy, and her makeup is perfect. My hair is wild no matter how much I brush it." She reached back, removed the band, and wrapped it back around her ponytail.

"Honey, curly blond hair has never been a liability in my lifetime, and it won't be in yours. All you need is a good haircut. You do look like your mother, and you'll age as well as she has."

"She doesn't have an ugly old mole." Elaine fingered a small black dot at the corner of her left eye.

"Ladies of my grandmother's day would have given anything for a beauty mark like that. My sisters and I used to paint them on when we played dress-up."

"Did you know we might have to sell the campground?" Elaine got up and started pacing.

"I thought the university was going to lease it," Annie said.

"I thought so too, but now I hear they aren't. I'll have to find out for myself what's going on." Elaine nibbled on the skin near her thumbnail with her teeth.

"Would it cost a lot to get the campground going again?" Annie poured more tea into Elaine's cup and patted the chair.

"More money than we'll ever see," Elaine, answered ignoring her friend's ministrations. "The Department of Health will ask for a voluntary closure, if we can't make the repairs. We've probably got until autumn to figure something out." Elaine sank into the chair once again and leaned back against the wooden slats.

"I wish I had some money," Annie said.

"No!" Elaine said vehemently. "We couldn't take your money. It would hurt Granddad too much. He's so sweet, but sometimes his pride drives me crazy."

"But how will you live if you have to sell?" A frown brought Annie's well-groomed eyebrows together.

"We'll have to move to town, and I'll try to get my jobs back. I'm not as worried about us surviving as I am about all the creatures that make Sacred Spring their refuge. Right now, there are several endangered scrub jay clans living in the pines on the ridge. Besides, I love the campground. I don't ever want to leave it."

"I understand how you feel," Annie said, "but maybe it's too big a job for one young naturalist all by herself."

"The only people who might want to buy the property will build a subdivision or worse." Elaine continued her discourse, getting more upset with every word. "That requires sidewalks, asphalt roads, patios, swimming pools. Where they lay cement or asphalt rain runs off into storm drains taking all the chemicals with it into the aquifer. It makes me furious!" Her fist slammed the table, rattling the china and causing tea to spill over. "Oh, I'm sorry. I'm up on my soapbox again." She carefully inched the cup back to the saucer's center.

"It's all right, you care, and that's what counts." Annie stroked Elaine's forearm as she had when Elaine was a small child in need of soothing. "I don't want you to sell out, either, but you must keep in mind that much as you hate the idea..." Annie paused to replace a spoon, which the display of violence had catapulted onto the tablecloth. "If you can't lease the campground or get a loan, I don't know what else you can do."

"I'm afraid we already have a buyer," Elaine said, rubbing her forehead with her fingers.

"Who's that?"

"I met a man named Hank Schaefer today. His corporation is interested." Her foot jiggled nervously as she launched into a description of their encounter.

"I know you feel awful about it, but if it's what God wants, you'll have to make the best of it. Why, you could get an apartment and live like a normal girl. You might meet somebody…a husband and children would take your mind off the environment. I hate to see you break your heart over it like this."

"I'm never getting married." This time Elaine finished the tea, then she carried her cup and saucer to the sink and washed them.

"Oh, now dear, you've said that before. A woman should marry."

"Then why didn't you?" Elaine twisted to face the older woman.

"I had a reason." Mystery had always surrounded that subject. Now Elaine became determined to know at last. Annie looked at her for a long time, and then said, "You're old enough to understand. The man I loved married someone else."

"Do I know them?" Amazed, Elaine could hardly wait to hear what Annie had to say.

"You know them. They lived in town a long time ago. He was a mechanic." Annie walked to the table, picked up an art deco framed picture, and handed it to Elaine. It was an exact replica of the one Ira had of him and Grandmother Belle on their wedding day. "Yes, you know them well," said Annie.

"Granddad is the man you loved? Why didn't you ever tell me?"

"Because, my dear, you were a little chatterbox and it wouldn't have been five minutes until you started asking questions. Ira always thought of me as a good friend, as did your grandmother. If he knew how I really felt, even now, he'd be uncomfortable and probably avoid me. I'd rather see him as just a friend than never to see him at all."

"But Annie, even though he did love Grandmother a lot, she died when I was three, over twenty years ago."

"Yes, but he never stopped loving her." Annie took the picture out of Elaine's hand and placed it back on the table.

"Don't you think relationships between men and women are complicated and confusing?" Elaine said, sighing.

Annie laughed. "I've spent a whole lifetime trying to figure them out, but there's one thing I do know: I never could measure up to your grandmother. She was perfect."

"Nobody's perfect. You've told me that a hundred times."

"No, of course not; but she was such a lady, so kind. She could put anyone at ease. She did things for people, like taking them food when they were sick and writing letters and visiting the hospital--the energy that woman had!"

"Did my mother like her?"

"She loved her...she was her mother." Annie got a faraway look in her eyes, and Elaine could tell she was thinking out the rest of her answer. "But they were as different as a mother and daughter could be. Monica always wanted to go to the big city, live on the fast road."

"I think that's 'in the fast lane,'" Elaine corrected.

Annie looked relieved when the shop bell rang, and Elaine knew with a sense of disappointment she would hear no more. The twin tornadoes, Scotty and Rags, burst into the room.

"They got past the china again without breaking anything," Annie observed, laughing and tweaking the cowlick that projected from the crown of Scotty's head.

"Hey, are we going get our licorice? We aren't afraid of that ole Raker, are we?"

"Got your money?"

"Yep." He dug in the pocket of the cut-off jeans and held out some coins, a few keys, and a limp frog. "Ah, he died. I was going to bury him alive for God. All he ever gets is old dead things."

"Get him out of here," Annie said, trying to keep a straight face. "Please don't put frogs in your pocket, and don't bury them, either. All God wants is your love and trust."

"Speaking of God," Elaine said, putting her hand on Scotty's shoulder but addressing Annie, "Do you think he cares about plants and animals and springs?"

"Well, sure he does," Annie answered. "Didn't he tell Adam to look after things on the Earth, and didn't he have Noah take all those animals into the ark? I believe he has given us the Earth to look after.

"Thanks for the tea, and especially for the talk." She gave the older woman a hug and stepped back for Scotty to hug her, too. "That Hank Schaefer is coming over tomorrow," she added.

"I'll be praying for all of you," Annie answered. She smiled mysteriously over Scotty's head.

CHAPTER 3

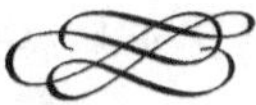

Raker still sat on the front porch of the store with his chair tipped back and his hat over his eyes. "Roll the window up part way and leave Rags in the truck," Elaine told Scotty as she got out, slamming the door behind her. The dog immediately bounded to the window and began to whine, but Elaine couldn't worry about the dog when it was going to take all her concentration to get herself and Scotty past Raker.

As she approached the front door, she watched him out of the corner of her eye. His long legs blocked the entrance. To someone who didn't know better, he looked as harmless as a cowboy snoozing off a morning's work. Yeah, she thought, he's about as harmless as a six-foot rattler. She raised her foot to step over him but when it was in mid-stride he spoke.

"Come into my parlor...."

"Hello, Raker," she answered in a cold tone, continuing past him. Perhaps the small courtesy would put him off. Scotty leaped over and taking a deep breath, Elaine grabbed his hand. She reached for the door handle. Quickly, Raker dropped the front legs of the chair. *Chunk!* In the same motion, he spat a stream of tobacco juice at her foot.

"Somebody ought to make him clean that up," whispered Scotty. Elaine tightened her grip on his hand and gave it a shake to signal him to pipe down.

"Excuse us, please." She pulled at the screen door and got it open a couple of inches before, but without getting out of the chair, he back-handed it, slamming it closed again.

"Hey, woman, look at me when you're talking to me."

She swallowed and held her breath, determined not to be cowed.

"Maybe you didn't hear me." She gave him the full stare, the frowning look she usually gave Scotty when he was being stubborn, the look, said her Granddad that could make a grown man cry. "'Excuse me,' means, 'get out of the way.'" The ominous buzz of a thousand cicadas started up in the trees behind the building.

"Oh, you want me to move. How's this?" He grabbed her wrist and pulled her onto his lap, imprisoning her in vise-like arms. He stank of stale sweat and his breath made her sick. Scotty pulled on her arm, meaning to help but it only made her feel as if she were being torn in half.

"Let me go," she demanded.

"Ah, babe, I want to rock and roll." Elaine's disgust was threatening to come right up out of her stomach and spew all over him. It would serve him right, she thought, desperately swallowing hard. He kicked Scotty's knee with the sharp toe of his boot and Scotty went down.

"Don't you dare!" She bent to sink her teeth into his arm. In the split second it took him to react, she tasted the sourness of his long sleeved Western shirt. He sprang from his seat with a scream of rage, dumping her onto the hard boards of the porch, and pain radiated from her tailbone to the top of her head obliterating all thought.

"I don't need any licorice. Let's go." Scotty scrambled to her side and tried to lift her up.

"No! I'm not going to let him get by with that." She grabbed Scotty's hand and pulled him into the store. Elaine scanned the darkening store for the owner. She saw ghostly shelves loaded with canned goods, and on the counter, tins of chewing tobacco sharing a glass case with pipes and pouches. She smelled the vinegary essence exuding from the pickle barrel, but there was no Mrs. Cumberly. "She must be upstairs," Elaine said, trying to think what to do next. She started toward the back of the store where the stairs rose to the next floor.

"You mashed my hat." Raker grabbed her around the waist from behind. "But what the heck, I'm a fair guy. I'll take it out in kisses." He squeezed her around the waist until she could barely breathe, but instead of fighting him again, she purposely went limp.

"Leave her alone," Scotty shrilled, rushing at the leering face. When Raker pushed her brother down, he had to relax his grip on Elaine and she spun free, but turned back with a swing of her fist. He ducked and started laughing with devilish delight. She tripped over Scotty and crashed full force against Raker. He cursed, lost his balance, and slammed into a pyramid of canned tomatoes. Elaine looked up just in time to see the top can wobble and the whole pile come crashing down. In a second, Raker was lying flat on his back in the aisle, out cold. She was shaking all over, but she and Scotty had won!

"Yes!" she shouted throwing her arms in the air in a triumphal gesture. As he stirred and moaned, a return of the panic she had kept at bay washed over her. She grabbed for Scotty, but the boy pulled away.

"I can get out by myself," he said.

"Well, hurry up and do it. We've got to get out of here before he wakes up." She turned and ran through the door propelled by the ancient urge for self-preservation. Running full tilt, she looked back as she crossed the porch. Surely, Scotty was right behind her. She never saw the approaching customer until their violent encounter flung her to the ground. Sharp pieces of gravel stung her cheek, but she just lay there trying to decide whether it was worthwhile to get up or not.

"I thought you were just mad at me, but it appears you have trouble wherever you go." She knew that voice! Her eyes flew open to the sight of a jeans-panted leg. Pushing up onto her elbow, she stared in bewilderment at Hank Schaefer, who sat with his legs splayed out in front of him and a dazed expression on his face.

"My brother's still in there with that man," she said scrambling to her feet. "I've got to see if he's all right. Could you please come, too?" She disliked the pleading note in her voice; but she admitted it would be nice to have someone with her if she had to face Raker again.

"You're hurt," he said, squinting at her in the rising moonlight. "You have a deep scratch on your cheek and it's bleeding."

"It's nothing," she insisted, though she touched her cheek and drew her finger away, wet with blood. "Why didn't you come out with me?" Elaine snapped at Scotty when he came out of the store. But he was sobbing and it melted her heart.

"Mrs. Cumberly came and I was going to get my licorice, but Raker woke up and took my money...and he called you a something and I don't know what it means, but I know it's bad." He let out a wail, knuckling his eyes, and mixed dirt and tears until he looked like a bandit-masked raccoon. "Really, I did want some candy, Laney."

"We'll see about that." Hank strode away with Elaine and Scotty behind him eager to see justice done. Mrs. Cumberly was now behind the counter, holding her hand to her throat, eyelids quivering. A furtive movement caught Elaine's eye as Raker vanished out the back door. Hank's gaze followed hers. "Was that the guy?"

"He done scooted," said the woman, "Good riddance to bad rubbish."

Hank started to turn away, but Mrs. Cumberly put up her hand to stop him. "Listen to me. It ain't a bit of use to go after him. He's hiding in them woods by now; you'd never find him. Regular wood's colt that one. He has no mamma, and his daddy is always carrying on. I have to say it, them Slocums is no good. Now take my kids..."

Hank's whole body radiated frustration as he walked to the back door and looked out. "I'm sure you have great kids," he said, returning to the counter, "but you really shouldn't let that man hang around here."

"I know it!" she answered, "but there ain't nobody around here can tell them what to do. They always been that way."

"Please give Scotty some licorice," Hank said, tersely. He reached into a pocket and withdrew some change. "Get whatever kind you want, kid," he said. Coins jingled as they dropped into Scotty's palm.

"We don't need your money." Elaine's thoughts played an old tape: Granddad saying *Never be beholden, Laney.*

"You invited me to help with a problem, remember? It isn't going to hurt to give the kid a couple of ropes." Hank held her gaze by lowering his head and looking at her from under his eyebrows while Scotty scooted the coins across the counter with a grimy forefinger. "Lover's knots, please," Scotty said. "One red, one black; Rags likes the red ones." Mrs. Cumberly handed him a coil of each in plastic wrappers. He tore open the black one and stuck a loose end in his mouth, chewing and feeding it in as it softened.

"Give Mr. Schaefer the change and offer him some of your candy," Elaine commanded. She had rarely been more embarrassed and now wished she had tried to handle the whole affair by herself. She hadn't been doing too badly.

"Keep the change *and* the goo." Hank waved the licorice-covered hand away.

"Say 'thank you,'" Elaine instructed.

"Thanks," the man said, obediently.

"No, I mean..." Elaine felt the heat of a whole body blush. Still shoving candy into his cheek, the boy managed to get out a muffled, "Thanks, mister."

"I have a first aid kit in my truck, Elaine." Hank said her name in a low, resonant voice that brought the flying shards of anxiety to a halt.

"No, really, I'm all right." Her body sagged with exhaustion from the nervous energy she had used. She wanted to trust him, to lean on him; but part of her wanted only to go home to her quiet sanctuary and forget her problems.

"Come on," Hank insisted. "Don't be so proud." Holding herself stiffly away from him, she gave in and walked with him toward his pickup. Scotty, a small waif with downcast eyes, shuffled at her side. Elaine drew him close.

"Don't blame yourself for what Raker did," said Hank. You stood up to him. Maybe he'll show some respect next time you run into him." Hank placed his hands under her arms, lifted her onto the tailgate, and hoisted Scotty up beside her, where they sat with legs dangling. The cicada rattle had settled into a quiet, steady thrum.

"Let me see that scrape. What happened in there, anyway?"

Elaine described the fracas from the time they arrived until Raker was laid out by a can of tomatoes. Hank laughed so uproariously she thought he'd split.

"Sounds like you're a woman to be reckoned with," he said when he stopped laughing. "I'm going to get my first-aid kit."

Scotty chewed until black food dye stained all around his mouth. Hank opened an antiseptic wipe and gently touched it to Elaine's face.

"It stings," she said leaning back.

"Nothing works like this." Hank drew the wand from a bottle of Merthiolate and touched her skin again. He then unwrapped a Band-Aid ®. When he finished, he looked into her eyes, letting quiet recognition pass between them as if they'd known and trusted each other all their lives. She couldn't help sighing as he kissed her forehead saying, "There now, it's all better."

"Stop," she said, rearing back.

"Haven't you heard of 'kiss it and make it well'?" he asked, grinning crookedly. He helped her down without letting her answer. "Okay now?"

"Yes, thank you." She touched the place he had kissed. "Actually," she said, with bravado strengthening her voice, "I could have handled it myself."

"You did handle it yourself," he agreed. "if you mean the confrontation, besides, every injured warrior deserves a corpsman.

While they were talking, Scotty had quietly disappeared. For a moment, panic fluttered in her chest, but she saw him huddled on the seat of their truck and hurried over. His head was buried in his arms, and his small body shook with sobs.

"What's wrong?" She reached in to caress his shoulder.

"I couldn't help you." He looked up, his tears making tunnels through the licorice on his face.

"Yes, you did. You were a big help. You got in his way, so he fell

down, and that was what gave us a chance to get away. You're a hero."
She ruffled his hair.

"He ran because he was scared of Mr. Schaefer. Thanks again, Mr. Schaefer," Scotty snuffled.

"You're welcome. I came for bread. See you tomorrow--bright and early. I want to get a good look at that campground."

He'd been so kind. Even though self-protective wariness had returned, she owed him at least a small measure of hospitality. "Well, all right, you can come, but..."

"Good," he said, "I'm looking forward to seeing both of you again. Thanks."

She saw the light in his face, heard the joy in his voice, and felt ashamed. He did seem like a good man. "If you're coming early, bring your bathing suit, and we'll have a swim in the spring."

"All right, sounds great! I'll tell my partner to bring hers, too." Elaine's temporary sense of well-being deserted her.

CHAPTER 4

Urr urr urr. Elaine jerked awake. Every morning at 4:00 A.M., the headlights of a passing train lit the campground like the rising sun and awakened Meringue, the big white rooster that lived in the hanging tree. Crowing lustily, he woke Elaine and Ira, but Scotty always slept through his loud serenade.

I should get up, Elaine thought, grabbing the brass rails at the head of the bed and stretching full length. The temperature would soar by midmorning on a day like this one and it was always better to work early while it was still cool. She lay watching shadows on the ceiling, thinking of the long hours ahead, until the roar of the train receded southward on its way to Miami. She would swim first--that would help keep her cool most of the morning. That man Hank Schaefer was coming to swim and to see the property. What kind of trouble is he bringing? she thought. Wonder if his partner is pretty. Why does he have to come into my life right now, anyway? Moreover, if he's going to be trouble, why does he have to be such a gentleman? She knew she was drifting back into sleep when the thought came, why does he have to be so good looking? A dreamy melancholy washed over her as she remembered his quiet voice and capable hands. Swallowing hard, she took a deep breath. I'll be remote, businesslike, and rational when I see him. Having made this decision, she pulled up the sheet and fell asleep again.

When the alarm jangled two hours later, she struggled from the twisted cover that had mummified her and staggered to the dresser to punch the stop button. She never dared have her alarm next to her because she was afraid she'd just punch it and keep on snoozing.

She passed Ira's room on her way to the kitchen. He knelt beside his bed with his Bible open on the worn, plaid spread. He believes every word, she thought, shaking her head. Even now, he would be receiving what he called "a word from the Lord." When he told her not to borrow money to fix up the campground, his "word" came from a verse in the eighth chapter of the book of Romans *"Owe no man anything but love."* That injunction certainly complicated matters now that the grant money was gone. Grabbing her bag of snorkeling gear from the back porch, she felt protest rising. I might apply for a loan anyway--after all, the campground is my responsibility. She quietly closed the screen door and headed for the spring. As soon as she got outside, her troubles melted in the glory of the fresh morning air.

Rays of sunlight penetrated the azure water, fracturing it into golden-rimmed squares of teal that undulated on the sandy bottom. She looked up to check on the eagles and there they were, enjoying a thermal above the tall trees. The leaves on the oaks were every conceivable color of green interspersed with red maple buds and silvery moss; they made a picture any artist would love to paint. If she ever prayed, it was to thank God for placing her here and to beg him to let her stay for as long as she lived.

It wasn't long before she heard the orange pickup truck pull in. Hank got out, wearing a pair of beige swim trunks with a towel draped across his shoulders; he was alone. When he paused to look around, his tall body telegraphed a message of restrained power that thrilled her. She knew he was searching for her and found it exhilarating. She waved then, suddenly shy, and lowered her eyes as he approached.

"Hi, kid." He gripped the ends of his towel with self-assurance. "Here I am, but I can't stay long."

"Where's your partner?" she asked.

"She said she had too much to do in the office. She'll come out with me next week...I think she said Tuesday. Will that be all right?"

Elaine didn't want her around, yet she nodded and said politely, "Anytime, sure."

"I won't look at the property without her, but I'd sure enjoy that swim. Thanks for inviting me."

"The water's cold, but once you get used to it, it feels great. It possesses holy and healing powers, and that's why they Seminoles called it 'Sacred Spring.'"

"Interesting," he said, listening intently.

Encouraged, she continued. "Ponce de Leon heard about it and came here in the early fifteen hundreds to see if it might be the Fountain of Youth."

"I think there's a Fountain of Youth in Miami." Hank's eyes shot sparks of mischief. "And I know there's a one in St. Augustine." He saw her start to protest. It wasn't fair to tease, but he felt so incredibly happy when he looked at this tall, lovely wood nymph with her Sheena-of-the-jungle hair and her star-sapphire eyes. He was looking at the most vivacious and mysterious woman he had ever seen. The females he encountered in boardrooms and at social gatherings couldn't hold a candle to her. I had better watch out, he thought. This is strictly business.

"Yes, I know other places claim to have fountains of youth," she said with no trace of humor. "Scientists know that many legends and old wives' tales do have a basis in fact." Elaine lifted her chin. "I swim in it all the time." She paused for effect. "You'd never know I was over a hundred years old, now would you?"

"Ha," he laughed. So she did have a sense of humor, after all. It got better and better.

"How old is your younger brother?" Hank asked, playing along.

"Him? He's a mere eighty."

"And your grandfather?" he led her on. She lifted one eyebrow and gave him a look of grave significance.

"Is that right?" His laughter boomed out over the pool and she joined him.

"What's important," she said, sobering, "is that you see the spring for the irreplaceable treasure it is. It's a second magnitude spring, which means that over thirty million gallons of water surge up out of the boil every day. Year-round the water temperature is seventy-two degrees. In the nineteen twenties, my great-grandfather turned the boil from a spreading swamp to a swimming pool by sandbagging around the edges and building a flue for the run-off. The water feels warm in cold weather, but on a hot day, it's icy. Are you ready to try it?"

"Yes, ma'am!" Long fingers combed back a lock of hair blown onto his forehead. "I hear this is one of the best springs in Florida for swimming."

As she slipped the strap of her mask over her head, it caught her nose with a jerk that brought tears to her eyes. Through the clear glass of the mask, she watched Hank flinch with sympathy. "Be careful." He touched her bare shoulder lightly. "Don't hurt yourself."

She put her feet into flippers and that made them look like big, clumsy duck's feet; made her waddle like one too. His chuckle followed her to the edge of the pool where he came to stand beside her, outfitted in the snorkeling gear he had brought. There in the silence of the peaceful morning, a rush of electricity passed between them, and she stood immobile, gazing down at the luminous mosaic on the pool floor while a cricket vibrated its rhythm and a mourning dove cooed softly. It was a moment she wished would never pass.

"It's prettier than a Tiffany window," Hank said lazily, his gaze following her own. Elaine wanted, oh so badly, to touch him, and she would not deny herself. Her palms registered the smoothness of his bronzed skin as she pushed hard and watched him fly into the water, arms and legs flailing.

Hank rose and started toward her, a laughing Neptune up from the depths--thank goodness, he was still laughing. She wondered if anything ever made him sad. She knew she didn't want to antagonize him, just keep him at an emotional distance. Icy droplets hit her bare legs as he rapidly scooped water, splashing her. "I'll get you for this, Elaine Donovan. Don't think you can escape my wrath!"

"You and what army?" she taunted, giggling.

Behind her, a screen door banged. Scotty had caught her daydreaming yesterday and cannon-balled her into the pool. Determined to retaliate, she'd been listening for him to come out, and this time she was ready. "Shh," she said to Hank, putting her finger to her lips.

Standing waist high in the cold water, Hank suddenly shivered. He watched Elaine throw back her shoulders and brace for he knew not what. Such a beauty and totally unaware of it, he thought. She reminds me of a peach I picked that Colorado autumn when I was fifteen. In his mind's eye, he saw the lovely fruit, white gold and russet backlit by sun—a diamond of moisture slid down its plump side before it dropped easily into his palm, heavy with sweetness when he bit into it. Never since had he tasted a peach as delicious, nor had he seen one...until now. He looked still deeper into the blueness of her eyes and saw a woman ripe for falling in love. He saw vulnerability and innocence in her face that refreshed him. Though he yearned to know her better, he feared for her. What if a man came along to woo her with false promises? He shook his head. No, he wouldn't trust anyone with her, not even himself. Look what happened to his sister with that Richard creep. Some men became beasts where virtuous women were concerned.

Elaine saw nothing of Hank's sweet torment because she was concentrating on Scotty sneaking up behind her. She could tell from Hank's change of expression when the right moment came to make her move. Now! She sidestepped neatly, throwing the boy off balance as he ran with his arms outstretched to push her in. She took pleasure in watching him windmill through the air. Rags barked. Clasping her hands above her head like a winning athlete she shouted, "Another notch for my snorkel! I got you both!"

Chuckling, Hank slowly waded toward where she teetered on the edge of the pool. Scotty surfaced at his side like a wet otter. "No fair. You tricked me."

"You got me yesterday." Suddenly she noticed how close Hank had come. Without warning, he grabbed her ankle and gave it a slight tug--enough to throw her off balance. She flew into his arms and from there, she hit the water and her whole body recoiled in shock. Bubbles cascaded before her eyes until the flippers steadied her and she was able to stand. She found that Hank and Scotty had retreated to a safe distance, slapping each other's hands in some kind of congratulatory male bonding that simply infuriated her. She waggled her finger at them. "You guys have had it."

"Come on, Hank, we had better get away from here," Scotty advised.

Never had the Australian crawl been so speedily executed as when the two of them swam away. She took off after them, but because they had such a head start, she arrived at the boil barely in time to see Hank's flippers disappear into the Z-shaped cave below. Frustrated, she floated on the swirling current, kicking to keep from being washed to its outer edges. As she stared longingly into the dark cave, jostled bits of fossilized shells shot by, tinkling in an underwater concert of miniature chimes. She, too, tried to swim down into the boil, she but kept popping back up like a cork. She could envision its hidden labyrinth of caves and tunnels, and biting her lip with apprehension, recalled a young friend who drowned in a North Florida spring.

When she went to visit his mother, the grieving woman showed her his room. "That SCUBA gear on the bed was Tony's. They told me he and his friends came to a big cavern," his mother said, "and they saw something further on that looked like a gazebo. They just had to go on and explore, but the first young man's flipper stirred the fine silt on the bottom of the cavern and it billowed into a whiteout. The kids couldn't which way was up. My Tony insisted the other two go out first. They had a line and they got out all right, but when Tony started, the line hung up underneath a rock and when he gave up on it and went on, he got lost. They found him bobbing around in there." Tears coursed down her weathered cheeks, and she shook her fist. "If I had my way, they'd dynamite all those springs so people wouldn't get trapped."

As she stared into the water, willing Scotty and Hank to return, Elaine felt the woman's agony. However, she reasoned, it wasn't the spring's fault. When nature hurts people, it usually happens because of human carelessness.

CHAPTER 5

*S*cotty had described the caves one evening when they sat talking on the back porch. "You can't see anything because it's real dark in there. The water swishes you around like a washing machine, and you keep bumping against walls--they're all knobby."

"But aren't the walls limestone?" she asked, wondering how dangerous the cave might be.

"It's smooth and kind of slick. It doesn't hurt, honest." She knew if they were slick, environmentally speaking, it meant the spring was already being compromised.

Now as she treaded water and peered into the darkness below, she fretted: could Scotty and Hank both fit in the first small cave, or would Scotty lure Hank into the tunnels beyond, where the two of them could become disoriented and drown? Heart palpitating, she waited, wondering what to do.

At last, patches of color appeared; Scotty came first, arms and legs pumping, straining upward. Hank rose directly behind him, face pinched with the strain of holding his breath. Both of them broke the surface gasping for air. "Whew!" Hank sucked in oxygen. "Why didn't you come down with us?"

Elaine had to spit out the end of the snorkel tube to answer. "I float--most girls do, you know."

Scotty swam between them. "Wow, that was neat, having somebody down there with me."

"You shouldn't drown our guests," she said, relieved to have him where she could nag. "People won't come to see you anymore." Knowing they were all right enabled her to acknowledge that she would have liked to share the deep-water adventure. Sometimes she wished she'd been born a boy. In spite of the cliché, it wasn't blondes who had more fun; it was usually boys.

"Come on, Scotty. Let's get this pool cleaned up. I have to open the restaurant soon." She finally gave him the smile he was waiting for.

"Let me help," said Hank.

"You probably have other things to do." Irritation crept along her nerves as she remembered the bulldozer and the downed trees.

"I want to. Please." He cocked his head, looking as if her reply had the power to bring him happiness or plunge him into the depths of sorrow. Her heart softened. What if he just wanted to stay here at her beautiful spring a little longer? She could understand that--even applaud his good taste.

"Oh, all right. You can help." A tremor ran through her, even though her body had now adapted to the cold water. How easy it had been for Hank to sway her, to change her mind with his charming manner.

"Pick up anything that doesn't belong," she ordered tersely. "Leave the fish, the sea grass, the petrified tree limbs, and the snails. If you see the five-hundred-pound millstone they threw in during the Civil War--leave it."

Hank squinted thoughtfully. "Are you sure somebody did that?"

"Yep," Scotty said. "Some Confederate soldiers didn't want the Yankees to grind grain for bread, so they rolled the stone into the boil."

"Nobody ever saw it again?"

"Nope," answered Scotty. "Granddad says it's probably still sinking--might even be in China by now."

"I'm sorry to disillusion you, kids, but if they'd dropped a stone that big, it would have blocked the boil and you wouldn't have this nice big spring. It must be just another legend."

How dumb of me, Elaine thought. I never even questioned the old tale. It's always been so much fun to believe in all the Sacred Spring stories.

"But an interesting one," Hank offered, seeing her disappointment. "I like it."

"We have a job to do. Let's go," Elaine said curtly. Lately it seemed the edifice of ideas, principles, and stories she had built was becoming tottery. She rinsed her mask out, stuck the snorkel in her mouth and swam slowly away, cruising like a shark to search the sandy bottom for trash. She spotted a wad of pink bubble gum stuck on a sunken tree limb and swooped to retrieve it. One athletic sock ringed with red and green did a sinuous Balinese dance along with the long tendrils of snake grass. A small school of sun perch kept pace with her, moving along curious and unafraid. When the day-people came, diving, splashing, and paddling around in inner tubes and floats, the fish would become invisible among the grasses.

As soon as her hands were full, she propelled herself to the bank with her flippers alone. Hank waited there with a hot-pink Frisbee in one hand and the ring from a pop-top can in the other. Beside him, Rags barked with excitement.

"Throw her the Frisbee; she loves 'em," yelled Scotty. Hank gave a backhand toss, sailing the disk toward Rags, who laid back her ears and ran leaping to grasp it in her small jaws. Even though it was almost as big as she was, she trotted proudly to Hank and dropped it in front of him.

"Now you've started something," Elaine said.

"Here, you throw it, kid. I want to talk to your sister." Hank climbed the ladder and handed the toy to Scotty. The hot sun beat down on their heads as Elaine plopped down beside him on the grass.

"From what I've seen today," he said, "I'm happy with the property and want to buy it. I'd prefer to build a subdivision, and I'm sure my sister, Jean, who is one of the partners, will go along with me. I'm not sure about Reva. She's a businesswoman, first and last. She always studies demographics. She's for building whatever will make top dollar. I have to tell you she's been talking about an industrial park. Since she's the other working partner, I usually honor her wishes. His face clouded. "We've been successful so far." He hesitated. "Frankly, my sister and I aren't..." he paused as if looking for the right words. "Put it this way: we may not care enough about making more money. Reva does. I'll bring her next time, and we'll see what she thinks."

Seeing his good mood turn somber as he talked about Reva gave Elaine a small but steady flicker of hope. If she could show him what an irreplaceable treasure the campground was. With his intelligence and obvious connections, if she could persuade him of the vital necessity to keep the waters of the spring pristine, there was no telling what might be possible. "Maybe we can try to be friends." She extended her hand. Instead of meeting her simple gesture with a handshake, Hank raised her wrist to lips that seared her water-chilled skin. A delicious shiver tickled her spine. She had absolutely no experience with men and longed to understand what was happening. Was he just naturally friendly and demonstrative, or was this a pass? More important, could he be trusted? Emotions churning, she snatched her hand away and stood up. Grabbing the mask off the top of her head and shaking out her hair, she took a few steps away. The familiar castanets of the cicadas thrummed through the park, laying a veneer of peace over her soul and somewhat easing her confusion.

"Do you have time to say hello to Granddad?" she asked, remembering her manners. "I know he'd like to meet you."

"I can come in for a minute, but then I have to get to work." Hank took the mask and snorkel from her fingers. "Here, I'll carry these for you."

The two of them strolled up the road toward the house while Scotty trailed behind, still throwing the Frisbee for Rags. Hank's truck sat in the shade of the biggest oak on the property. He reached in through the window and brought out a tidy roll of clothes that looked small in his big hand. Two blue jays scolded as the two humans passed under the tree. Hank and Elaine smiled at each other.

Taking Hank around to the back of the house, Elaine began to see it through the eyes of a stranger. Oh, how she wished they had fixed the sagging roof and replaced the peeling paint on the lap siding with a new coat. Weeds thrust their seeded heads above the ragged bushes around the foundation. Time for weeding had been an unobtainable luxury lately. The screen door squeaked a long, drawn-out protest. She knew she should have fed it some oil in the last few months. It closed behind them with a bang as they walked across the porch into the kitchen.

Ira stood at the counter, a butcher's apron over his overalls. The smell of fresh-ground coffee came to her eager nostrils as he measured it into the basket of the battered aluminum pot. "That smells so good." She kissed him on the cheek. "Make enough for us to have some too, please."

"I already did." The familiar *poof* as Ira lit a burner on the ancient gas stove reminded Elaine how dear all the old appliances were to her. How amazing that they all still worked!

"Hello, young fellow." Ira and Hank shook hands warmly as they were introduced. "You're shivering, son. You got dry clothes in that there bundle? Change in Laney's room."

"Granddad, no!" Elaine implored. "How about Scotty's?"

"He's got so much junk in there you can't hardly get in the door."

"Then..."

"I just mopped my room." Ira stated flatly, ending the discussion.

"Oh, all right. Wait here a minute," she conceded, hurrying away to see if she had left anything in sight that could embarrass her.

CHAPTER 6

$\mathcal{E}$laine's room looked more like the bedroom of a teenager than that of a grown woman, yet she loved the worn, pink spread that covered the bed. Matching curtains billowed at the open window. She closed it, and the curtains settled to their job of providing privacy.

A desiccated corsage of rose buds clung to the post of the cheval mirror, souvenir of the only real date she'd ever had--with a good friend rather than a boyfriend. With a shrug, she reminded herself that not every girl has a campground to run, a brother to look after, and a grandfather who guards her from the clutches of scheming men.

In college, she was too busy to date. Hank might find that hard to believe; he probably slid through with no effort. She walked over to the wicker rocker and pulled her ancient teddy bear to attention. When she was a child, she had kissed his face smooth. Shorts and a shirt from the floor went on over her wet bathing suit before she grabbed an ancient "Save the Whales" tee shirt and tossed it in the closet. She gave a final look around to make sure no underwear lurked in a corner. How mortifying that would be!

As she straightened her dressing table, she paused to study the photograph of Monica that stood there. Her mother's head tipped back in a sensuous pose, long blond hair spilling down her back like a shimmer of yellow satin. I don't look like that, Elaine thought, do I?

She plucked a tissue from her dressing table and used it to dust everything she could reach. She rearranged three birds' nests sharing a shelf with her favorite books, *Girl of the Limberlost* and the one she most often dipped into before going to sleep at night, *Golden Apples*, by Marjorie Kinnan Rawlings. A book of poems by Robert Frost completed the small collection. Hank had waited tactfully outside the bedroom door.

"Come in," she said at last. "The coast is clear." The room seemed to grow smaller and shabbier as he entered.

"Granddad and I will be on the back porch; would you have time to have coffee with us?" He nodded and she guessed he was mentally recalculating his calendar. She pulled the warped door shut and leaned against it for a moment to give her tap-dancing heart time to slow down.

Elaine and Ira toted the battered aluminum percolator, thick white mugs, and a plate of toast to the picnic table. Hank came out, rubbing his hands together briskly. "Hot coffee sounds good!"

"Sit down, son." Ira pointed to a spot on the redwood bench next to Elaine.

"What a pleasant place," Hank said, looking around. Elaine's gaze followed his. To her, the screened wooden porch where they sat was the best part of the house. She loved the way hanging plants trapped sunlight in their leaves and shaded the pots of carefully tended African violets below. Pothos sent its leafy spirals up the supporting beams, and a ficus she'd been nursing since high school towered over a pot of sturdy aloe.

"Elaine tells me you put a trailer on your building site," Ira said. "Why don't you move it over here? We could give you a mighty good rate, and you'd be able to swim with the kids whenever you wanted."

"Granddad!" Elaine said, shocked at the way Ira seemed to be shoving her in Hank's face. Didn't he know it wasn't good to mix feelings and business? "He doesn't want to move his trailer over here!" she said adamantly.

"Oh, I might." Hank looked at her from under lowered brows and saw the slow shaking of her head. "Guess not. Maybe I can take you up on that swimming, though," he said.

She looked him in the eye, hoping he'd get the message that she didn't want him coming around any more than he had to. She didn't want to fall in love because you couldn't be your own person if you were in love, or so she believed.

"We ought to take you on a canoe trip so's you can see the rest of the property," Ira went on, undaunted. "An overnighter. It ain't that the property is so big; it's just that once we get in the river, we got to navigate a curvy stream before we come to a landing where we can load the canoes and truck them home."

Scotty arrived, holding aloft a balsa-wood airplane and making motor noises with his lips. When the plane dipped over Ira's head, he made a grab for the boy and began to tickle him. Scotty dropped the plane to squirm and giggle until he was out of breath. At last, Ira set him down, letting him stagger to a bench. "Granddad," he said, "when I grow up, I'm going to tickle you until you can't stand up."

Ira laughed. "It's a deal--if I'm still around." Elaine's scalp tingled. Why did he have to say things like that? What would they do without him? "You have to stay for a long time," she said. "That's an order."

"When can I drive the riding mower?" Scotty addressed his sister. "Can I do it pretty soon?"

"I'm not sure you're big enough," she said, loath to put him in a position where he could get hurt. I'll think about it."

"You can help me today," Ira said.

"Doing what?" Scotty jumped up. "I'm a good helper, I can do anything, can't I, Laney?"

"You can learn to do anything you want to do." She, too, rose and started to clear the table. "I'm sorry, but my breakfast crowd at the Old Mill will be banging on the door soon. They're awful when they're hungry."

"What are we going to do, Granddad?" Scotty hopped on one foot, then the other. He took the last triangle of toast and stuffed it in his mouth.

"I'll give you a lesson in driving the mower. We have to pull the trash trailer with it today; and if you do good, I might let you mow someday. After all, that's how we learn, ain't it? *Line upon line, precept upon precept.*" Ira looked meaningfully at Elaine, and she knew she'd have to squash the smother mothering.

"I'll teach him that tractor ain't no toy," Ira said reassuringly. We could always use another hand around the campground, she thought. I only wish he weren't in such a hurry to grow up.

"I've got to be going, too." Hank interjected. The two men shook hands again. "Thanks for the coffee and for your time, sir. It's a beautiful piece of property. I'll be looking forward to seeing more of it. Goodbye for now, Elaine." She took his hand, and wanted never to have to let go of it.

"Come see the Old Mill, then I'll walk you to your truck," she said, breaking away through sheer will power. When they got to the mill, Elaine heard an ominous creaking and flinched as Hank studied the huge dead branch still attached to the oak above. It was so dry and full of holes she knew it could let loose at any time.

"I'd get that pruned before the first hurricane this year," he said. "If it gets blown off, it's big enough to knock the roof in. The place could use a new roof too." He scrutinized the shingles. "It doesn't look that good."

Although she had said much the same thing to her grandfather many times, the suggestion infuriated her. "Maybe you don't appreciate historic places." She glared.

Hank stared back at the fascinating woman with the ever-changing moods. She'd be warm and open one minute, then suddenly her disposition shifted, surrounding him with a cold wind of disdain and chilling his bones. Now she was angry again, yet he had said nothing unkind. They'd been having a good time. He shook his head and decided to keep the peace by explaining what he meant. "Elaine, that branch..."

"Oh, I know all about it! We'll prune it as soon as we can. I'd appreciate it if you'd keep your advice to yourself. Do you think that you're God, and you can come in and tell everybody what to do?"

"Let's get one thing straight right now, Elaine Donovan." He stopped walking and turned to face her, his mouth a firm, straight line and his deep-set eyes blazing. "I have too much respect for God to allow even you to say such a thing. My goal is to provide places for people to live--beautiful places, affordable places. Stop trying to make me out to be some kind of villain. Is it my fault you have to sell?"

Elaine was speechless. It wasn't her fault, either. It wasn't! A large mosquito landed on Hank's arm and she slapped it hard.

"Ouch!"

"Mosquito," she muttered, showing him the blood from his body via the insect.

"You've wanted to do that, haven't you?" He turned and walked off. She scurried to catch up with him. The smack of her palm against his skin had released her fury, but she couldn't let him leave until she'd had her say.

"You may think the campground is run down. But that's how I like it, and it's none of your business what I do with it. You don't own it yet, and you have no say over my actions. Stop giving me advice."

She saw the cords of pent-up anger standing out on his neck, yet she couldn't stop herself. By the time they reached his pick-up, she was so frustrated she fairly screamed at him. "You see that other oak over there?"

"Even a clod like me couldn't miss a tree that big."

"That's a Civil War hanging tree, but you'd probably cut it down," she said in a low voice now dripping with ice.

"You'd like me to hang from it, wouldn't you?" He gazed up into the branches, his voice, like the off-key tolling of a distant bell, permeated with sadness. He opened the truck door and got in without looking at her.

"Maybe I would." Now that she was calming down, she, too, felt heavyhearted.

"Thanks for everything. I did have a good time," he said.

Near tears, she braced herself for one last shot. "Just don't think you're coming in here to take over. That's all."

He started the motor and gave a cheerless salute before driving off.

Elaine muttered aloud as she started back for the Old Mill. "That man is so annoying. He thinks he can turn my whole life upside down. I'm never going to talk to him again unless I absolutely have to."

An adolescent peacock strolled by, his plumage only a promise in the natural backpack of unfurled feathers high on his rear. He looked up, expecting his usual handout of sunflower seeds. "Shoo!" she said. He scarpered down the road on legs that seemed too long for his body.

By late afternoon, Elaine's work in the restaurant was finished. She set the chairs upside down on the tables, where their jutting legs reminded her of a denuded forest, then mopped the floor, locked up, and headed home. As she hurried past the pool, she saw Mr. and Mrs. Braithwaite, small pear-shaped people who were the camp's oldest, most faithful and today, only, campers. Mrs. B.'s head, encased in a fifties-style rubber bathing cap, came out of the water while Mr. B. waited for her with an open towel. Elaine paused to greet them.

"Have you had a good swim?"

"Oh, yes, dear." She rolled the cap up. "I can't hear in that thing. The water is so invigorating."

"Did you know that we might have to sell out?" Though touched by the woman's swift look of sympathy, Elaine hurriedly stepped backward to avoid a soggy embrace. Undeterred, Mrs. B. hugged her cool body against Elaine's steaming one.

"Oh, my dear, we're just so mad. Why, there's nothing at all wrong--we love it here. It's comfortably primitive. We've camped all over the world, and this is the cleanest place we've ever been."

"That's not really the problem, though." Elaine nodded at Mr. B. who smiled back vaguely. Elaine wondered how much of their conversation he was actually following and reminded herself that some people might not be interested in her troubles.

"Isn't the campground your only means of support? What would you do if they closed it down?" asked Mrs. B.

"Maybe the health inspector will get ideas," put in her husband, raising his eyebrows briefly and chuckling.

"Seriously, Mr. B., I hope somebody gets a few ideas about how to save the campground, as much for the need for pure water in Florida as for all the threatened and endangered animals."

"If there's anything we can do, please let us know. Mr. B. is used to being active, and I like to see him busy and staying out of trouble." Elaine began to edge away, knowing well that the woman could talk the rest of the day away without seeming to draw a single breath.

"Thank you; I'll keep your kind offer in mind." Before she reached the house, the keening sound of the bulldozer filled her ears. She heard the sharp beeping of the back-up signal and in her mind saw the yellow machine and the man with the reddish hair and green eyes who operated it. She shoved the picture away. It was the sound of the machine, not the man, that triggered turmoil in her soul. Let's keep that straight, she said to herself.

Ira stood at the kitchen sink with a pained expression on his face and tears running down his cheeks.

"What's wrong?" she cried, alarmed. "Has something happened to Scotty?" Before he could answer, Elaine sniffed and looked down--he was peeling onions. She burst out laughing, relieved. "Why don't you let me do it?" she asked.

He wiped his cheek with the back of the hand that held the knife. "Don't you want to get your evening swim now? You do enough cooking down at the Old Mill. Scotty's waiting in his room, counting his key collection." Her grandfather paused, brows knit in a deep study. "Laney, there was something else I meant to..." He nodded to himself as his blue eyes looked sadly into hers. "Yeah, that was it--we'll most likely have to sell to Hank's company."

"No!" she cried, putting her hands over her face.

"Now, honey, we might have to. We're for sure going on that canoe trip so they can get the lay of the land. The Braithwaites have been asking for things to do. We could let them take care of the place just for a couple of days. Annie would help if they needed anything."

Elaine clamped her jaws together,

"Now don't be mulish," Ira admonished. "You know you don't always get your way. Life ain't like that."

She walked to Scotty's room with dark fantasies clouding her mind--of the clear pool choked with building debris; her campground stripped of trees; a dead eagle on the riverbank, its muddied feathers rocked by the lapping wash of a speedboat. She'd seen the dynamited boil at that other spring. All that remained was a small opening crowded with cattails and weeds, from which, instead of a good strong surge that filled a pool and ran like a river, water bubbled weakly, stayed for a moment and then soaked into the ground.

In the pool, Scotty tried to get her to play, but she wasn't in the mood. She doubted if she'd ever be free to have fun again. Who could be happy when the web of their lives was about to be ripped to shreds by the winds of adversity.

At least she was cool by the time she went back to her room to dress. Some fragrant talc fluffed all over her body would help her stay that way. The sound of the bulldozer continued to deliver its sinister message. She ought to go back over there and confront him again. She grabbed some lacy under things from a drawer. They were way too scanty and fancy. Why didn't her mother come and see her instead of sending all these things? It had been five years since her last visit. If I could afford to, she thought, I'd ignore all this and buy some practical and comfortable things.

The smell of frying hamburgers made her stomach clench with hunger. In the kitchen, the clock ticked peacefully; and as Scotty and Rags dashed in, the past suddenly returned with them--when she'd held a two-year-old boy crying for his vanishing mother as a taxi pulled away from the house.

"Wash your hands," she ordered.

Scotty obliged, but managed to leave a large grimy spot on the towel. She sighed, exasperated. It took so much work and training to turn a child into a civilized human being.

"What can I do to help?" she asked Ira.

"Get them potatoes, honey."

Before she could pick up the bowl of potatoes, Scotty stuck in his finger, scooped up a large blob of mashed potato and melted butter, and popped it into his mouth while the butter ran down his chin. When he spoke, Elaine had to ask him to repeat. "I and Rags chased a armadillo, and I got hold of its tail, but it wiggled away." He ran out to the porch and sat down at the table. Rags followed, disappearing underneath, and laying her head on Scotty's dirty feet.

Elaine carried out a tray with a pitcher of tea and glasses "There's no need to frighten the armadillos," she told Scotty, despairing of success as a mother.

"They can't be scared of us. We won't hurt them."

"You know they're slow and can barely see. The animals trust us. We need to protect them, not chase them all over the campground. Leave them alone."

Ira came out with the hamburger steaks. "Sit down, Laney; you've had a busy day." He sank onto the bench. "Scotty, you can ask the blessing."

Scotty steepled his hands and bowed his head. A grin spread across his face. "Do you think God was laughing when we chased the armadillo? Those things look so funny when they crash through bushes."

Against her better judgment, Elaine smiled. "You're incorrigible. Say the prayer."

When Scotty finished, "God is great, God is good, let us thank him for our food," he grabbed the bowl and piled salad on his plate. "And you can't do anything with me neither." He'd heard her say that. "Please pass the hamburgers."

Feeling restless after dinner, Elaine wandered the house before settling at last with pillows propped at a comfortable angle on the couch. She turned on the lamp and stretched out to study one of her nature magazines.

"Hi, whatcha doing?" Scotty flopped on the braided rug beside her as lightning lit up the room.

"I'm reading about Florida panthers; they estimate that there are no more than 80 left in the wild."

"How come?" He looked up from scratching the dog's ears.

"Most of them have been killed on the highways." She showed him a picture of a large buff-colored feline.

"You sure worry a lot about animals."

"I know." She squeezed his shoulder, and they both fell silent in their small circle of lamplight while thunder rolled in the distance. "Scotty, don't you ever worry about anything?"

"Yeah," he said, "sometimes."

"What do you worry about?"

"Right now I'm worried about that guy, Hank."

"Hank? Why?"

"Laney," he said, sighing, "I kind of like him, but I don't know about you. Do you like him or do you hate him?"

"You shouldn't hate anybody. I know I don't treat him well some-times, but it's a grown-up thing. You wouldn't understand."

"But how do I..."

"Put it this way--don't get to liking him too much."

"How come?"

"Because he won't be in our lives for long." Rags jumped up beside her and snuggled down. Elaine laid her hand on the dog and felt muscles and the pulsing of her heart. This little dog was so alive. What a gift life was.

"Why don't you want Hank to buy our campground?"

"The first thing is the spring. We could lose it all together if we aren't careful. Remember those Tarzan movies we watch sometimes?" the boy nodded. "Six of them were filmed at Silver Spring in the 30s and 40s."

"What's the 30s and 40s?" he asked.

"A long time ago. Can you be quiet and listen for a minute?" She touched him on the chest with her toe. "Silver Spring was prettiest of all the springs. It was so clean and clear that you could see the bottom as if it were right under your canoe, even if the water was twelve feet deep.

"Then many people moved to Florida and they all wanted to water their lawns and used more water for the outsides of their homes than for drinking and washing on the inside. I think small farmers are responsible and some of the big ranches are too, but not all of them take good care of the water we have.

"Parts of Florida don't get as much rain as they used to, and nasty stuff called nitrates from fertilizer run into the fresh water aquifer under the sand and soon algae and weeds start growing. Remember when I told you about the canaries they had in the coal mines to let them know if the mines were getting dangerous for people to be breathe in?"

"Yeah, Laney, the gasses built up and if the little bird fell off the perch, dead, it meant the people should get out of the mine before they got poisoned, but I thought you were telling me about the spring."

"The springs are our canaries. What's happening to them can tell us about things that could cost us our health and eventually our lives. Our spring is still good and we need to do all we can to keep it that way."

"And our spring is a habitat for all kinds of bugs, birds, and animals and some of them are threatened and some of them are endangered and some of them are of special concern."

"Right! What a good boy you are to remember all that."

"How does it hurt to build houses, though?"

"More yards, more wells to suck the water out of the aquifer mean less water for the springs."

"Yeah, I get it, Laney. But Mr. Hank is so nice and he likes me."

"I know, sweetie, and you've never been around any man except Granddad. And he's so good for us and so good to us, but it would be help if you knew someone about the age your daddy would be."

"My daddy is, you mean. He's not dead."

"Okay, you're right. Well, why not think of it like this: if Mr. Hank builds a subdivision," Elaine began a patient explanation, hoping to help him understand, "where will the armadillos live, and what will happen to the eagles?"

Scotty's brown eyes were big and sober. "We wouldn't have any place to live, either, would we?" He brightened. "But we'd have lots of money...and I could get a motor bike, and we could buy Rags a new red collar, and we could get a computer and a TV and, a Nintendo DS 3d, which is what I really need."

"We wouldn't have the campground, the pool, or our house to live in. We'd probably have to move into an apartment in town--but you don't need to worry. You can like Hank as long as he's around. Remember that if we sell, we'll move away and never see him again."

"Okay, Scotty," Ira said, coming to stand at the foot of the couch. "It's time for bed. You got a big day tomorrow."

Knowing Scotty would go to bed more easily if he thought she was being sent to bed, too, Elaine rose and went to her room. Rain spattered on the roof, and a faint breeze lifted the curtains. She got into a soft seersucker nightgown that had once belonged to her grandmother. Wearing it was like wearing love.

Until the storm broke, the night air would hang heavy with moisture. Somewhere in the park, a chuck-will's-widow threw its clear, three-note call on the night air. Sleep would not come. She rolled onto her back.

Did Hank sleep well in that little box of a trailer on the edge of the woods? Did his humming air conditioner shut out the soft night sounds? Did he sleep on his side or on his back? Did he sleep the deep, dreamless sleep of a hard-working outdoorsman? Did he snore as Granddad did? She giggled and began to relax.

CHAPTER 7

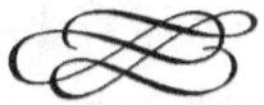

Tuesday morning, a shaft of sunlight followed Elaine into the Old Mill and she braced the door open with a wedge. She ducked when a blue-and-green dragonfly zipped in and buzzed across the room to batter itself against an impassable crack of light between the shutters.

Catching its pencil-like tail, she held on while the struggling insect's wings continued to beat the air. As she carried it toward the door, the tiny head swung around, and the insect closed paper like jaws around her finger. It didn't hurt but almost surprised her into letting go.

"Hey, watch it! Don't you know when somebody's trying to do you a favor?" She laughed at the small creature, so fierce in its own defense, and yet so helpless.

Giving it a toss, she watched its glittering wings helicopter into the thin layer of mist over the pool. Clouds fluffed in a blue sky as the eagle soared above the trees. What a glorious day!

Heat would soon crawl into every corner of the old building, but the rainstorm last night had wept away humidity and filled the air with sparkle. Besides, Hank was coming back today, and in the intervening days, she'd almost forgotten her anger with him. She wasn't looking forward to meeting his partner, Reva, though. She felt like a country bumpkin.

Following the routine she'd adhered to every summer since she was sixteen and first started to run the restaurant, she opened the shutters and allowed sunlight to pour in. Its spotlight fell on the iron wheel that reached from floor to ceiling and on the huge, round-bottomed pans used at the time when the mill ground sugar and grain.

Perspiration began to dampen her forehead, reminding her to start the paddle fans suspended from the ceiling. As she set them whirring, a stack of yellow napkins fluttered up like a flight of swirling butter-flies. She retrieved them hurriedly.

The shadows of the fan blades glided over an array of old photographs on the walls. She liked the Model-T Fords parked in a line. She envied the people in old-fashioned bathing suits that crowded a floating platform in the middle of the pool.

Her favorite photograph was of a man clasping a straw boater to his heart while gazing at a woman in an ankle-length georgette dress at the red-tiled Spanish pavilion. In the background, a small group of tuxedoed musicians played violin, cello, saxophone, and piano. That was the same piano Annie had now.

Hearing tea-dance music in her head, she quick-stepped between the tables, She knew evening parties also took place in the old lodge, now a near ruin back in the woods. Sometime, she thought, I'll take Hank around and show him the real glory of the place. Maybe then, he'll understand why this isn't just our home or a sanctuary for birds and animals, but is a piece of history, as well.

Customers would soon arrive, and she had a lot to do. Because this was the beginning of summer vacation, daytime business was better than ever. Though few tourists came to Sacred Spring to camp overnight, on holidays, vans full of locals drove out from Orlando and the surrounding towns to eat pancakes, swim, fish, and float down-stream in rented canoes.

The lawn around the pool was a popular spot for afternoon naps on beach towels. Sometimes diving instructors brought their classes out for practice sessions. They dressed in their shiny wet suits and jumped two by two into the spring's boil.

After measuring coffee and water into the machine, she pressed the button and set it burbling. While she mixed blueberries into whole-grain batter and filled pottery pitchers, the fragrance of brewing coffee filled the room. She loved the smell, loved the fan-stirred air, and loved the early morning tasks so familiar and dear.

She carried a stack of place mats into the dining room and laid out a few for the first customers. Each table, handmade of golden pine, had a griddle installed in the center where customers cooked their own pancakes.

When she was first learning to read, Granddad had helped her decipher the message printed on the mats. "Old Mill Pancake and Sandwich House. Natural, stone-ground grains make our pancakes the best and most healthful in the world." Across the bottom, it said, *"Parts of this mill date back to 1840."*

As she bustled around, Elaine wondered why there were so few overnighters. Perhaps tourists wanted to stay closer to Disney World. She knew only that she couldn't pay her bills out of the income from the restaurant alone and that she couldn't afford to repair the corroded electric wiring and plumbing throughout the campground.

The sound of splashing and joyous shouts broke into her musing. Through one of the big-screened windows, she saw Scotty and Rags swimming in the river. "Hey, get out of there!" she yelled. "Go swim in the pool."

Years ago when Scotty first came to live at the campground, the river run had been safe. Back then, alligators had been listed as "threatened." With conservation, they multiplied, though, and she'd seen many of them sunning on the banks or cruising in the run itself. They were now so numerous, a statewide draw was held for permits to cull them. Their proliferation was a great testimony for conservation.

She watched until Scotty obediently climbed out of the run and raced to the pool. Satisfied, she returned to her chores, getting out a huge maple-syrup can and filling pitchers for each table. The screen door slammed, and there he was, dripping water on the floor and shivering. "B-boy, I saw the bi-gg-est b-bass in the run!" He crossed his arms over his chest and gripped his ribs with hands splayed for warmth.

A wave of protectiveness broke over Elaine as she saw how blue his lips were; he always got so cold in the seventy-two degree water. "Please don't swim in the run, "Alligators love to eat dogs--and children. You know that."

"They wouldn't eat me, I'm too skinny." He tossed his head as she boxed at his ear, pretending she'd connected. "Ow!"

Scotty swiped his finger through the sticky sweet on the side of the pitcher and sucked noisily. "Can I pour some? And can I have a motor bike? If I had one I could get a paper route and help pay the bills, then we wouldn't have to move." She patted his goose-fleshed arm.

"Thank you. I love you. Now go on up to the house and dry off so you don't catch your death of cold."

"Wait." He slid back the lid of the old-fashioned ice cream freezer and took out a small package. "Can I have an ice cream bar?"

"I can't believe it." She tightened the lids on the syrup pitchers. "You're standing there shivering, turning blue, and asking for ice cream?"

"Well, can I--please?"

"May I. No, put it back. It's too early. You might be able to have one later. Granddad's going to town, and I have a busy morning ahead of me. Sometimes I think we need to hire some help. If we don't get the grass mowed pretty soon, it'll be up to our knees."

"Laney?"

"What?"

"You sure are a grouch."

"Go!"

As people started coming in, she forgot about Scotty. Expecting

Hank and his colleague any minute, she kept an eye on the parking lot. Her vigilance was rewarded when a maroon Mercedes whispered to a stop, followed by the now-familiar pickup truck. Hank walked over to assist a woman from the car.

CHAPTER 8

*H*ank's partner--he had called her Reva--was a city woman for sure. Her gleaming-white sheath set off the rich tones of raven hair feathered around her face. She waited while Hank ran up the stone steps of the house.

Elaine wondered at the contrast in their clothes; Reva looked all business, but Hank was dressed in jeans and a moss green shirt that matched his eyes. Elaine saw her grandfather appear in the doorway and watched as Hank retraced his steps to speak to Reva. He pointed at the Old Mill, where Elaine stood waiting at the shadowy kitchen window. The woman listened briefly and vehemently shook her head.

A customer claimed Elaine's attention and by the time she hurried back, Reva was tapping up the walk in her three-inch heels, and Hank had disappeared.

The precarious shoes reminded Elaine of the time she modeled for a university benefit. She had staggered down the runway, trying to keep her balance. The decidedly unsympathetic director accused her of sampling the champagne, a drink she had never tasted. Laughing at herself, Elaine relaxed, banishing the growing tension she just realized she had.

Unlike Elaine, this woman stepped as lightly and gracefully as if born to high heels. Though obviously not Asian, she resembled the geisha doll in a glass case at Annie's, meticulously dressed, with hair coiffed by expert hands.

Elaine was not surprised to see that her long, polished nails matched her burgundy Mercedes perfectly. Neither the flashing diamond ring on her engagement finger nor the discreet earrings were unexpected accessories. Of course a woman like Reva wore diamonds on weekdays--diamonds every day, why not?

Elaine scurried to open the wooden door. Taller by several inches and much bigger boned, she felt clumsy beside the other woman's dainty femininity. She took an involuntary step backward as Reva approached, raising eyebrows precisely tweezed into graceful twin arches.

"I'm Reva North, here with Hank Schaefer," she said with a trace of southern drawl.

As Elaine introduced herself, she couldn't help staring at the neat head, wishing her own mop would stay half as smooth. Even as she thought about it, her carelessly pinned-up knot loosened and fell, but there was no way to repair the damage. All she could do was slip the barrette into her pocket with the grocery list and run nervous fingers through her curls in a futile attempt to tidy them.

"Would you like coffee, Miss North?"

"Please." The woman marched to a table without a further word. She plucked napkins from the holder and wiped the seat before laying her case down and scooting in beside it.

"Cream and sugar?" Elaine asked politely as she did all unfamiliar customers.

Reva rolled the combination lock on the case, leaving Elaine to wait for her answer. Elaine glimpsed a computer pad. Reva extracted a handkerchief and dabbed at the tiny droplets of perspiration forming on her upper lip. "I hope I don't look like a person who uses either," she drawled.

"No, well, I don't know what a person looks like who...." Elaine gulped, feeling foolish and extraordinarily warm, herself. She straightened. "Lots of people drink it with both. I do."

Reva's gaze traveled over Elaine's body, head to foot. "Yes, I see," she said, making Elaine feel fat suddenly, even though she had been slightly underweight all her life.

"I'm going to die of the heat," Reva said with a pout of her lip-sticked mouth. "Don't you have air conditioning?"

"No, it's too cold for people coming in from the pool," she said. What she did not say was: We can't afford it.

"Please bring the coffee and see if you can't get Hank down here. I need him now."

Not wanting to leave the restaurant unattended, Elaine rang "no sale" on the cash register and palmed a quarter for the pay phone.

"Granddad," she said into the mouthpiece, "Send that man down here; you can talk to him later." From experience, she knew they would be deep in conversation by now. Ira enjoyed company. He thoroughly agreed with Will Rogers: "I never met a man I didn't like." Life was complicated enough without Hank and her grandfather becoming buddies.

A family of regulars came in, the smallest girl riding happily in her father's arms. Elaine laid out menus and paper plates and leaned over to plug in the griddle.

"Coffee for us, milk for the kids, pancakes, bacon, and eggs," said the attractive young man in tee shirt, shorts, and athletic shoes. His wife smiled apologetically at Elaine as she pulled the corner of a menu from the baby's mouth. It came out bent and soggy looking. Elaine hardly dared ask if they wanted cream and sugar for their coffee.

She managed to get Reva's mug of pitch-black liquid onto the table before several other couples arrived. Steam hissed while hungry customers waited for puddles of batter to turn into pancakes.

The sound of the riding mower out by the wall came buzzing through the growing hum of conversation. Granddad hadn't planned to mow today. Surely he isn't letting Scotty...she thought. No, Granddad probably decided to do it before leaving for Annie's.

Covering the distance between kitchen and tables with brisk steps, she mentally stored a list of orders...one egg...two eggs...sausage...bacon...pancakes for six.

"Miss!" Reva spoke suddenly at her elbow. All the neatly cataloged items scattered like crystals turned in a kaleidoscope.

"I'm still waiting."

"He should be here any minute. I called the house, and my grandfather said he'd send him down. I'm sure they got to talking." Elaine attempted to stay calm in spite of the Mexican jumping beans in her stomach.

"Hank will talk to anybody. Bring me some more coffee then--in a clean cup." Reva glided back to her seat. Healthy anger at the woman's arrogance replaced Elaine's timidity. She almost felt grateful to her for helping her to get angry enough to stand up for herself.

As she was washing mugs in the sink under the window, Elaine at last saw Hank leave the house and head toward the Old Mill. Purposeful strides brought him quickly into the hot, noisy restaurant. He paused and looked around and she realized how hard it was to see when you just came in out of the sun. She started toward the booth with fresh coffee and realized that Reva had spotted him. "Hank." She waved at him. "Hank, darling, over here."

A frown creased his forehead as he headed toward her, passing Elaine without seeing her. The clean, spicy smell of the Florida outdoors followed him, triggering Elaine's memory of what Helen Keller wrote about the scent of young men, *"Fire, and storm, and salt sea,"* the blind and deaf author had said. A blush rose when she remembered the rest of the quote. *"It pulsates with buoyancy and desire. It suggests all the things strong and beautiful and joyous and gives me a sense of physical happiness."* Though she was still trying to stay angry with him, she recognized what Helen Keller had been writing about.

She watched Reva rise on tiptoe and wrap her arms around Hank's neck. The lush lips approaching his as she tried to pull Hank down to her caused Elaine to avert her eyes, but the small girl who had come in with her parents said, "Look, Mommy, soap opera!"

Elaine set Reva's mug down with a thump and felt Hank's eyes searching her face. "Hello, Elaine," he said cheerfully. "Would you mind bringing another two mugs and sitting down for a minute?" His expression reflected neither annoyance nor pleasure, so she couldn't tell how he might be feeling about Reva. His businesslike tone, when he invited her to join them, matched her mood exactly.

"I'm working," she replied, shaking her head.

As she poured Hank's coffee, Ira came to the counter, halting further speculation. At this moment, his presence was the calm in the center of whirling emotional turmoil. He wore his best overalls with a crisp work shirt--a product of their last clothes-shopping trip to Orlando two years ago. Its pale blue color set off his silvery hair, and his eyes looked brighter after a night's rest. "I told Scotty he could use the riding mower before I go to town," he said.

"But he's too little," Elaine answered. "I don't trust that mower."

"Got a list?" He never liked her to challenge his decisions. As she dug it out of her pocket and handed it to him, he relented. "You can't protect him forever, girl. If he's going to grow up to be a real man, he has to learn to do a man's work. I told him to be extra careful on that slope out there." He gestured toward the steep bank that came down against the back of the building. To forestall further argument, he continued, "I'll be stopping to see Annie."

"Tell her I'll see her again soon."

"Guess I'd best meet Hank's lady friend." He set off, stepping carefully between the tables. Smiling, Hank slid over to make room for him. Elaine followed as if pulled by a magnet. Setting Hank's coffee down, she started cleaning off the next table so she could hear as Hank introduced Granddad and Reva.

"Your property isn't too bad," Reva said, shaking hands. "Hank told me you'd like to take us on a canoe trip so we can see more of it. I think that can be arranged."

"Ain't my property; it's Laney's. She inherited it from her daddy."

Elaine stole a furtive glance at the booth. She now thoroughly regretted the stubbornness that had impelled her to refuse Hank's invitation to join them. She saw Reva touch Hank's hand. "Sometimes I chastise Hank for thinking small," the black-haired woman said. "He wants to build a few of his perfect little houses, but I think we should put up an office complex or an industrial park. It's time to do something big!" She pinched Hank's thumb playfully. "That's where the money is, sweetie, you know that."

Hank balled his hand into a fist with the thumb inside. "We'll talk about it later."

"We don't want no more buildings of any kind; there's enough already," Ira said. "But I know we won't have a say about it if we sell." He sounded subdued. "I'm going to take Annie to town now. You young folks got to do some talking with Elaine." He raised his hand in farewell. "Pleased to meet you, Miss North."

Elaine went to the door with Ira and gave him a hug. He squeezed her quickly in return. She waved a silent goodbye and moved to the cash register where the last breakfast customers were ready to pay. She heard the mower again, but was too busy to give it further thought.

Hank and Reva continued talking, their gestures evidence of lively discord. They were waiting for her, but she refused to sit down until every bit of her work was finished. She grew more and more irritated as she cruised the room, tossing paper plates and napkins into a black plastic bag. She thought about the purpose of the visit. An industrial park, indeed; who did these people think they were, coming from wealth and ignorance to ruin her life.

Now she heard the roar of the mower as it worked its way down to the tricky part of the bank. Maybe she should go out and supervise. Suddenly there was a tremendous *whump* as the mower crashed against the outside wall. "That was Scotty!" Elaine cried. "He's had an accident...somebody help me!" She tore out the door without looking back.

CHAPTER 9

*E*laine sprinted around the building, listening for Scotty's cries or for anything that would tell her he was still alive. All she heard was a laboring motor overlaid by shrill barking. Rounding the corner, she found Scotty crumpled against the tabby-stone foundation, blood streaming from his forehead. The mower lay on its side chugging uselessly. The strength drained out of her, and she had to stop, sagging against the wall. The shooting pains she felt when she came upon an injured animal streaked down the backs of her legs.

"Oh, dear God!" she cried, unaware she had uttered a prayer.

She hovered dumbstruck while Hank knelt to feel Scotty's wrist. He had heard her plea and quickly complied. "Get some towels to stop the bleeding," he commanded. Hearing, but unable to respond, Elaine just continued to stare. Hank rose and gave her a quick shake. "Towels, Elaine," he said. "Now!"

As she focused on his face, panic receded. She raced to the kitchen and grabbed a handful of clean dishtowels. She couldn't get back to Scotty fast enough; but as she turned, Reva blocked her way--dark eyes flashing.

"What's going on out there?"

Elaine pushed past without answering. She gasped at the amount of blood flowing through Hank's fingers as he applied pressure to the wound.

"Is he...?" She handed him the towels, shouting over the mower's noise.

"We'd better take him to the hospital. I can't tell how badly he's hurt, but he's probably got a concussion." As he glanced beyond her, she pivoted to follow his gaze. "Go back inside, Reva," Hank said. "You know you can't stand the sight of blood, and I don't need you passing out on us." Reva's hand flew to her mouth.

"Elaine, turn off that mower, and then take her inside. Get her car keys while you're there, will you? And don't forget to lock up the restaurant." He now held a thick cloth pad against Scotty's wound.

"Reva," Hank said. "Since Scotty's unconscious, we'll need extra room. We'll take your car and you drive the pickup to the office."

"I hate that truck," Reva muttered, as she stomped back toward the restaurant with Elaine at her heels. It seemed an eternity before she dug the keys out of her purse. When Elaine reached for them, Reva childishly jerked them behind her back. "Now you tell Hank not to let any blood get on my upholstery."

Elaine held out her hand, fingers wiggling impatiently until Reva slapped the keys into her palm. After consulting the list of emergency numbers posted by the phone, she telephoned ahead to alert the hospital.

She called Annie's, but there was no answer. Ira refused to have a cell phone so it was down to her and Hank. Picking up more towels, she hurried back to the man and boy, chastising herself for not giving Scotty the ice cream he had asked for earlier. I may never get another chance, she thought.

She stood by the car, waiting while Hank settled Scotty on the back seat, then watched with gratitude as he got in and gently cradled the boy's head. Rags hopped in, but Elaine impatiently shooed her out knowing she'd crawl under the porch and sleep.

"Get going." Hank ordered. "I'll keep the pressure on the wound and maybe the bleeding will stop." Ordinarily, the high-tech perfection of the Mercedes would have thrilled Elaine. Now, though, she barely noticed how easily it started, how quietly it ran, how smoothly it took the bumps on the way out the gate.

"Turn on the AC," said Hank from the back seat. "We'll all be more comfortable."

She looked at the dashboard full of lights and numbers and shot a quizzical look into the rear view mirror. Hank leaned over the seat and pointed. "See that small square?"

She pressed where he indicated, and the display showed seventy-two degrees. Seventy-two, the year-round temperature of the water in Sacred Spring's clear pool. If only they could be splashing in the pool right now, instead of rushing to the hospital fearing for Scotty's life.

Her throat was tight with unshed tears. My little brother...life would be so empty without you. She glanced again into the mirror and met Hank's eyes, eyes that reminded her of sun-kissed moss.

"Are you going to be all right?" Hank's hand resting on her shoulder brought flutters and she tightened her grip on the steering wheel.

Would Scotty grow up to be a big man like Hank? She remembered holding her brother when he was only two and helping him wave as their mother left for the airport in a taxi. No matter how Elaine stared, willing her mother to turn and wave, the back window of the taxi remained blank.

Pain from gripping the wheel forced her to flex the fingers of first one and then the other hand. She decided to try not to think, not at all, until they got to the hospital and found out how Scotty was.

It took an hour to drive to the Orlando hospital, but Elaine and Hank found little to say. Elaine pulled up under the portico of the emergency entrance and let Hank out with Scotty in his arms. The boy's legs dangled as the man walked. Elaine peeled off to park the car.

When she came back, Hank met her at the door. "The nurse is looking him over now. Admissions want you to fill out some forms." He took her to the desk and stood close as she scratched words and numbers in the blanks on several pieces of paper.

"Are you his official guardian?" The receptionist asked.

"Yes," Granddad had changed it when he had his first stroke after Elaine turned eighteen.

"What method of payment do you prefer, Miss?" The thin woman behind the counter inquired.

Studying the floor Elaine frowned. Her bank account wouldn't cover any method of payment. One thing she knew for sure...Scotty must be treated. "Well, I..."

"We'll take care of all that later." Hank said. "Here's my ID, and here's a check. Does that cover it?"

"Oh! Mr. Schaefer, sir. Yes, sir. I've heard of you; your grandfather started this hospital."

He took Elaine's arm and led her away from the desk. Heads together, backs to the clerk, he whispered, "It's all right; I'll let you pay me back--someday--if that's important to you."

"I'm so embarrassed; I don't want to be a charity case."

"What's money for if not to help a friend?" Hank smiled. "Sit down. They'll tell us something about Scotty's condition in a few minutes."

On a chair cloned from the one Elaine sat in, an old man drooped his head with his fists clenched between his knees. When he looked up at her with sad eyes, she wondered who belonging to him might be in the hospital. A wife? A beloved son? Compassion urged her to smile at him. His eyes brightened in response, but the light faded into hopelessness before its reflection reached his mouth.

"I've got to call Annie and see if they got back yet," she told Hank as he came to join her.

She reached into her pocket, feeling for the tips that usually weighed it down, before remembering she had transferred it to a small glass piggy bank. She liked the old-fashioned bank because she was forced to keep saving until it was full. Smashing it to get the slowly accumulated twenty dollars it usually held was a ritual she always enjoyed. She could then buy a record for Granddad; a toy or clothes for Scotty; and if she was careful, a book for herself from the used bookstore in town.

Her empty fingers stayed curled in her pocket as she made an effort to control her wandering thoughts. "I hate to ask...," she began reluctantly.

Seeing her dilemma, Hank handed her his cell phone. "It's okay, honest."

It felt good to be looked after, especially by someone so obviously delighted to help. Hank was a busy person, and she knew the time spent with her must have been costing him a great deal. As she dialed the well-known number, she looked up at the clock above the telephone. Noon. Granddad had probably had time to do most of his errands.

At Annie's lilting, "Hello?" the words gushed out as she explained about Scotty's accident. Annie said she and Ira would start for the hospital that minute.

Elaine returned to the row of blue chairs and met Hank's glance. "They're on their way."

She handed him the phone then suddenly began to tremble as an ice cube shaped lump formed in her chest. She could scarcely breathe around it. Abruptly, she turned and walked away, fighting for control over her emotions. She paced--nine steps past the room that held her brother, seven to the soft drink machine at the end of the hall, and sixteen back to Hank. He watched her make several turns, but eventually rose and reached for her hand. It trembled in his like a trapped butterfly.

"Elaine, don't worry so." His words and the compassion in his eyes lifted the sluice gate, and tears coursed down her cheeks.

"I shouldn't have..."

"It wasn't your fault." Hank pulled her into his arms."He'll be fine; boys are tough."

"Why did we ever let him get on that mower?" she said against Hank's chest. "He's too little."

"Elaine..." he said her name tenderly, rocking her in his arms.

In the warmth of Hank's concern, her fear and frustration began to melt. Tears for having failed to take care of her family, tears of sadness at the thought of giving up the campground; tears of loss because this man who held her so gently belonged to someone else, endless tears soaked the front of Hank's shirt. Almost imperceptibly, she became aware of the springy mat of hair under his shirt.

He pressed her head to his chest repeating, "Shh, you'll be all right," as if she were a child.

She didn't feel like a child as a tingly, pleasurable sensation exploded in her diaphragm and spread to the fingertips that wanted above all things to touch him. Taken by surprise, she jerked away. "Your shirt's all wet," she said to excuse her abrupt withdrawal. "I'm sorry."

"It'll dry." Hank reached into his back pocket and handed her a clean white handkerchief.

She wondered who did his laundry; surely not that partner of his. That one didn't look as if she'd know a washing machine from a coffee urn. Elaine stared at Hank, suddenly seeing him as the stranger he was. Are you going to marry a woman who doesn't do your laundry, who won't cook for you? she asked silently.

"What is it?" he inquired, unaware of her inner monologue. "Are you okay?"

"I'm sorry about making a scene." She sucked in a deep, ragged breath. "It isn't like me."

"I know that much about you already," he said. "You'll be all right. You're a resilient woman. I have faith in you."

A woman. She couldn't recall anyone ever having called her a woman before. In ways she hoped he couldn't sense, she was beginning to feel like a woman, indeed, and wasn't quite sure she liked it.

An intern stepped out of the emergency room and came over with a lopsided grin and a "Wow" gleam in his eyes; something about it made her extremely nervous. "Miss...?" he queried.

"Donovan," she said curtly.

"Miss Donovan." He seemed to lodge the name consciously in his brain. "You can see the young man now."

"I'd like to see him, too." Hank spoke behind her as she opened the door to Scotty's temporary quarters.

"Are you a relative?"

"Close friend." Without stopping for permission, Hank followed Elaine behind a curtain into a cubicle that reeked with disinfectant.

Scotty lay on a white, padded table with a gleaming bandage around his head. His freckles stood out against his pale face. He clung as she took his hand in both of hers. "What happened?" he asked.

"The mower threw you, and you hit your head...how do you feel?" Elaine said.

"It hurts." He touched the bandage; then his gaze fell on Hank. "What's he doing here?"

"He brought us to the hospital. Wasn't that good of him?" She wanted him to thank the man. Scotty's slow nod made it obvious how much his head hurt when he moved.

"Yeah, but where's Granddad?"

"He'll be here soon." She bent to kiss the freckle that stood out plainly on the tip of his pale nose. "I'm so glad you're all right, little brother. Maybe we should wait until you're older before you do any more mowing." He strained upward, trying to get off the table.

"I made my mistake, and now I got to climb back on that tractor; because if I don't, I might get scared of it. Remember? That's what Granddad says. He spoke with all the forbearance an eight-year-old could muster for the thick headedness of an adult.

She pushed gently on his chest with the flat of her hand, and he lay back down. She glanced at Hank, who had moved to a chair against the wall. Turning the pages of a magazine, he paused to examine a picture.

"Hey, Hank," she called, "did you ever have an accident like this?"

"Funny you should ask."

"Tell us," Scotty begged.

"I was looking at this picture and it just reminded me." He strolled over to show them a photo of a dark blue, snow-topped mountain. "My accident happened on a mountain like this. Our dads..."

"Our...?" Elaine inquired.

"Reva's dad and my sister Jean's and mine were partners in the construction business. Our families spent most of the time together when we were young."

"And did you go to the mountains?" Scotty asked, eager for a story. Elaine was delighted to see him looking healthier by the minute.

"Every summer." Hank nodded. "We went to a dude ranch in Colorado to work and ride horses and swim in the creek. The ranch kids called it a 'crick.'" He paused. "Most of the time our dads had to stay in Florida working and running the contracting business, but sometimes my dad would fly to Colorado in his small plane to visit. He'd take me up in the mountains on horseback, and we'd pitch camp beside a beaver dam. We'd get up and start fishing at sunrise when the air was cool and crisp. And the view--watching the sun pop up over the snowy peaks--takes your breath away."

"I want to go," Scotty said sleepily. "I can hear this story better sitting up." He struggled to rise.

"No. Wait till the doctor comes back," Elaine commanded.

"When Reva and I were twelve, she asked me to take her to the beaver dam." Hank had a faraway, remembering look in his eyes. "Our mothers had gone shopping in town. I'd never been to the high country without Dad, and I didn't think it was a good idea; but Reva insisted." He shrugged. "She was sort of used to getting her way, so I let her talk me into it. My sister wanted to go, too, but I figured one girl was enough to look after; so I left her with the ranch owner's wife."

"You wouldn't have to look after Laney; she can do anything." Scotty's eyes sparkled with interest. As Hank patted the sheet covering the boy, Elaine noticed how square and clean his nails were.

"Your Reva doesn't seem like a person who needs looking after, either," she said. Without thinking, she fitted her own hand where his had been patting Scotty.

"My father told me many times that I was responsible for the girls because I was the eldest and because I was a boy. Watching out for them became habit. It took Reva and me half a day to get near the timberline where the beaver dam was. We had fun over lunch and fished awhile until I caught a creel full while Reva caught nothing. She was furious and decided to get even."

"Then what happened?" asked Scotty. He sounded so excited that Elaine wondered if hearing the story might be too much for him.

"She challenged me to a race down the mountainside and immediately whipped her horse into a run. Dad taught me never to run a horse downhill, but what could I do?" He shrugged.

"I'd taken her up there and I had to look after her. The sun was going down, and I knew our moms would be home soon and starting to worry. The horses wanted the corral and their suppers."

There was a small silence as Hank hesitated. "We were doing fine until the trail forked. I was leaning to the right in my saddle and my whole body was ready to go in that direction, but when Reva suddenly veered left, my horse followed. He went left, I went right, and I flew out of the saddle and landed on my tailbone."

"Ouch!" Scotty said.

"Right, ouch." Hank grinned at the boy and shot a smile in Elaine's direction. "Reva and the horses went on without me and by the time I finally limped home, everybody was talking search and rescue. Boy! You don't think I felt like a total idiot? I have never underestimated the power of a woman since."

"Great story." Scotty clapped his hands.

"You'd better rest," Hank said. "Your sister and I will see about breaking you out of here."

"Do you still feel responsible for Reva?" Elaine inquired, walking with him into the hallway.

He pondered. "I guess so, although she never asks for my opinion. One of the last things my father said was, 'Take care of our little girls.' Reva was never a little girl to me, but I guess she always was to Dad, and like I said, I guess I'm in the habit of thinking of myself as her keeper."

"Did your dad die?" Elaine asked, wanting to know everything about the tall man walking beside her.

"Jean was 17, and Reva and I were in our early twenties, when our parents flew up to Colorado for a weekend." He lowered his head and cleared his throat. "They crashed the Bonanza on Pike's Peak in a sudden down draft."

"How awful." Elaine felt a rush of sympathy as she remembered the agony of losing her father when she was very young.

He closed his eyes, pain flickering across his face. Elaine knew he had told her as much as he could for the moment.

She heard a commotion and looked down the hall to see Ira and Annie rushing toward them. The intern scurried after them, white coat flapping. Annie's blue polyester dress felt deliciously soft as she enfolded Elaine in her arms, but Ira's rough overalls rasped her skin when he hugged her.

"Is Scotty all right?" Annie asked.

"Come in here and let me show you something," the intern broke in. They trooped back into the examining room. "See here?" He snapped an X-ray onto a light panel mounted on the wall. "He's got a hairline concussion." Elaine could see a faint fuzziness where he pointed.

"And look here." He plucked a penlight from his jacket pocket and turned to shine it into first one and then the other of Scotty's eyes. "One pupil is large and the other is small. He'll have a whopper of a headache for a while, and we had to take a few stitches. Head wounds can be alarming because the blood vessels are so close to the surface that they bleed profusely."

"Can we take him home now?" Elaine asked.

"May we," Scotty corrected her, and Elaine knew he was on the mend, for sure.

"I don't see why not, but you'll have to bring him back and have him checked tomorrow exactly at this time."

"Why exactly?" Hank inquired with one eye squinted and an edge of belligerence in his voice.

"I'll be on duty then, and I can do it personally." The young doctor ignored Hank and pointedly addressed Elaine. "Obviously, that's important because I'm the one who treated him today." He winked at Elaine.

"Sure!" Hank's tone clearly conveyed his disbelief in the quick and ready explanation.

A nurse installed Scotty in a wheelchair, and Hank pushed him into the hall while his entourage flocked after.

"Why don't you go stay with Jean so you don't have to drive out to the campground and back again tomorrow?" Hank asked Elaine, who walked close beside him. "My sister would love to have you. She and the baby and the housekeeper are the only ones in that big house, so there's plenty of room." Elaine was tempted, remembering wistfully that she had never had time for a good friend. Somehow, she knew she would like Hank's sister very much.

"Thank you, son," Ira broke in, "but it ain't our way to be beholden. Elaine will have to open the restaurant tomorrow for the breakfast people, like always. We'll come in together."

Elaine hoped he wouldn't find out just how beholden they already were. He didn't believe in letting anyone help--not even her mother-- and he would be embarrassed if he knew Hank had paid the bill because he had put off buying medical insurance.

Ira's old truck looked decrepit next to Reva's sleek car. "I'll run Elaine and Scotty out to the campground," Hank volunteered. "But first I have to trade cars with my partner."

"Annie and me will head on home then. I'd be obliged if you'd give the kids a ride. There ain't much room in our little truck." Granddad stuck his hand out to shake Hank's. "We do appreciate all you done for us. I imagine you had to pay the hospital bill, but we'll get that back to you, won't we, Laney?"

So...he was aware, after all. "Maybe Mother..."

He shook his head to stop her. She remembered him saying, "Your mother's a big success, but she doesn't handle money too good and she usually ain't got any." He looked at Hank. "How's about having supper with us when you get there? Elaine sure makes a tasty stir-fry."

"Love it if it's all right with you. Elaine?"

Determined to distance herself from the dangerous happiness of knowing that he'd be around a while longer gave her, Elaine spoke coolly. "It's the least we can do after what you've done for us.

"You don't owe me anything." A look of hurt flickered in his eyes, telling her he'd rather be welcomed for himself.

After they got Scotty settled in the back seat, Elaine, limp with fatigue, relaxed her head against the headrest.

"Would you like some music? Reva has streaming." The glorious strains of "Jesu, Joy of Man's Desiring" filled the car. Elaine wondered just how much time Hank spent in Reva's car. She closed her eyes as the music began to saturate her mind. His next words shattered her peace.

CHAPTER 10

"This morning at the Old Mill seems like a long time ago," said Hank.

"You're not going to talk about buying my property again, are you?" Now that the crisis was over and she knew that Scotty would be all right, she didn't have the strength for another argument.

For an instant, he turned his head away as if he were annoyed, and then went on unheeding. "Reva's got some ambitious plans, but I'd like to persuade her to stick with the idea of a simple residential development."

Elaine clenched her jaw as she acknowledged that he was going to talk about it whether she wanted him to or not.

"I know you don't want to sell, but what else can you do? It will take a lot of money to keep going." She wished he'd leave her alone; maybe if she didn't answer. "Anyway," he said, "I hope you'll at least consider selling to us. You may not have any other offers."

"I can manage."

"You'll have to do it sooner or later." Though his voice was gentle, she cringed at his certainty.

"I'll think of something."

"Did you ask the bank for a loan?" His gaze left the highway for a moment to examine her face, genuine concern in his eyes.

"Yes." Elaine pressed shaking fingertips to her forehead. "But we aren't making any money, so how could we repay a loan?"

"Is that what they said?" Beyond the apparent self-interest with which he had begun the conversation, Hank's quiet voice indicated he empathized with her. She studied his face, appreciating the clean straight lines of nose and jaw.

"You know how banks are, they expect to be paid. We've never borrowed money before, so we had no credit history. They wouldn't accept the campground as collateral because it's too far from town and the tourist attractions, and they don't see us doing enough business to support ourselves, let alone repay a loan of the size we need.

"Granddad isn't much help because he thinks God doesn't want people to go into debt. I know all the businesses do it. You probably do. So..." She took a deep breath. "Even though I applied for a loan against Granddad's wishes, it looks as if it was a waste of time after all, except that now I know where I stand."

"That's tough," he said, nodding.

"They canceled the field study because the private company that pledged most of the money changed its mind." Her fingers made nervous circles on the soft leather of the car seat. He frowned as if something unpleasant had suddenly occurred to him. Whatever it was, she realized he wasn't going to mention it.

"Sorry," he said, "but you're right. This isn't a good time to talk about it. Why don't you put your seat rest back for a while? Pull the handle at the side." He continued to frown, immersed in a fog of concentration as he watched the road.

She relaxed back but images of Scotty's pale face and Hank's green eyes kept her mind in turmoil. Think happy thoughts, she told herself. Deliberately, she called up a picture of the spring run and the eagle's nest with the babies in it.

She thought about the young male peacock with his funny strut. Music came softly through the speakers and soothed her. When the motion of the car ceased, she awoke to the sight of a handsome glass high-rise glittering in the late afternoon sun.

"It didn't take long to get here," she said, rubbing her eyes.

"You fell asleep," he said with a smile that made his eyes crinkle.

Scotty began to stir, and as Elaine twisted around, she saw that his color had further improved. "The doctor said he should get plenty of rest," she said.

"Where are we?" Scotty asked.

"This is Reva's office in Orlando." Hank got out and opened the back door. "Come on, you two. You can wait in my truck while I take Reva's keys up."

As Elaine sat on the truck seat, she gave a yelp and pulled a block of wood out from under her. On it was a list printed in heavy black marker: "1. Order trusses. 2. Call plumber. 3. Call electrician." She showed it to Scotty, and laughed up at Hank. "Hasn't anybody ever told you about that newfangled stuff called paper?"

"I know all about it." He grinned, taking the inscribed block from her and laying it on the dash. "I always have these around, so I use them. I'll be right back."

Ten minutes later, Hank was starting the truck, with a frown creasing his brow.

"Is something wrong?" Elaine asked.

"It's nothing, Reva's mad again. She lit into me about where I'd been—all that, you know. She accused me of shirking."

"She was probably upset that you were with me."

"Look, kid, it's not your fault. I never know what's going to set her off."

"Oh?" In spite of his pique and sensing that she shouldn't pursue the subject, curiosity overcame her. "It must be hard to work with someone so unpredictable."

"Sometimes," was his only answer.

The motor sounded rough; it was beginning to look as if she wasn't the only one with things that needed fixing. The thought was somehow comforting to her. Certain she wouldn't get any more information out of him, Elaine decided to drop the subject, but that didn't mean she couldn't think about it. He obviously had compassion for the troubles of others, but was reluctant to talk about his own.

As they headed onto the highway, Elaine pondered. If he didn't like Reva, why did he continue in partnership with her? Was he really the gentleman he seemed? How could a girl tell if he was being chivalrous or if he really liked her? Realizing it shouldn't matter either way, she took herself in hand. *Quit it, you dope,* she scolded herself. *He's strictly a business acquaintance.*

"I'm hungry." Scotty shattered the brittle silence.

"That's a good sign. We'll be home soon, and I'll get you something," she said. Her thoughts fluttered down for a landing, and settled again on Hank and Reva.

Elaine lightly touched his hand on the steering wheel. "It's our fault she was angry. I'm sorry. Thanks for taking us to the hospital and for helping in so many ways. I will repay you as soon as I figure out how."

"My pleasure." He moved his hand out of reach. "And I don't need your money."

"We will pay." She had no business touching him. "One way or another, we'll get it to you."

At last, they pulled onto the tree-lined drive that ran through the campground and ended at the house. The long day full of pain and conflict was over; they were back where they belonged. Outside, Elaine reached down to scratch Rags' ears as the dog greeted them by bounding and yipping. Hank carried Scotty into the house in his arms.

"I can walk, honest," Scotty said. Hank held firm as he tried to wiggle free.

The ancient kitchen appliances stood on the clean but pitted linoleum as they had for all of Elaine's life, making the kitchen look out-of-date and cloaked in poverty. Annie was busy at the sink, which Elaine knew from experience was steel over laid with paint and so rock hard it would shatter a china plate in one bounce. Ira hurried in, and with misted eyes took Scotty from Hank.

"Put me down," the boy demanded, but no one paid any attention to him. Unable to speak, Ira tightened his arms and squeezed his beloved grandson until he cried out.

"Come on in, Hank. We'll drop this boy on the couch and I'll show you my record collection." Ira disappeared into the hall without waiting for the younger man. Hank went after him. Elaine soon heard Scott Joplin's "Peacherine Rag" tune and knew they'd settled Scotty and started going through the old discs.

"Remember, Annie, when Granddad used to threaten us with ostracism if we touched his records?" Elaine asked.

"I surely do, darlin'." Annie laughed, shaking her head. "You didn't even know what that meant."

As the music stopped, Ira's voice began a familiar litany. The two women smiled at each other. "Now, son, you are careful with them records; if you break one you get ostracized."

"That would be bad," Hank said. "I sure don't want to be ostracized--not from around here, anyhow," he chuckled. "What's this one?"

The strains of a melancholy love song filled the air, and Annie sang a few words. "I'll be seeing you in all the old familiar places." Then she said, "Those sad old songs...soldiers leaving their loved ones, girls working on assembly lines and missing their fellows."

"I'd hate to be so dependent on a man that I couldn't enjoy life without him," Elaine commented with asperity.

She checked to make sure there were ice cubes in the upper compartment of the wheezing refrigerator. It really was a museum piece! Small and yellowed, it had an art-deco molding around the door. It wheezed every time it came on and threatened to quit altogether whenever they had an electrical storm.

The trays were there, but she wasn't sure how she was going to dislodge them from the thick layers of frost. She usually brought ice up from the restaurant. She took flatware and dishes out to set the porch table, thinking the whole time about love and war. "Granddad went to war, didn't he?" she asked, crossing back into the kitchen.

"Yes, he was in the infantry. Your grandmother and I kept each other company while he was gone. I'd saved up some money, and I bought the old house over at Living Spring. Whenever we had enough gas coupons, we put your mother in the car--she was about five--and went to estate sales to buy antiques.

"Belle helped me set up my business. We didn't have many customers, but we stayed busy trying to fix up the house. A lot of it never got finished, though. Some things are easier with a man around."

"I suppose they have their place," Elaine agreed reluctantly. "Right now they seem to be giving me a lot of trouble. Speaking of men, I'd better go check on our casualty."

"Belle read parts of his letters aloud, and I'd write to him sometimes." Annie went on reminiscing as if Elaine hadn't spoken.

Scotty lay on the couch with his hand trailing over Rags on the floor. Elaine looked once again at a part of the house through Hank's eyes. The thin curtains hung crookedly because she hadn't got around to repairing the rod pocket. The floor was free of sand, but the rug the dog lay upon was badly worn. I'll bet he thinks we're poor, she thought--because we are--Her shoulders slumped with weariness and discouragement.

"Laney, what's 'ostracized'?" Scotty asked.

"The blow to your head didn't hurt your hearing, did it?" she teased. She bent to kiss his cheek and to stroke Rags. "If you don't know what ostracized means, you'll be afraid to touch Granddad's collection."

"I wouldn't touch it anyhow."

"Not unless somebody left you alone with them. I know you and your curiosity--and those things are practically irreplaceable. Now lie still and be quiet. You may come to the table when we're ready. I love you."

When she looked up, she saw that Granddad and Hank both turned to watch her and a strange image came to mind, they're like sunflowers turning to the sun, she thought. She went back to the kitchen, but Annie shooed her out. "There's time for you to shower while I finish cutting up the chicken. Go, you'll feel much better."

"I should be doing the cooking. After all, it's our house, and you're the guest."

"Honey, I haven't considered myself a guest in this house since Ira moved in with you when you were only three. You can do the stir-frying at the last minute. Go on, now." Annie flapped her apron as if shooing a rooster off the porch. Elaine went.

In the only bathroom they possessed, she let the rusty water run from the shower head until it cleared. Then under the hot spray, the tense muscles of her back loosened. She sudsed and rinsed her hair, wrapped herself in a towel, and scurried down the hall to her bedroom.

She pawed through all the drawers. Her hair fluffed as it dried, curling around her face and tickling her bare shoulders. She decided to leave it free of its barrette for now.

Sitting at the back of the dresser a seldom-used bottle of perfume seemed to beckon. Removing the stopper, she inhaled the luscious, woodsy scent. As she dabbed behind her ears, a memory of herself at seven enveloped her.

Mother had come for one of her rare visits, and Elaine was thrilled that they shared a room, even though Monica would have preferred to be alone. She recalled a creamy satin nightgown with spaghetti straps. "Come here, darling. Let me show you something."

The little girl shyly approached, head down, as the beautiful woman held out a perfume vial. When she bent to smooth some behind Elaine's knees, a curtain of soft blond hair cascaded over the child's face; Mother's hair, with a fragrance all its own.

"A touch there," she said, before stretching out Elaine's slender arm, "a tad in the bend of each elbow, and a smidgen behind your ears. There."

She straightened and smiled at her daughter. "Those are your pulse points. That means every time your heart beats, it sends fragrance into the air like a secret message." She gave Elaine a quick hug. "Don't ever use too much, and be sure always, always to take a bath before you put it on." She handed Elaine the vial. "And for Pete's sake, don't save it. Perfume doesn't last forever."

Elaine closed the bottle and set it back on the dresser. Although she seldom bothered, she was well schooled in using cosmetics as well as perfume. She rummaged in her dressing table to find the still-unopened makeup kit her mother sent last Christmas.

Satisfied with the color in her cheeks and the way mascara intensified the blue of her eyes, she moved to the closet. It was full of clothes from all over the world. They arrived at the Crossroads Post Office so regularly she couldn't keep up with wearing them all.

A tiered, voile peasant dress in variegated shades of violet caught her eye. She fingered the hand-crocheted ruffle around the low neckline. I'll wear this, she decided; it will help me stay cooler. I hope Hank likes it.

She slipped her feet into gold sandals to compliment the hoop earrings Mother had said were pure gold and proper accessories for any outfit she had. This isn't like me, I've never cared how I looked, she marveled.

In the long, cheval glass her eyes sparkled, her lips swelled plump and red, and the dress glowed as if it were a hibiscus drenched in light. Her shining hair framed her face like a halo. The image hinted at another, unsuspected, Elaine Donovan whose voice wanted to break into an aria of celebration, whose feet wished to leap in an exuberant ballet, and whose arms yearned to hold someone.

Because there was no one there, she threw her arms around herself and danced across the room, catching glimpses of the full skirt as it rose and fell in a circle of feathery waves.

She returned to the back porch where Ira and Hank talked over half-empty glasses of tea. Scotty sat next to Ira, listening. Hank sat facing the door, his broad shoulders leaning into whatever story the old man was telling. She paused, willing them to look up. When they did not she moved to the end of the table as if Hank were steel and she was a magnet. Had she known what he was thinking, she might have quailed. Even so, the chemistry between them made her shiver with excitement.

Hank had seen beautiful women in lovely dresses before, but never had the sight caused pain to shoot through his chest almost like a heart attack.

Elaine saw his hand move over his chest in an involuntary gesture as if he were in pain. The intensity of the hunger in his eyes startled her. Ira's eyebrows headed for the ceiling and he too clutched his chest. "I thought for a minute you was Belle," he quavered.

Elaine felt a blush start at her toes and sear its way to the top of her head as Hank slowly stood. In that instant, she experienced the power inherent in womanliness for the first time. If she didn't break and run like a deer in the meadow, her life would change forever.

Without taking his eyes from hers, Hank gently brought her hand to his lips and held it there long and lingeringly. The same dizzying pleasure she had experienced so briefly in his arms at the hospital enveloped her. She pulled away reluctantly.

Ira cleared his throat. "Um, maybe Hank here, would like some more tea, Laney."

Annie came to her rescue by slipping the neckband of an apron over her head and tying it in back. "Come and do the stir fry," she said. "You do it so well, but you mustn't get any on that pretty dress."

In the kitchen, Elaine stood sautéing strips of chicken and struggled to recapture her equilibrium. Dreamily, she removed the chicken and slid fresh vegetables hissing into the hot oil. Stirring, she closed her eyes again, feeling Hank's lips warm her skin. What's the matter with me? she wondered. I act starved for love, but how can I be? Granddad loves me. Annie and Scotty do too.

"It's time to take the skillet off the fire," Annie reminded her. Elaine lifted the big pan and spooned vegetables onto a plate of rice, chastising herself for daydreaming instead of tending to the meal.

"Will you ask the blessing, young man?" Ira requested as they sat down at the rustic table.

"Lord," Hank prayed softly, "thank you for these dear people and for your goodness in every part of our lives. Thank you for this food, and bless the hands that have prepared it. Amen."

Elaine looked down at the beautiful colors of the meal: green broccoli, orange carrots, fluffy white rice. Butterflies, however, had taken up residence in her stomach and they sure weren't hungry. She laid down her fork and listened as the men launched into a discussion of her future.

"Tell us about this here subdivision you're starting next door, son." Ira's coarse white eyebrows bristled, standing out in every direction, antennae set to capture Hank's words.

"Well, sir," he began with a happy grin, "it's going to be the prettiest place you've ever seen. We'll have lakes, waterfalls, cedar-chip paths; and we're leaving enough woods for the kids to play in safely.

"In our plans, a wildlife corridor runs through for wildlife to travel from one wilderness area to another and down to the river to drink. We have plans for townhouses, single-family homes, and condominiums. That way there will be something for people in all stages of life.

"I'm hoping we can build an assisted-living complex for progressive needs, which will incorporate into the rest of the community. Residents can walk to the grocery store and library, and kids can ride their bikes to school. That way we'll leave a smaller footprint on the Earth, reduce fuel consumption, and cut down on traffic.

"Each section will have its own natural swimming pools and waterfalls, and we'll build playgrounds with sturdy wooden equipment. We're leaving the big trees--oak, palm, and maple--and even putting in tulip poplars." He looked at Elaine. "I know you were upset when you saw me bulldozing, but all I took out was scrub oak and hickory. The big trees are still there. Didn't you see them?"

She nodded, remembering the deep jungle behind Hank's bulldozer, but not wanting to acknowledge how overwrought she'd been on the day they met. "I guess I saw but..."

"Let the man go on with his story." Ira held up his hand to forestall an argument. Glad for his assistance in keeping control of her emotions, she heeded his admonition.

Hank smiled apologetically, as if he disliked seeing her corrected.

"Within walking distance, we'll have a town square with benches where people can sit and talk, shops and restaurants. We hope to encourage the kind of community involvement towns had years ago. I'm sure you'll like it." He watched her over the rim of his glass as he sipped his tea.

"Sounds like a place where we could live happily ever after." Ira's eyes twinkled as he nodded. "Yes, sir, you got a good plan there." His tone told Elaine that he had more or less gone over to the enemy, and she wondered why.

The idea of being powerless to keep Sacred Spring Campground natural and pristine, with a few repairs, of course, made her stomach ache, and now Granddad was weakening. Other than losing her loved ones, her greatest agony would come from having too many people on her land and watching the spring clog with debris, never to flow again.

"I'd like to extend onto this place, building fine homes for the families pouring into Florida."

CHAPTER 11

The edge of the picnic table bit into Elaine's ribs as she leaned forward to follow the conversation. Stomach churning, she wondered, *what's going on here?*

Granddad's welcoming this man into our lives as a friend. Until the past few months, Ira had taken care of all the thinking and planning for the family, and she'd been content to follow his lead. She marveled at the contrast between the apathy that had been creeping over him and the liveliness he displayed as he basked in the company of the young man across from him. She wished it would last, but feared it would not.

Granddad has looked after things all these years because he loves us, she thought, *but his strength is gone. Even if he's not aware of it, he's ready for someone else to make the decisions. It's only right; after all, Dad didn't leave the campground to Granddad, he left it to me and I should take up my responsibilities and give him a rest.*

Thinking about it now, she realized she'd already taken over most of the decisions. Her deep sigh caused Hank to glance up with obvious concern.

Silence fell as everyone except Elaine enjoyed the food. She knew that Ira and Scotty would become more than ever dependent until Ira *went home,* as he called it, and Scotty grew up. Pain pierced her heart at the thought. *Then what will I have--nothing!* She barely saw Hank nod his thanks when she poured more tea into his glass.

"You have a fine family, Mr. Thompson," Hank said, ending his own short reverie. "Someday I hope to have one of my own like it." He looked straight into Elaine's eyes as he spoke.

A tightness in her throat warned that tears were lurking. She escaped into the kitchen, where she found herself staring blindly into the open refrigerator without knowing what she had come for. In her mind's eye, she saw the flash of a solitaire diamond on the slim hand of an elegant dark-haired woman.

How could I ever think Hank might be interested in a girl like me? I have no style or sophistication. Even though he drives an old beat-up truck, she chided herself; *he's a rich man from a society family. He can have any woman he wants.* She slammed the refrigerator door just before remembering the ice she'd come for and had to open it again. The remaining aluminum tray she wrestled out of the freezer stuck painfully to her hand and she had to run cold water over it to get it unstuck.

Perhaps if Hank can come to understand the history of the camp-ground and grow to appreciate its beauty, perhaps if he can understand how our water supply is being slowly compromised and can acknowledge the necessity for natural habitat, maybe he will come over onto our side. He's smart and knowledgeable; he might even help us figure out what to do and help us do it. I don't think I'm too proud to ask, she thought.

Pulling the lever to separate the ice cubes produced a loud crack that brought her focus sharply to the task. Back on the porch, she plucked ice from the tray with tongs and dropped it into Hank's glass.

"Thanks, Elaine. You make good southern tea." Hank turned back to his conversation with Ira. "How long have you been at the camp-ground, Mr. Thompson?"

"Been here..." He looked at the ceiling and stroked his chin. "Oh, twenty years or thereabouts. It's a good life, and I love my grandchil-dren." He gazed at each of them in turn. "Laney was very young when her daddy was killed, and her mother didn't want to run the place, so Belle and me left retirement and moved in.

"It sure is a pretty place." Hank spoke to Ira, but looked at Elaine. For some reason, his appreciation was different from that of other men. He seemed to look into her soul and liked what he saw there. Maybe when he saw into the soul of the campground, he'd help make things right.

"Pretty, yes," Ira repeated. "In the old days, we had five or six times the frogs and scrub jays we got now. Those noisy things used to drown out our singing at the old-fashioned camp meetings we held out here on Sundays. You was a little girl then, Laney, remember?"

"We've had some good times." She remembered the pavilion filled with people sitting on wooden chairs and fanning themselves with what she called "Jesus fans."

"It's a fairly large property, isn't it, sir?" Hank asked.

Granddad took another serving of stir-fry. "One hundred acres, most of it woods." He chewed gingerly as if his teeth needed to be refitted. "Back in there," he gestured toward the deep woods, "we've got sand pine--it needs high, dry land--and lower, stands of palm, cypress, and live oak. You'll find a little bit of everything, even wild orange trees back in them woods."

Elaine shuddered, remembering how bitter these wild oranges were. Some of the old Florida natives used them as meat tenderizer.

"I'll let you taste one if you'd like," she said with a wicked little smile.

"We were planning to build a boardwalk over some of the swamp like the state parks, but we haven't got around to it," said Ira.

"Maybe I can do something about that." Hank rose. "A fine dinner, ladies. I thank you."

"You ain't leaving are you?" Granddad's brows beetled together as he looked up at Hank. "You want to see the place, don't you?"

"Sure, but you folks are probably busy," Hank answered.

"Laney can show you around some now, and in a couple weeks, when we're sure Scotty's healed up, we can take you on a canoe trip to see the rest of it. How's that sound? We can take the tents and have us a high old time. We ain't done that since before Laney started college."

"You mean an overnight canoe trip?" Hank asked.

Scotty's excited voice rang out from the couch. "I want to go!"

"You better rest, son," Ira shouted back, his voice filled with amusement.

"I can't hear you," Scotty answered.

A chuckle bubbled up from Hank's throat. "It's so good to enjoy a real family again."

"I don't know what I'd of done, without these kids." Ira's voice seemed to be giving him trouble. As she listened to the two men, Elaine wished she could be around these dear people forever. Especially Hank, she thought, before she grabbed control of her wandering mind.

"I'd appreciate a canoe trip so I can see how much of the land is buildable and what kind of arrangements I need to make. I have a good consulting firm to run interference with the Environmental Protection Agency and see that we adhere to all the rules." He rocked back on his heels, suddenly filled with childish buoyancy. "I'd love a short tour now."

A glimpse of the adventuresome boy inside made Elaine wonder if perhaps building houses failed to satisfy all his desires; maybe he needed more of a challenge in his life.

"We can leave early on a Friday morning and come back Saturday evening." Ira rubbed his hands together in anticipation.

"What should I bring?"

"Nothing, son. We have all the gear we need. We'll take two tents, one for the boys and one for the girls. You want to come, Annie?" Ira's eyes shone.

Annie had been quietly listening. "I would love to, but my old bones refuse to sleep on the ground anymore."

"Then leave them old bones at home, and come on anyhow," Ira said with a chuckle. "To tell the truth, mine don't like it any more than yours do, but I got a yen to take one last trip down the river."

He inspected his plate with a pensive expression. "Meantime, you two best get going while it's still light enough to see. I wish we'd had the money to restore the old hotel. You'd have loved her in her time. Ain't much wrong a passel of money couldn't fix; needs a new roof, but the marble floors and the walls is still in good shape."

"You go on," Annie said. "Ira and I can handle the dishes."

Elaine pinched the tops of the four iced tea glasses between her fingers to carry them to the kitchen. Hank picked up his plate and followed. "You don't have to take me around now. You must be tired after such long day. I know you don't want me to buy the place."

"We might as well get it over with. I won't be able to rest until I know what's going to happen."

Ira came in and set a pile of dishes on the counter. "Annie and I will wind up the Victrola and do the washing up to ragtime music."

In the now-crowded kitchen, Annie squirted soap into the dishpan and turned on the faucet. "Better let us. Ira doesn't make the offer very often." Elaine understood how much Annie wanted to be alone with Granddad. All these years, she'd had only scraps of his attention. She empathized with how much more Annie must have wanted from the man she had loved secretly for so long.

"Shall we take a walk then?" Elaine asked. Rags, whose scrabbling feet tapped across the slick linoleum as she danced in circles, provided the answer.

"She heard 'walk,'" said Granddad, laughing. "Now you got to take her. Some critters just don't know how serious life is getting to be." In spite of herself, Elaine let a bubble of happiness rise into a smile.

"Can't I go, too?" came Scotty's plaintive voice.

"Another time," Ira said, and motioned for them to head out.

As Hank and Elaine strolled the dirt road toward the pool, more ragtime music poured into the night. With the notes nibbling at her toes, Elaine felt an almost uncontrollable urge to dance. Tree frogs added their high-pitched peeping, and the occasional *garumph* of an alligator drove the melody forward like bass tones in the evening's ensemble.

Rags roamed ahead, cruising the edges of the road for the familiar smells of opossum and raccoon. They skirted the pool and walked to where the water rushed through a flume into the river. "Would you like to cool your feet?" Elaine asked. She had been given a gift of time and felt no sense of rush whatsoever. She sat down on a platform over the rushing stream and took off her sandals.

Settling beside her, Hank removed his shoes and socks and rolled up his pant legs. Unlike the visible parts of his tanned and muscular body, his long, bare feet looked pale and somehow vulnerable. "Whew, that's cold!" he gasped.

"It feels good though, doesn't it?" Elaine concentrated as silvery clouds stood outlined against the gray-blue sky. As they sat quietly dreaming, together, yet apart, a flock of white birds settled to roost in one of the big oaks on the riverbank. Soon a flock of cattle egrets filled all the nearby trees. Whole branches drooped from the weight of them.

"Would you look at that?" Hank said softly, his voice full of awe. "I've never seen so many in one place."

"It's their favorite spot," Elaine murmured.

"It's so peaceful here." Hank swished his feet without splashing.

She fell silent again, wanting to grasp these few moments of tranquility and hold them in her memory forever. Tomorrow would be time enough to take up the endless battle to save the spring. As the birds settled for the night, their number reflected in the river as if it were a crumpled mirror.

"Granddad always said life was like this river," she mused. "It moves fast, so fast it makes him feel like he's floating off with the current. The older I get, the more I appreciate what he means."

Hank nodded. "I remember my dad reading us something similar from the Psalms. *Life is like the flower on a blade of grass.* Nevertheless, I want time to do something special, something the Lord asks me to do."

"Your dad read the Bible to you?" Elaine asked. "Granddad used to read it to us every morning after breakfast, too. I wonder about what the Lord wants, though, don't you?"

"Well, you have no idea where you might be if he hadn't kept you and your grandfather and Scotty together. He's obviously kept you healthy, and in spite of your problems, I sense you've always been happy. Am I right?"

"Yes, you're right. I do have a lot to be thankful for."

"Looking at the spring, I'm thinking about The Flood. Did you know that in the story the waters came up out of the Earth as well as down from Heaven?" she said.

"Now that I know a bit about how springs work, I can believe it," he answered.

"Maybe Sacred Spring gushed out for the first time back then and just kept right on going. I love the idea of its antiquity. The whole park is steeped in history. Once a plantation owner bought it for the price of fifty black women," she said.

She felt him tense beside her, his voice sharp with disapproval. "Slaves?"

"Yeah, I don't believe in people owning other people either, but that's not the point. The point is a man was willing to spend a lot of money to own it. It shows how highly valued its beauty was even that long ago." Elaine's feet had gone numb, so she pulled them out of the water and wrapped her arms around her knees.

"I agree with you that it is beautiful. I'm not sure of its current value in terms of money. We're a good ways from town, but I'm willing to take a chance that the outskirts will move this way." He too withdrew his feet and sat balancing his heels on the boards.

"On the other hand, Sacred Spring is the kind of place they're calling 'the real Florida' and I'd hate to see it spoiled." He turned his head as he spoke, absorbing the evening's pure tranquility. "You know, it's likely that the EPA won't even talk to me. They're getting strict about places like this. Look there," he said quietly, pointing at a green heron walking across a lily pad, its sharp bill aimed at the water.

"Fishing," Elaine explained with a smile.

"I guess it's time for the old hotel." Hank got up reluctantly and pulled her to her feet. They took a path twisting between tall pines and headed into the woods. Barefoot and carrying their shoes, they stepped onto the dry pine needles covering the trail. Thick bamboo made a canopy over their heads.

"Ouch!" he said. "First you freeze my feet, then you make pincushions out of them."

"We'd better get our shoes on." Elaine put her hand on his arm to steady herself as she slipped into her sandals.

Hank then sat down on a fallen tree to pull on socks and tie his shoes. As she watched him concentrate, she felt a silken thread of commitment reach toward him as tenuous as the first filament spun by a spider for a new web. She pulled on it and it broke, but she knew it would be nothing for it to spin itself into existence again.

I'll probably have to give up his friendship about the same time I lose the campground, she thought, so I'd better not get used to having him around.

"The hotel is right around that bend." As the trail curved back toward the house, the beat of ragtime music got louder in the humid air. She led the way into a tunnel of softly rustling bamboo.

CHAPTER 12

$\mathcal{E}$laine and Hank emerged at the near ruins of the Mediterranean style hotel, which her grandfather, when he was stronger, had spent many hours trying to keep in repair.

The three of them had worked in the gardens, but now periwinkle and lantana inched up between cracks in the sidewalk, and wild grasses crowded the beds. The air was redolent with Confederate Jasmine blooming in wild profusion. Bird-of-paradise blooms jutted above clumps of fern, and wild grapevines cascaded over the picket decrepit wooden fence, their tendrils reaching to climb and bind everything in their path.

"Come see the veranda," Elaine invited, leading Hank onto the path around the building. It brought them to a long porch in the back. "How do you like this?" Elaine, happy for a family heirloom to show, crouched to brush away the dust and Hank stooped to smooth the pink and cream tiles.

"Beautiful. Is it Tennessee marble?" He looked up at Elaine inquiringly.

"Yes it, how did you know?" Before he could answer, she called his attention to the lintel above the French doors. "That came from Spain."

He gave a low whistle. "Hmm, look at that deep azure. Someone invested plenty of love and money here. Was it built in the late twenties?"

"Great-grandfather Donovan built it in 1927. He wanted to make the park a playground for wealthy people. Alas for us," she turned her mouth down in what she hoped was a comical pout, "he lost all his money in the Great Depression. If he had fulfilled his dream, we'd have a fabulous resort now and everything we need to keep the spring clear and clean."

Hank stopped to examine one of the doors. "Imported mahogany," he commented. He almost purred with pleasure at discovering the fine wood. Though he pushed the door carefully, reverently, it responded with an arthritic squeal of protest.

"The hinges need oiling," Hank commented as he stood back for her to go first. "I'm surprised it still works as well as it does, though. In most places as old as this one, either the wood swells or the hinges rust solid, and you can't work the doors at all."

"Granddad took good care of it through the years," she answered. "He can't manage it now." They were passing through the lobby with its tabby fireplace. I guess he wanted to use something from Florida."

Hank said, "Sand and millions of tiny coquina clams with their leached lime as glue. Right?"

"Come this way." She led him into a room where a long marble counter dominated a vintage ice cream parlor set about with wire chairs and round tables. "They imported this marble from Italy--the counter is sixty feet long."

"Magnificent," he said, smiling and running his hands over it. "Wonderful."

"It is, isn't it? I've always loved it, especially when I think of the guests who came here all dressed up and having a wonderful time together." Her sense of well-being overflowed as she took Hank's hand to lead him along. "This way to the grand ballroom."

"There's more?" Hank felt Elaine's slender hand nestling confidently in his and felt as if a small bird had landed there, knowing he would not crush it or hurt it in any way. His knees wobbled a little and his heart pounded, but he made his hand steady.

A wide expanse of marble covered the ballroom floor. Peeling gold-leaf whorls decorated the walls. Dust motes waltzed in the last rays of the lowering sun.

"See the dais in front of the big fanlight window? That's where the chamber orchestra plays." Hank gave her a strange look. "Oh, I mean played. I pretended that the orchestra played for me. I have a photograph of the musicians. Can you hear the waltz?"

"Sorry, all I hear is your Granddad's ragtime," he answered, chuckling at her fancies. His tall, muscular body swayed.

Elaine sensed a tightly coiled excitement in him, and a sudden exultation fired her imagination. "Waltz or Ragtime, I see a room full of women in light summer dresses and men in dinner jackets sweeping and turning."

"Those dinner jackets are hot. How about we open a window?" Hank whispered, playing along, not wanting to disturb the phantom dancers.

The light threw shadow stripes across the floor. Hank helped he open several sets of doors and a cooling breeze rushed in to brush the chandelier prisms and set them tinkling like the shell fragments that came up from the boil.

A bolt of lightning cracked the sky while they lingered. "One thousand one, one thousand two, one thousand three," Elaine counted before the thunder boomed. "It won't break for a while," she announced, not wanting to go home. She tried desperately to think of some way to hold his attention, but her wits failed her. "Hear the chuck-will's-widow?" The night bird sang softly, its call barely audible.

"Sometimes they keep me awake at night," Hank said, looking into her eyes. Rags trotted into the ballroom, head up, ears perked. She was satisfied that she had chased all the wild creatures back where they belonged.

"Go, Rags!" Elaine shouted, playing the game the little dog loved so well. Rags became a dynamo speeding around the large room, her back paws skidding out from under her at every turn, while Hank's booming laugh satisfied Elaine's need to know he was being entertained.

"Storm crazy." Elaine laughed and slipped her arm companionably through Hank's.

He leaned away, no longer trusting himself with the smallest contact. "This is a fine place," he said hastily.

The physical rebuff stung like a slap; she released his arm, and spoke to cover her confusion. "Joplin's music always makes her crazy." Not knowing what else to do, she began to chatter. "Granddad put on a new roof when we first came here. He had plans like my great-great-grandfather." I sound so dumb; she thought angrily, but she continued in spite of a growing anxiety.

"Great Granddaddy came first as the promoter and developer of Sacred Spring." She smoothed her electrified hair as she strove to speak calmly. "Back in the 1800s, he published a promotional sheet. I love all the old-fashioned language in it." She hoped Hank was interested.

"Like what?" Anything to keep her talking so he could look at her. Everything would be all right as long as he didn't touch her.

"The waters of Sacred Spring, being of miraculous mineral composition contain healing properties that promote beauty and good health far beyond the years most people usually live. A few of the results from daily swimming in the spring and drinking its waters are: flower petal skin, both in the feel and in the fragrance; vitality instead of debilitating fatigue, especially by heat; and complete healing for the liver, kidneys, pancreas, stomach, and intestines, which results in deliverance from common ailments such as catarrh, biliousness, rheumatism, consumption, crysipelas, and palpitating heart."

"You memorized all those hundred-dollar words?" Hank found himself laughing again and hoped Elaine would not think him a fool.

She nodded and continued her litany, knowing that if she stopped, she'd have either to start all over again or give way to overwhelming giggles. "Nervous disorders, including depression, phlebitis, and boils!"

He chuckled. "Does it?"

"Does it what?"

"Cure all that?"

"Of course. Long before my great-great-grandfather came along, the Seminole Indians called it 'Sacred Spring' because they always felt better after they swam or bathed in it. They believed it had miraculous healing powers. She straightened her shoulders. "I personally attest to being cured of 'fatigue by heat' every day."

"You really love the place, don't you?" Hank took a handkerchief from his back pocket, wiped his forehead, and put it back, as unprepared as Elaine was to acknowledge what had been building between them.

"It's our home."

In a brief silence, the sound of cicadas and crickets welcomed the coming storm. "Bird Brain Ragg" echoed softly through the undergrowth. This time, try as she might, she couldn't resist moving a little to the music.

"You're having a good time," said Hank. "Do people dance to that?"

"I do."

"How can you? It's an uneven beat."

"Didn't you folk-dance in elementary school?" He gave an affirmative nod. "Then you can do it. You have to put in a little bounce--like this." She showed him her Charleston-style steps.

Hank slid his arm around her waist and took her hand in an old-fashioned waltz position. At first, he held her at arm's length, but then had to draw her close for the sake of balance.

He held her so tightly that Elaine had to melt all the way into him so as not to trip and throw him off balance. Even though Granddad frowned on dancing for religious reasons, she knew that Hank's was the one pair of arms in which she belonged.

Rags nipped at their heels as they circled the ballroom doing a quickstep. She barked frantically when they spun out of reach. Hank's laughter counterpointed Elaine's as the two of them, driven by melody and catapulted to heights of silliness, spun around the smooth floor seemingly without effort as though they were whirling dolls on a cuckoo clock.

All at once, common sense set its ambush, and realizing her emotions were nearly out of control, Elaine held back, trying to slow the spinning carnival ride. Hank's eyes widened in surprise as her steps faltered and he felt the two of them falling.

He flung out one arm while the other tightened protectively around her waist. The transcendent joy of the dance became a clown act as they caromed off the wall and slid gently to the floor, laughing so hard they couldn't stop.

Rags ran to lick Hank's face and he handed her to Elaine. The marble floor felt cool, so they stayed where they were to rest for a moment.

"Rags, sit!" Elaine put the dog down and the dog obeyed, tipping her head in a lopsided pose, totally mystified by the strange behavior of her Elaine. The puzzlement renewed their mirth to the point where they couldn't stop laughing.

"She can't...figure why we're...making these...funny noises," Hank gasped.

Elaine wiped her eyes. "Why are we?" They cackled and snorted, immersed in hilarity. Hank straightened against the wall while Elaine struggled up beside him, all strength drained.

"Whew, you're fun to be with, Elaine. I'm so glad we met."

She sobered, pleased and flattered, and yearned for more honey from his lips. Was she beautiful? Witty? Talented? Charming? Anything, as long as it came from him.

"Do you know that song?" he asked, suddenly veering away from another personal observation.

A quieter melody came to them on the evening mist. In the fading light, his expression was only a blur. In spite of her disappointment, Elaine murmured the words to the slow, sweet song. "I'll be with you, in apple-blossom time."

"Your granddad likes those old songs," said Hank.

"Not only old songs, but old ways too. He has kept that mechanical record player so he can still have music when the electricity goes out.

He can fix whatever goes wrong. Annie said a man was looking for one of the original Columbia consoles for his collection and kept upping the amount he'd pay, but Granddad wouldn't sell for any amount of money."

"Old ways are comfortable for most people, but the world moves on, and if you don't move with it, you lose out," Hank said.

"Maybe what looks like progress really isn't progress at all, though." She dreaded what was coming next. It was an inflammatory subject, and she knew that once they began on it, enchantment would end.

"Yes?" he prompted with the lightness gone from his voice.

"It's simple. Anybody ought to be able to understand it." She moved a few inches away.

"Explain it to me, then. I guess I'm a dummy."

"Sometimes true progress means leaving resources alone so flora and fauna survive and that means mankind can survive."

"I understand, and I agree," he said. "But what do you propose to do with all the people who are moving down here? Are you going to keep all this beauty and clean air to yourself?"

"Don't be silly." His accusation stung. How could she ever persuade him? "I'm not saying we keep everyone else out, I'm just saying let's be careful with what we have here."

"Haven't you ever heard of mitigation?"

"I know what it is. It's what happens when you take wetlands that have existed for centuries, fill them in, then take dry land, and dig out ponds and swamps to create more wetlands. Does that make sense to you?"

"Well, sure, if it's where you want to put your community. That way, everybody wins."

"If you turn Sacred Spring into a subdivision how will you get a new spring? Even you can't do that, can you?"

"I may not be able to build here at all, but I'd like to try, and believe me, Elaine, I will do everything possible to protect the spring. Your only alternative is to close up the campground and let it sit empty. That would not be good for it, either. And can you afford it?"

"No." She shook her head, all happy feelings wiped away.

"Do you pray about things like this?" His hand slid over hers on the cool floor. He gave it a gentle squeeze.

"No, I have to learn to make decisions for myself. I've depended on others far too long. I know Granddad and Annie do, though."

"So I will," he said.

"For me or for yourself?" She slid her hand out from under his.

"Both."

"You can't pray for both of us to have what we want, our dreams just don't go together. We want totally opposite things."

"Not really. You care about habitat and so do I. What you say makes sense. I'd like to see if I can find out what God has in mind." He sighed. "He usually has a third alternative you'd never think of in a million years. Say," he looked around, "this ballroom would make a great recreation room."

"A recreation room!" She rose in a quick, fluid movement and stood glaring down at him. "I suppose you'd cover the walls with plastic paneling and the floor with cheap carpet."

A brief flicker of lightning showed her the anger on Hank's face. He got to his feet and said deliberately, "I don't operate that way." Thunder rolled ominously close.

"Oh, no? What about bulldozing trees with birds' nests in them?" She found herself shaking with anger.

"I didn't mean to knock it down." He tried to catch her arm as she turned to walk away. "Please, Elaine..."

She fired a volley over her shoulder. "Don't touch me. This is still my property and I want you off."

Knowing he couldn't hold her by force, he desperately sought for something that would stop her. She could be so infuriating. She simply would not listen when he tried to explain that he wanted what she did. He tried to listen to her; why didn't she do the same for him? "We can't keep arguing like this," he said to her back. "We're going to have to communicate and decide what to do."

"Forget it. You're impossible to communicate with. You'll have to decide how to sweet talk somebody else out of her property." She knew her attitude was unreasonable even as she sank deeper into the stubbornness that seemed to be her only refuge. Raindrops pattered on the roof as more lightning lit the ballroom and a great peal of thunder cracked nearby. The rain sounded like a freight train as it started to fall in earnest.

"Let's go back to the house," he said, starting out. "I've got to get busy tomorrow ruining everything," he said through clenched teeth.

Elaine rushed to close the French doors, but they fought her like wild things in the raging wind and rain. Hank came to lend his weight, and together they got them closed. She ran out the way they had come in. On the trail, Hank moved quickly to keep her in sight. "Elaine, please, don't run away." He shouted, "Talk to me!"

She childishly put her fingers in her ears and scurried back through the thick bamboo tunnel, which somewhat protected her from the rain. As soon as she reached the track to the house, she splashed quickly through one puddle after another, leaving him to make his own way the best he could. At the heels of her beloved mistress, Rags ran too, unafraid and having fun, though the puddles came up to her belly.

CHAPTER 13

*T*wo weeks passed before Elaine heard from Hank again; two weeks of gray clouds and spectacular shows of thunder and lightning—two weeks of depression and despair and not understanding what was happening to her. She dragged herself from the house to the pool and from the pool to the restaurant.

A few customers trickled into the Old Mill, but Mr. and Mrs. Braithwaite remained the only steady campers. Her mood darkened even more whenever Scotty and Ira sat with their heads together planning the canoe trip. One day Mrs. B. showed up at the restaurant in a white uniform with her gray hair netted and her feet in nurse's shoes. Elaine showed her around, let her work an hour or so, and was mildly amused when she refused pay, but gleefully pocketed tips.

Ira invited Elaine to have a cup of coffee with him after the breakfast rush. She looked forward to a heart to heart talk with him as she carried steaming mugs to the screened room at the back of the Mill.

Scotty squatted on the ground outside, taking things off his bike with pliers and wrenches and throwing them into a pile. He reveled in being outside with his beloved little dog after a week in the house. Perhaps she'd kept him a bit longer than necessary, but it was better to be safe.

Ira sipped the hot coffee and placed his mug carefully on the uneven boards of the picnic table. "What's wrong with you lately? You been moping around like a hen what somebody stole her settin' eggs."

Before she could answer, Scotty and Rags bounced in, the boy's arms black to the elbows with grease. Granddad grabbed his cup and lifted it out of reach before Scotty's filthy fingers could close around the handle. "No you don't, son. That'll stunt your growth."

"Look at your hands," Elaine said disgustedly.

Scotty obligingly looked and hurriedly rubbed greasy streaks onto his shorts. "I'm ready to put it back together, Granddad, but I might need help because I can't remember where all the parts go."

"Aren't you supposed to know all that before you take it apart? And please get that dog outside. If the Health Department stopped by, we'd be cited. Go wash your hands and finish up so we can have a swim," Elaine scolded.

"I wanted to fix the bike fast." He ignored her string of orders and answered her question. "You have to learn to work quick if you're going to make any money as a mechanic." He peered longingly at the freezer just inside the door.

"I'll be out in a minute, son, I got a few more things to say to Laney."

"Granddad, can I have an ice cream?" he asked.

"All right; then wait for me outside." Ira's serious expression shot fear into Elaine's heart. Now she was going to get the third degree, and she might have to admit some things she didn't want anybody admit, even to herself. "You going to tell me what's wrong?" he asked again.

"I don't know. I just feel tired all the time and like there's no use in doing anything."

"Honey, I'm getting old and I'm tired myself. You know I won't always be here to look after you kids."

"You're just trying to make me feel better." She gave a tight little smile at her own wry joke as she stirred sugar into her coffee.

"If we sell out, we'll be able to afford to buy one of them nice condos in town. Scotty can learn things in a bigger school that he can't learn stuck way out here—things he'll need to know to survive in this crazy world. You could really start to use your education or even get your doctor degree. Now wouldn't that be something? Dr. Elaine Donovan.

"You're sure smart enough to do it." Looking directly into her eyes and seeing the pain there, he paused. "Honey, I'd just hate to go off to Heaven and leave you and Scotty alone without getting these things settled."

"But I love it here," she cried. "I love you and Scotty and our way of life. I don't want anything to change. If we can hang on, I might be able to do some serious research right here. Isn't that what education is for: so you can do something worthwhile, something lasting?"

"But, you got to remember, you can't get too hooked on saving this old world. Someday it will be gone, and there'll be a new Heaven and a new Earth or the old one will be fixed up nice. Do you ever think about that?"

"People my age don't want to think about things like that. Our lives are just getting started." She looked away from the compassion in his eyes. "We're not ready for the end of the world."

"I know, Sweetheart, and people your age are usually thinking about getting married, too. How about that? I'd like to see a couple of great-grandchildren crawling around before I go, but it don't look like you're ever going to meet anybody…unless you already have?"

"Don't you see that nobody wants me?" she said, letting a trickle of true feelings slip out.

"Now, that ain't reasonable," Granddad said. "What about that nice Hank feller? He's taken a shine to you, hasn't he?"

"Why do you say that?" He'd caught her attention. Elaine focused sharply on every nuance of what Ira was saying.

"I can tell by the way he looks at you with his heart in his eyes."

"You're mistaken. He's got some kind of a thing going with that partner of his."

"Not if he's the man I think he is." Ira smiled. She wondered if he were teasing, but she took the bait.

"What do you mean?"

"She's a pretty lady, and she's smart as a whip, but there ain't no contest between her and you. That young man deserves someone who would treat him gentle-like. He's got a real big heart."

"I don't want to get married." She could hardly get the words past the elation that fluttered in her heart. Could Hank really need her as Granddad said? What a glorious but impossible thought.

"Everybody wants to get married, darlin'," he said gently.

"Then why didn't you ever remarry?" she asked.

His shaggy head bowed, and she felt ashamed for being so direct and taking her frustrations out on him. She could hardly hear his lowered voice. "Now I'd be the one nobody would want, decrepit old fogey like me."

"I know someone who would—if you wanted her."

He looked up and grinned. "How'd you do that? We were talking about you, when all of a sudden I'm the main subject of the conversation." He took a final swig of coffee and got up. "Got to get that bike together." He walked out, and for the first time in her life, she found herself more confused after one of their talks than she had been when it began.

A week later, on a Monday evening, the phone rang. Elaine hurried through the darkening house to the front office to answer it. Reaching for the heavy black receiver, she glanced out the picture window. In the obsidian shadows at the edge of the pool, all was still and silent.

"Hello, Elaine, it's Hank." Her knees buckled at the sound of his deep voice, and she sat down quickly in the big leather chair, breathing slowly and deliberately.

"Are you still talking to me?" he asked after a pause.

"Yes," she whispered. "I'm talking to you." Her thoughts tumbled in chaos. And furious with you, and dying to see you, she thought, but did not say.

"Listen, I'm sorry I was insensitive. I do understand what you're going through. In many ways, I agree with you. Wilderness and sources of water should be paramount."

Cupping the phone as she would a jeweled chalice, she tried to control the quaver in her voice. "It was as much my fault as yours. Granddad's always telling me I need to learn to be more patient, not flare up so easily." She tried to laugh, but it sounded more like choking.

"We're okay then?" He sighed audibly. "How is Scotty?"

"Fine; his only problem now is that he took his bike apart and he and Granddad can't get it back together."

Hank chuckled. "I didn't call before because, to tell the truth, I was afraid you wouldn't want me to." She could hear the smile in his voice. "I've missed you; can't get you off my mind."

"Oh." Wonder at the knowledge that he'd been obsessed by thoughts of her too, filled her soul. She kept quiet, waiting to hear more.

"Would you come to church with me Sunday and then we could go to brunch? I owe you a meal, and I want to discuss the camping trip."

"Sunday's our busiest day."

It was his turn to say, "Oh," and she heard dismay in his voice. "There's no way you could make it?"

"I suppose I could get some help."

"Great! I'll take you to one of the hotels over by Disney World. They're truly beautiful and the one I'm thinking about has a delicious buffet. I think you'll like the atmosphere. That always seems important to a woman."

"All right." She didn't wish to discuss Reva's preferences.

"I'll pick you up at seven. That way we'll have plenty of time."

As she gently placed the receiver in its cradle, Elaine wanted to sing and dance, to weep with joy. She sashayed down the hall to her room and started rummaging in her closet.

What would Mother wear? Ah, the silk dress with the blues, purples, greens, and pinks of a peacock's tail that Mother sent with sandals to match would work fine.

Elaine spread the full-skirted dress over a chair and got out her grandmother's turquoise crystal earrings. She remembered the day Monica took her to have her ears pierced. At fourteen, she'd quivered with fear, but the two of them had so much silly fun that when the time came, she sailed through it. She put the earrings back in the velvet-lined jewelry box, closed the lid, and gave it a pat.

For the rest of the week, she thought constantly about Hank. He was on her mind while she mixed pancake batter and poured it into serving pitchers. He was there in spirit when she laid out the place mats and when she transferred foil-wrapped cubes of butter from the refrigerator to the tables where they immediately began to melt.

She swept the house, the restaurant, the picnic pavilion, the bathrooms, the bathhouse down by the pool, and the cement walk around the pool. Hank's handsome face and strong body invaded her dreams, in which he talked softly to her, listened avidly, and even held her in his arms.

Each morning when the rooster crowed, she gave up all attempts at sleep and stepped into a hot shower, scrubbing until her skin hurt, trying to wash away the soft, warm sensation of heightened physical awareness with which she had awakened.

The day Hank was to come for her, Elaine dressed carefully. With her makeup applied the way Monica taught her, she pulled on a satin slip and slid the luxurious silk dress over her head. When she was ready, the hands on her Big Ben alarm clock still only pointed to five o'clock. Wandering from room to room, she leafed through old textbooks, walked down by the pool, fed Rags who had left Scotty's room to investigate her restlessness, and went down to the peacocks. By then it was five-thirty and she decided to go on line and do a bit of research about what was new with conservation of springs.

Fifteen minutes later, she tiptoed into Ira's room to see if he was awake yet. He was, but he knelt next to the bed with his open Bible and she had to wait until he finished talking to God so he could talk with her. Once she started chattering, she couldn't stop; and when he saw her need of company, he went to the kitchen to make coffee.

Hank arrived as promised after what felt like a million years of waiting. His dark suit and striped tie made him look like a dignified businessman, but Elaine thought perhaps she preferred him in more casual attire. I'd be more comfortable, she thought, if we were going for a swim.

CHAPTER 14

"*D*id you have any trouble getting someone to mind the restaurant?" Hank asked after walking her to his truck. He turned the key and the motor sputtered to life.

"No, the Braithwaites seemed glad to do it, and I bribed Scotty to help them."

"Elaine," he said his voice husky, "I'm glad you could come. I've been counting the hours."

She noticed that his hands shook slightly on the steering wheel--a man so filled with self-confidence shaky as a schoolboy on a first date. They stuck to small talk all the way across the city, but both of them found it fascinating and satisfying. To each, the smallest detail about the other was important. Elaine responded with enthusiasm when Hank mentioned his sister. "Tell me all about her."

"Jean likes people, but since that thing with Richard, she isolates herself. Her doctor says she has post traumatic stress disorder." He looked thoughtful. "I guess she doesn't know what to say to people. Someone took advantage of a sweet, innocent kid who was bereft and confused."

He seemed to assume she knew what he was talking about, but how could she? He chuckled and shook his head. "As little as my niece is, she loves to make people laugh. Turn a camera on her and she becomes an adorable little clown." Hank chuckled. "I did tell you Reva was going to church with us, didn't I?" He parked in the lot of a high-rise condominium. "I don't know why I slipped and told her I was taking somebody."

"I didn't know," she said quietly.

They rode to the top floor and stepped out of the elevator. A uniformed maid showed them into a stark living room dominated by black leather and chrome. A gigantic slash of red dominated one wall while the other was all window squares looking at balconies of other identical buildings.

"Miss Reva asks you to sit down, *por favor*," the maid said, looking up at Hank from under straight black bangs and an old-fashioned ruffled maid's cap. "She will be ready soon."

"This is Maria," Hank said. "Maria, this is my good friend, Elaine." The two shook hands while Hank stood by smiling.

"How have you been?" he said. "Is that boy of yours still doing well in school?"

"*Si*! When you told him he can be a builder like you, he decides to study his math and English. I am so proud of him. *Gracias, Senor,* for giving him a dream."

"He's a bright kid. He'll do well," Hank said.

A voice came from another room and Maria's eyes grew large. "She need me. Goodbye, Mr. Schaefer, Miss Elena." She scurried away.

They sat on the hard couch, waiting, and each silent in thought. Elaine absorbed every detail of the room: the shining bars that made up the furniture, the metal pots and canisters that decorated the glass-topped tables, and a few more bright paintings on the walls.

Next to her on an end table, a small dagger gleamed with jewels. She supposed it was a letter opener. She hoped it wasn't a weapon. A violent sneeze took Elaine by surprise. She thought it must be the heavy odor of sandalwood hanging in the air.

"Bless you," Hank said, grinning at her. She wished they were back at the campground, outdoors, instead of shut up in this elegant but stuffy apartment.

Reva swept in, and once again, Elaine had to admire the beauty that had launched a fresh assault on her self-confidence. With her gleaming dark hair in a smooth pageboy, alabaster skin totally without blemish, dark eyes reflecting the topaz necklace she wore in the hollow of her throat and matching suit, she was formidable.

Elaine glanced at Hank, who seemed oblivious. They both stood as Reva approached. She raised her face for a kiss, but he ignored the gesture. "Say hello to Elaine," he said. The pursed lips rearranged themselves into a pout as Reva nodded curtly in Elaine's direction.

"We need to get going," Hank said. "It'll be hard enough to find a place to park as it is."

Reva plucked an envelope bag from a credenza. "I'm ready. I suppose you brought your truck?" At Hank's nod, she suggested, "Let's take my Mercedes, we'll all be more comfortable, and really, sweetheart, it looks so much better at church."

While Hank parked the car, the women waited in the foyer of the church. When he came back, they entered a lobby and then went into the church. The ceiling stretched as if to encompass heaven.

Elaine craned to examine a balcony halfway up that must have seated over a thousand people. The hum of conversation competed with a lively musical offering from a small orchestra. An usher showed them to cushioned chairs near the front, where Reva motioned for Elaine to go in first.

Elaine looked around in time to see Hank's hand stay Reva so he could move in next to his guest. With his solidness beside her, she breathed the fragrance of fresh bouquets at the front and unexpectedly felt her spirits lift.

A thin young man bursting with energy took the podium and introduced. "Now let us sing 'The Doxology,'" he said. Voices quieted, hymnal pages rustled like dry leaves, and two thousand voices began, "Praise God from whom all blessings flow."

Hank leaned close. "We sing this one first every Sunday. It gets us into the right frame of mind for worship." As he spoke, his breath gently stirred the tendrils at her temple and she sighed with contentment.

Studying her, Hank noted how the lashes of her half-closed eyes shadowed her cheeks. How angelic her smile seemed. He inhaled her clean, outdoorsy smell and longed to touch his lips to the smooth wrists that held the hymnbook she had plucked from the back of the pew in front of them. He longed to draw her close, so close that the heart in her lithe, graceful body would beat against his. Wait a minute! I shouldn't be thinking of such things in a church service. My mind should be on God.

Her lashes swept up, inviting him into the depths of sapphire eyes. Yes, he realized with joy, my mind should be on God, and it is. Only God could have made a creature as lovely, as mysterious, as wholesome as this woman here beside me. He bowed his head. Thank you, Lord.

He looked at her again. She was frowning now. What was she thinking about with that sharp mind of hers? He hoped it wasn't the campground again. He wondered how there could be so much contention between them when they were plainly meant for each other? What is it that even in the best of times, takes her away from me? Why do we fall into arguments at the slightest excuse?

Reva's arms were folded over her chest and her sharp fingernail nudged him to pay attention.

The song leader now asked people to greet one another. The buzz of talk grew louder as everyone stood and began to hug and shake hands. Hank shook hands with the man behind him. Duty out of the way, he reached for Elaine. She leaned against him for a second before he reluctantly let her go. Maybe a better question would be what makes her open herself for brief moments, and then shut me out again? If only I understood women.

The Bible reading was so well done that Elaine could picture the whole story. Children came to Jesus, but the disciples told them to go away. He took the children in his arms and told his companions never to turn little ones away. Elaine could fairly feel herself enfolded in the arms of the Lord, and it felt a lot like being in the arms of the man who now sat next to her. The preacher spoke of God as a father who loved his children and of an open, easy relationship with him. He said God could direct a life much better than any human being could. Elaine sighed. If only it were that easy--just turn your life over to God--I can't do that. I have to grow up and make decisions that affect the rest of my life--and Scotty's and Granddad's, too. I can't use God as a crutch.

"All that business about trusting God," said Reva, while they waited for Hank to bring the car. "Hank believes it, but I don't. I believe the part in the Bible that says, "God helps those who help themselves." Elaine nodded distractedly as she watched for Hank. She knew Benjamin Franklin had actually said that. But maybe, as much as she hated admitting it, maybe in this one thing Reva and old Ben were right.

When Hank drove up, Reva moved to settle herself in the front seat next to him. She stretched her arm across the seat, allowing Elaine to see the gold filigree bracelet she wore.

"Hank, honey," Reva said fingering the hair on the back of his neck, "you need a haircut." Elaine was embarrassed for him. She liked the way his hair looked, curling softly just short of his collar. "I wish you'd told me sooner about going out to brunch. I have an appointment with one of our investors. I can't get out of it, but why don't you come with me? He hardly believes you exist."

"Most of the time you don't want me around when you're talking to investors." He pushed her hand away. "You'll do fine; you always do."

When they got to the condominium, Hank settled Elaine in the truck and accompanied Reva up to her place. As soon as he returned, they set out for the hotel--without Reva, Elaine thought with a thrill of elation. Elaine had passed up breakfast in favor of saving room for the famous brunch she had heard about from tourists who came to Sacred Spring.

CHAPTER 15

As they turned off the Interstate, Elaine admired the masses of deep red coleus that lined the road without a weed in sight. They must have an army of gardeners who edged and weeded twenty-four hours a day. Hank pulled up to a small guardhouse tended by a stout woman in uniform. "Morning, Mr. Schaefer," she said, waving the old pickup through as if it were a Lexus.

Underneath the broad portico, a parking attendant in Sepoy costume bowed to Elaine and opened her door. She could picture herself as an Eastern princess in a sari descending from a sedan chair. Gently squeezing Elaine's elbow, Hank guided her into the hotel and through several spacious, deeply carpeted lobbies.

A mirrored elephant in a display of East Indian works of art caught her eye, but Hank hurried her along and down a curving stair-case. They entered a large, open room flooded with sunlight from floor-to-ceiling windows.

Near a waterfall cascading down the front of a smooth, shiny piece of dark green marble, a young man in a tuxedo played show tunes on a baby grand piano. The splashing water and the musical notes mingled, adding to Elaine's heady feeling of happiness. Areca palms and Boston fern grew in planters everywhere, while outside, taller palm trees leaned forward, peeking in the windows.

Elaine offered a silent, *thank you*, to Monica for sending her the Paris silk she now had on. It was the prettiest dress in the room, and certainly appropriate.

The hostess led them to a table set with heavy silverware. Elaine admired the woman's skill as she removed pleated napkins from the tops of stemmed glasses and laid them with a flourish next to gold-rimmed plates. She then filled thin china cups with fragrant coffee from a nearby cart. "Help yourselves to the buffet when you're ready," she said.

For Elaine, the sight of the laden tables was a feast in itself. Silver warmers held smoked salmon, Eggs Benedict, and Canadian bacon. She looked at Hank quizzically when she saw a pile of rolls with strange, puffy tops.

"Brioche," Hank said, "and these are croissant." He picked up one of the puffy ones with a pair of tongs, laid it on his plate, and offered to get one for her. "I think you'll like these."

As they moved down the buffet, they came to a life-sized ice swan glistening in the center of a luscious-looking array of sliced melon, wedges of pineapple, grapes, and oranges. "The chef must be quite talented to sculpt a swan like that," Elaine observed.

"They use molds." Hank's eyes twinkled, and Elaine watched closely to see if he might be laughing at her. Maybe he wasn't, but she'd have to act more sophisticated. She was such a rube, in her own estimation.

Noticing that Hank's plate was piled high with delicacies, she looked at her own and found that she had taken more than she could eat, but suddenly her appetite leaped and she decided she'd give it her best try. Even more than physical hunger, she felt a compelling need to communicate with her companion on a deeper level than ever before.

She quietly hummed along with "My Blue Heaven" as they returned to their table. The waitress came to warm their coffee as she sat down. Hank patted her hand, enjoyment written all over his face.

"Do you think we'll have this much fun on our camping trip?" he asked.

"It's not nearly as fancy," she said. "What do you think?"

"Of course we will." Smiling, he popped a grape into her mouth.

Carefully controlling her voice, she continued, "The Boy Scouts are booked for the weekend, so I don't want to leave the Braithwaites alone with that many kids, even though the Scouts have their leaders, so can we possibly go on Monday or Tuesday?"

He stroked his jaw between thumb and forefinger. "That might be a bit hard for Reva."

"Reva? Is she going?" Elaine felt as stunned as if somebody had punched her in the solar plexus.

"I can't make any decisions without her approval. She makes most of the real business decisions. All I do is build. Isn't it all right if she comes?" When she didn't answer right away, he looked up at her with concern. "Is something wrong?"

"No." She shook her head denying the truth with a smile.

"What do you want us to bring, really?" Something was wrong, but Hank figured if she didn't want to tell him, there was no way he could force her to talk.

She was so lovely with her sparkling blue eyes; she was like his sister, Jean, in that way, unspoiled. That small mistake about the ice sculpture had endeared her to him even more. But, he thought, I shouldn't get too sentimental over her. I must keep my mind on business. We'll give her a fair price for her property and that will be that. She'll probably hate me, though, he thought wistfully.

"Don't worry about bringing anything. We have," she counted off on her fingers, "tents, a propane stove, lanterns, flashlights, can opener, bug spray... everything."

"If you're sure." He laid his napkin beside his empty plate.

They talked about their lives again, all the way home in an attempt to learn everything that had happened in the years before they met. Hank listened in such an animated way that Elaine felt witty and beautiful.

At the campground house, Hank walked her to the door where Ira and Scotty waited for a visit with them. When she heard how well they had done along with the Braithwaites, Elaine found herself inexplicably miffed that they had done so well without her.

For the rest of the week, she moved in a bubble of radiance: the thought of the wilderness, the clear, fast-flowing spring run, the canopy of stars—with Hank beside her—was delicious. She tried to ignore the fact that Reva would be an omnipresent and unwelcome guest.

On the day of the trip, Elaine's family was still asleep when she tiptoed through the house to study the sky from the office window. The weather would be the difference between enjoyment and misery. If the gray clouds that now filled the sky should linger, they would shade the river and make the trip cooler.

On the other hand, a long day of clouds usually meant a long night of rain. If the sun came out and they stayed in the middle of the stream where there was no shade, it would probably fry their poor little brains. Well, sun or shade, she'd need plenty of sunscreen. She went back to her room and slathered it on then slipped into a bathing suit, cut-offs and a red tee shirt. With practiced ease, she lifted her hair and twisted it into a ponytail, which she secured with an elastic band.

Ira was sleeping later every day. She worried about him; maybe she should have taken him to see Dr. Potter before they started out. Standing by his bed, she called softly, "Granddad, it's time to get up. We're going camping with Hank today."

He opened his eyes slowly and struggled to focus as Elaine waited. "Laney girl." She saw his long legs stretch our under the sheet and watched him wince from the pain of arthritis. "At first I thought you was Belle." The skin around his eyes pinked with unshed tears.

"You've been tired lately, haven't you?" she asked, sitting on the edge of the bed. "Are you sure you feel like going?"

"I've got to make that jaunt one more time," he murmured. "Let me get these old bones moving." The bedsprings creaked as she stood up. "You need new pajamas," she said.

"Collar frayed? Could you turn it like your grandma always did? I surely do like these pjs.

"Frayed not," she joked. "I don't know how to sew. I'm not very useful, am I?" She tried making light of it, though she felt sad. No one should have to work so hard or go without so much in old age. "Annie could teach me to turn collars, darn socks, and sew on buttons," she said, knowing she would never ask. She patted his shoulder. "I'll wake Scotty."

"You go along." Ira slid his legs off the bed. "I'm ambulating fine now."

Elaine went to the kitchen and measured coffee into the percolator. She heard it start to bubble as she checked the packages of food piled on the table. Scotty came to stand at the sink and wolf down her cereal before offering to help her.

"Those lightweight nylon tents Mother sent you and Granddad for Christmas are on the porch. The sleeping bags take up too much room, and it's too hot for them anyway, so we'll take a couple of sheets for each of us. Can you get all that and stow it under the canoe seats?

"Okay," Scotty said. "Which canoes do you want?"

"The yellow one, but leave the blue one in case someone wants to rent it; it's more stable. You and I will use the red one. It's downright dangerous for anyone who hasn't gone down the run in it at least half a dozen times.

Hank and Reva arrived as Elaine returned from checking with the Braithwaites at the Old Mill. Reva, in white walking shorts and a crisp green-and-white striped shirt, wore immaculate white athletic shoes with green stripes down the sides. Monica would approve. Elaine wondered if Reva had a pair of hundred-dollar shoes for every garment in her closet. I hope she doesn't expect them to stay white, Elaine thought.

Quelling pangs of jealousy, she led them into the kitchen and poured cups of coffee. "You look nice, Reva," she forced herself to say. It was true but Elaine wished politeness had not dictated that she say it.

"Hank helped me find this outfit when I told him I wanted to look especially good for him on this trip." She moved close to Hank who stood with his back against the counter. "We don't get away together like this very often."

"Howdy, folks." Ira came in and reached for the coffee pot. He nodded to Hank and Reva. "We're about ready to go." He rocked back on his heels like an eager teenager, slopping coffee onto the floor. As she tore off a paper towel and knelt to wipe up the spill, Elaine could tell he felt better now that he was moving around. She pointed at the bags of food. "You can take these and go on down," she said. "I'll be right there." Her emotions were running wild and she needed a moment to herself.

"We'll go along then," Hank agreed. "I've got a kit, and Reva has a couple of bags. Shall I stow them too?" He carefully scrutinized her expression. The green fire in his eyes made goose bumps rise all over her body.

"If there's room," she snapped.

"Are you sure you don't want me to come back for you?" She shook her head, telling herself she might as well try to stay detached because this trip might be the last time she'd see him—until they closed on the campground.

Hank and Reva set their empty mugs down, picked up their bags, and followed Ira out. Elaine wondered if Hank had any idea how she felt. She wondered if humans exuded anything as potent and unseen as the pheromones moths used to attract mates.

Being near Hank made it difficult to keep a clear mind. She found herself wanting to please him, wanting what he wanted, and resenting Reva's intrusion into her life. Tension seized her by the neck and twisted downward gripping her shoulders in stiff bands. No matter what happened, a chapter of her life was closing.

Pausing a moment outside the back door, she gazed at the house intending to fix every detail in her memory; but then she was forced to see the peeling paint, the sagging porch, and the faded shingles on the roof.

We need to run the mower, she thought, ashamed of the weeds growing around the doorstep. She heard the creak on the dead branch on the oak that grew over the Old Mill and lowered her head in desperation. I just can't keep up, she thought.

"You okay?" Hank had approached silently. Opening her eyes, she saw him standing before her, his face filled with compassion. "What's wrong?" he asked.

"Nothing."

A frown creased Hank's forehead. Since they were committed to spending two days and a night together, he wanted to avoid an argument.

"Well, I am a bit worried about that gigantic branch over the Old Mill." There was no use telling him all her troubles, she thought. That one thing should be enough to distract him. "I'll have it lopped off one of these days." she said as if he had spoken. "Meanwhile," her voice was brittle, "no major storm has ever hit this area, so I'm not really too worried."

Hank touched her shoulder. "Now that you're brought it up, it wouldn't take a major storm to knock that branch through the roof. Why don't you let me fix it?"

"Maybe someday." She shrugged off his hand, uncomfortable with the intensity of his gaze. "The others are waiting, shall we go?"

CHAPTER 16

Ira, Scotty, and Reva stood waiting down by the river. As Elaine and Hank approached, all three began to talk at once.

"Let's go, the sun is coming out and it's getting hot," said Ira.

"Can I steer, and may Rags go too?" asked Scotty, pulling on Elaine's arm.

"I'm going with Hank," Reva stated in a flat voice that demanded compliance.

"All right," Elaine said. "Here's what we'll do. Granddad, please get in the yellow canoe with Hank and Reva. They aren't used to the spring run, so they'll need you to steer."

"Scotty and I are taking this one, and yes, Rags can go." Rags jumped into the red canoe and Scotty ran ahead and stood behind it ready to push it into the water while the dog faced the spring, head to the wind, like the masthead on a ship. "Shove them off first, then us," Elaine said.

"Would you mind sitting in the middle?" Elaine told Reva when she noticed the small woman had arranged herself ramrod straight in the back of the yellow canoe. "We need experienced paddlers at the ends."

"Are you sure this thing won't tip?" The boat trembled as she began to crawl forward.

"Not if we're careful," Ira answered. "No shenanigans, kids." He shook his finger, smiling with mischief.

"What does that mean?" Reva asked with a scowl as she awkwardly made her way to the middle seat on her hands and knees.

"They like to fool around; throw snake grass at each other and such." Tenderness rested on Ira's face. "They enjoy turning canoes over."

Reva's dark eyes widened. Though what he said was true, Granddad's attitude was that of a gleeful jokester sticking pins in Reva's pride. "They were always a lot of trouble, those over-turned canoes, I mean, everything and everybody spilled out, and then we had to dive for some of it, if it was heavy, that is. Some things floated okay. Can you float, young lady?"

"Oh," Reva shuddered and darted a mistrustful look at Elaine. The message was clear, *don't you dare!* Ira chuckled.

"Put on your life jacket, it's under the seat," Elaine said. "You'll be fine." She hated to admit it because it seemed mean, but she relished Reva's discomfort. The woman obviously belonged in a boardroom or drawing room, not out on the water where the wrong move could be life threatening. We'll watch out for her, Elaine vowed.

Scotty pushed the yellow canoe off the sand, then pushed the red one and jumped in before it was fully in the water. They took up their paddles and moved out into the current in perfect synchronization. They always tried to stay in the center, away from the masses of water lilies and sawgrass that could hide cottonmouth moccasins and alligators. Scotty held them on course by using the paddle first on once side and then on the other.

"There's one," the boy said, indicating an alligator sunbathing on a sand bar. As the creature slid into the water, Rags sprang up onto the seat next to Scotty, barking wildly.

Elaine twisted around to order the dog to lie down in the bottom of the boat. She smiled at the sight of Scotty perched on the back of the canoe in his swim trunks, his happy eyes and joyful grin the embodiment of boys and summertime.

"That was only a six-footer," he said. "Look over there." Several gators lay together on a sandy bank. "We got lots more now than when I was little, don't we?"

"They were endangered then," she answered, her back to him as they paddled. "Now people are endangered if they aren't careful around them."

"I'll draw one of those licenses to hunt when I grow up," Scotty announced. "That's called 'culling.'" She supposed somebody had to keep the gators in check, but she hoped she'd never have to kill a gator or anything else.

"You don't shoot them in the head if you want to take them to a taxi…" Scotty paused.

"Dermist."

"Yeah, taxidermist, because their whole head is bone and it will explode and the stuffing guy can't fix it to look like it oughta."

A silence fell and finally the sense of peace that always came to Elaine when she was on the spring run came over her. Water drops made a splashing every time she stroked into the river with the oars, keeping the canoe on course.

The sky had cleared to deep blue with cloud puffs stretching across the horizon like strings of popcorn. As the canoes floated on a slower current for a while, Elaine lifted her face to a cooling breeze. Cicadas thrummed, pulsed, purred, and fell silent in turn. Red-winged black birds clung to cattails along the bank calling to each other like kids playing with their voices.

The scenery offered an infinite variety if an observer knew what to look for. Palmettos, which looked like palm fronds coming straight out of the ground, and pines, grew on high ground, while the places where sable palm grew meant the land was low and boggy.

Taller palms, because of their shallow root system, had fallen to the banks, but continued to grow. If she found she needed to stop the canoe, she knew she could catch hold of one of the small oak, hickory, or sweet bay branches that grew within reach of the boats. It was dangerous, though, because highly poisonous cottonmouth moccasins loved to sleep draped over the branches in patches of sunlight.

Her heartbeat quickened. There were two fat ones now. In a stupor from the heat, they lay motionless and nearly invisible, looking like dirty clothes that didn't quite make it into the hamper. With only an instant's hesitation, Elaine decided not to point them out. Scotty would want to paddle closer so he could knock them off and watch them fall into the water. If they landed in a canoe, however, everybody would have to vacate immediately. Reva sure wouldn't like that.

If the snake came into the water after them, they didn't stand a chance because those snakes were master swimmers and could bite underwater just as easily as on land.

They rounded a bend and saw raccoon fishing at the water's edge. She imagined that the bandit eyes in the furry face were looking at her reproachfully as the canoes swept past. Fluffy, ringed tails like his too often flew from the antennas of pickups with oversized wheels and gun racks.

The other canoe came abreast as the stream widened. Hank had removed his shirt and his powerful muscles stretched and expanded as he paddled. She had to admit she still didn't know much about this tall, confident man, not nearly as much as she would like to.

What a picture she made, Hank thought, sitting so straight and proud with her blond hair shining in the sun. "It's prime land, all right," he said, knowing he was already beginning to care more about her than about her property.

Look at those shapely arms, browned by the sun, smooth and strong as they moved with the paddles. Her sky-reflecting eyes gazed shyly back across the water. She was a tremendously vital and exciting woman, totally without artifice, whose manner told him plainly that she felt out of her element in the company of men older than ten or younger than seventy. He turned his gaze back toward the scenery and gave a deep sigh. Too bad life couldn't always be like this.

For the next couple of hours, the five people in the two small boats paddled on, lost in a steamy but tranquil dream. It was about noon when Scotty's wail broke the silence. "I'm hungry! When are we stopping for lunch?"

"Yeah, Miss Laney. I'm starved, too," Hank teased.

"How about the hummock over there? It looks firm and dry," Elaine said.

"Yeah, and look, a lagoon to swim in." Scotty's wiggly enthusiasm caused the boat to rock.

"I'm burning up, too," she answered. "But we've seen several gators. I don't think it's safe."

"Ah, Laney, we always swim on a canoe trip," Scotty whined.

She looked around the small lagoon and saw no sign of the fearsome beasts. After this, she would probably never be back; and she did love swimming in spite of the dangers. Echoing Ira's longing for one more time, she told Scotty, "Okay, but just for a minute. Now paddle!"

Elaine and Scotty paddled fast and hard in perfect synchronization, driving the canoe up onto the bank. As they came to an abrupt halt, Elaine jumped out, gave the painter a tug, and safely beached it further up. "How about you, Reva?" The other woman gripped the sides of the canoe as Elaine jerked it forward. "Would you like to go in the water with us?"

"No thank you!" she shuddered. "I'm staying right here."

"You and Granddad can watch the food." Elaine double-looped the lines around the roots of a tree. She was hurrying now, looking forward to plunging into the cold water.

"Come on, Hank." Scotty jumped out of the canoe and started bouncing up and down, making the islet tremble. "I can make my own earthquake. How come?"

"A hummock's mostly roots and tightly packed vegetation—not much solid dirt. You can look around in a little while. Sometimes hummocks have ancient Indian mounds made of discarded shells. You might find a relic."

"I think we'll get rid of these little islands," Reva announced as she pulled her cell phone from the pocket of her shorts and started jabbing keys. She studied the device and announced, "It'll cost plenty, but their configurations ruin the *feng shui* of the stream."

"Whoopee!" shouted Scotty, ignoring Reva's comments and Elaine's dismay. He took a running leap that ended in a splash. Rags followed and started swimming fast with her head high to keep her nose and ears out of the water.

Elaine peeled down to her bathing suit and splashed through the shallows into the delicious coolness of the lagoon. She rolled onto her back to float and watched Reva trying to talk Hank out of his swim. Doing a quick flip, she jackknifed and swam underwater, reveling in the iciness that was quickly reviving her energy.

A disturbance made her look through the water in time to see Hank's legs, his muscular torso, and his scrunched up face coming down. When all three heads bobbed up, Elaine thought of otters, those incorrigible playboys of the swamps.

"Whoo, this feels great!" Hank shouted lifting his hands in the air.

Elaine absorbed his happiness and made it her own. Euphoric, she was about to challenge him to a race when Reva screamed.

Searching frantically for the source of the distress, Elaine spotted an alligator cruising down the run heading for their lagoon. Rags paddled blissfully, unaware of her mortal peril. By looking at the length of the gator's snout, Elaine estimated the total length of the beast at about fourteen feet—a ton of appetite driven by a brain smaller than a potato chip.

"Hank!" she shouted. However, he had already seen and headed for the boy, who had set out to rescue Rags.

"Don't go near her!" Hank yelled.

"Get over here, Laney girl, and grab a hold of this." Ira called from the bank. Black fear for her brother's life overcame Elaine's ability to think as she headed blindly toward where her grandfather stood making a loop in the end of a coil of rope. When she realized what he planned, she breathed a prayer of thanksgiving that they had brought the thick, strong rope.

"Throw it to Hank," Granddad ordered

That wasn't what she intended at all. The creature could easily snap off Hank's strong brown arm or decimate a long, lean leg. "No, I'll..."

"Hurry up!" Hank shouted.

Attracted by Scotty's thrashing movement, the huge animal turned and cruised smoothly and soundlessly toward the boy. Elaine would have to obey. Hank was closer. Adrenalin pumped through her body, making her responses sure and swift. She threw the rope. Hank caught it and glanced at Ira for further instruction.

"Loop it around the snout!" Granddad yelled.

Hank swallowed hard and Elaine began to thrash and yell in order to distract the reptile, almost losing her nerve when it turned toward her, displaying its diabolical grim.

She looked into its pale yellow eyes with the slitted black pupils down the middle. Such a beast would be thick-headedly confident that whatever it wanted, it would have. No land animal in the swamp was bigger; surely, nothing ever escaped it. Oh why, had she decided they could swim today? She felt sick with fear and regret.

"If that alligator hurts one hair on Hank's body," Reva screamed, "I'll sue you until you can't even squeak!"

In one quick, fluid motion, Hank slipped the noose around the snout and yanked it tight, sealing shut the fearsome jaws. Elaine knew the lower mandible was weak on a gator, so it was now anatomically impossible for him to break his mouth open. Just as the beast's reflexes took over, Hank pulled hard on the rope, one end of which Granddad had attached to a tree.

"Okay, son, get away from him now. He'll do the rest." Hank moved away and true to instinct when caught or trying to drown prey, the beast rotated like meat on a spit, wrapping itself in the rope. Hank grabbed the dog and they all headed for the bank to watch as the gator began to sink.

"It's time to pull that critter out now; we don't want it to drown," Ira shouted as he hauled on the rope. "It's still against the law to kill them, not like back in my day."

The mummified body was immobile, but Hank and Elaine joined Ira in pulling it in like a big fish. It soon laid half in and half out of the water. From the end of its snout to the pointed tip of its tail, it was exactly the same length as the red canoe.

Ira pulled a hunting knife out of the scabbard at his side. "Get in the boat, kids."

"What are you going to do?" Elaine asked.

"Hack off a mess of gator tail for supper." Ira grinned, and Elaine knew he was teasing. "No, honey, I'll just cut this here rope, and we'll be on our way before he figures out he's free and comes after us again. I bet this is one mad behemoth."

"But, Granddad," Scotty piped, "we didn't eat our lunch, yet."

"Son, if you don't want to *be* lunch, jump in that boat."

Hank touched Scotty's shoulder. "We'll find another hummock and this time, we'll stay out of the water."

"Stop running your mouths, I'm cutting the rope." Ira walked over to the gator's side, hunkered down, and sliced through the coils. He stepped back quickly while the gator was still whipping back and forth trying to get free.

Hank pulled Ira out of danger just before the animal's tail could hit his leg and break it. Elaine felt another stab of fear as she saw how colorless Ira's face was becoming. She walked beside him to the canoe, not visibly supporting him, but there in case he needed her.

"Are you all right?" she asked.

With visible effort, he roused himself and held her off with a wave. "We got to get out of here. He'll be free in a minute, and he ain't seen nothing to change what little mind he's got about coming after us. Thank you, Hank for all you done," he said. "You're a brave man."

"I must say the same for you, sir." Hank saluted before clambering into the canoe and shoving off with Reva hanging on to the seat with all her might. Looking back, Elaine saw the big alligator struggling to crawl farther up onto the beach, shedding strands of rope as it went.

After they beached the canoes downstream, Elaine hauled the small cooler out from under the seat and rummaged for sandwiches. "That's funny," she muttered, pausing with one in her hand.

Both canoes should be loaded to the gunwales, but there's too much room. Something's missing. Why didn't I notice before?

She ran over her mental checklist. Food box, utensil bag, sheets and blankets, tents, tents! No! Maybe they were in the other canoe, but they wouldn't both fit. Maybe there was one, then. Putting the food back in the cooler, she scrambled up to look in the other canoe where she found one tent, but only one. She moved aside some baggage.

"Scotty!" she yelled.

He and Rags came running from where they had been playing close to the water. "Where's the other tent?" she asked, her voice rising slightly.

His eyebrows drew together. "Oh, yeah. After I loaded the one, I had to count my key collection in case anybody stole any while we were gone. I just remembered the other tent right now."

"You didn't pack it? Scotty! I trusted you." She sighed. "Now what? You can't put men and women in the same tent."

"How come?" he asked. "That's a big tent. We can all get in it."

She shook her head despairingly. "You don't understand."

"Don't be mad. Us men can sleep outside."

"Yes," she said, trying to be patient, "but it's going to rain."

"Then why can't we all sleep together? Wouldn't that be cozy? You like cozy, don't you?" She shook her head. This wasn't the time to explain about propriety.

He shrugged, giving up. He wouldn't get the obviously interesting nugget of information right now. He could tell, however, from the agitation exhibited by his sister that it was worth pursuing in the future. "When are we going to eat? I'm hungry," he said.

She drew a long, slow breath and let it escape in an audible sigh. "Here, hand these around," she said, giving him a stack of sandwiches. "We'll worry about the tent later."

"Are we going to get chiggers? I hate them worse than ticks because they get under your skin and itch bad."

"I hope not." She schooled herself to patience. "Go on now, hand out the food, and I'll get the bug repellent."

When lunch was over and they were again paddling instead of floating along on the current, Elaine saw the distant sky as a gray steel curtain, descending upon the last act of a play. Where they were, the sun was shining, but in one spot on the horizon, a wide column of lighter gray seemed to fall to earth like silvery folds of chiffon. That meant rain no more than five miles away, about where they would camp for the night. Please dissipate so we can pitch a dry camp, she pleaded with the clouds.

Hank looked across as the canoes floated side by side. "These springs are awesome," he said, fracturing her worried concentration. "It must be deep here, but the bottom looks like its right up under us."

"I'd guess it's about twelve feet," she answered, studying the moss-covered limbs lying in the depths below. "Those branches down there look like petrified wood."

"You suppose they were blown off in some prehistoric hurricane?"

She nodded, feeling sleepy in the afternoon humidity. "Hurricanes are great pruners."

"Look!" he whispered. Three soft-shell turtles, stacked like fallen dominoes, sun bathed on a log. As the canoe glided by, they slid off into the tannin-brown water: plop, plop, plop. "Weren't they great?" Hank's voice was low, but jubilant. "Heaven must be like this."

"Yes," Elaine whispered in full agreement, knowing that his company was a major part of her feeling of well-being and security.

In the late afternoon, they came upon a tall, feathery cypress. "This is where we camp," Elaine said. "That tree is called Methuselah; it was a sapling when Christ was born."

"Over two thousand years old?" Hank breathed.

"They found a bristlecone pine in California that was three thousand years older than that." Elaine noticed she had everyone's attention. "Guess how they found out how old it was." No one answered. "They cut it down and counted the rings."

"What a terrible waste," Hank said.

"That's what I'm trying to tell you."

"I know, Elaine, I know."

This wasn't the time to spar. "Well, we're here now. Let's get unpacked," she called. As they ran the boats onto the bank, Reva stepped out first--into rich dark soil called "muck" that spread a black line halfway up her white shoes. Elaine watched with dread as Reva balanced on one foot and held up the mucked one for everybody to see.

"It's disgusting. How can any place be this filthy? Get me a handkerchief." She snapped her fingers and her squire, Scotty, fetched Granddad's, which he obligingly held out.

"Here, let me help you," Hank said at her side.

"Why did she come if she hates camping so much?" Elaine asked.

"She's okay," The bronzed muscles in his bare chest and back rippling, he lifted the tent onto one shoulder. "She just isn't used to roughing it."

"The mosquitoes will be biting pretty soon. Would you like me to bring your shirt?" Elaine didn't care about Reva any more.

"No, thanks. They don't like me--something about my body chemistry. Besides, if one did, it would give you an excuse to wallop me again. You'd like that wouldn't you?" He grinned, showing even white teeth.

"I sure would," she said, forced to laugh. "But seriously, if I'd known they weren't actually biting you, I might not have smacked you so hard."

"Sure." His glance was doubtful.

"Well, mosquitoes eat me up."

"That's because you're so yummy," he said. She decided that as hungry as he looked, she'd better get the campfire going and cook supper.

Reva sidled over to join them. She moved close to Hank, took his other arm, and placed it around her waist. "I won't be able to get the mud off my new shoes, and I certainly can't imagine people doing this camping stuff voluntarily," she said in disgust. Elaine ground her teeth as she watched them walk away.

After a supper of delicious homemade stew, Hank pulled a harmonica from his pocket and sat down next to Elaine. She remembered her cousin Nick playing his guitar on family campouts. With delighted anticipation, she poked a stick at the coals and watched sparks fly as Hank's mouth caressed the small musical instrument.

She loved sitting near a fire listening to an instrument played close and sweet with wood smoke rising like incense into the twilight. Now the sweet mournful tones of "I'm So Lonesome I Could Cry" slowly found their way, one-by-one into the deepest recesses of Elaine's heart.

A glacier of repressed feeling, which had been accumulating over a lifetime of self-control, began to melt, causing the sweet release of tears to flood her being. The feeling reminded her of the deluge of tears when she was a child and had fallen, and skinned her knee. She ignored the hurt until she arrived safely within Granddad's arms, where she was able to let go and simply soak up his love and warmth.

Hank's heart wrenched at seeing her hunched over with her arms wrapped around her knees, crying as if she would never stop, but something told him to keep on playing. When she began to look up again, he palmed the harmonica. "Request time," he announced.

For almost an hour, he played every song his audience named in a lively competition to find titles he might not know. They couldn't stump him. Elaine wondered where and how he had learned so much by heart. Elaine and Reva sang along establishing a truce as long as the music lasted. Elaine would have been happy to sing a few more songs and go to bed, but Scotty paced around the fire like a caged panther.

"Let's go for a walk." He stopped at her side and looked down, waiting for an answer.

"I'm not going anywhere," Reva declared. "It's the dead of night. Hank, you stay here with me."

"What's going on?" Ira stirred on his pallet, and Elaine realized he'd been asleep.

"We're going for a flashlight walk, Granddad," Elaine answered. "You want to go?"

"Yep," Granddad said. Hank jumped up to steady him as he rose, bracing his hands on his knees. "Thanks, son."

"Come on, hurry!" Scotty urged. "I heard something over there. We got to try and catch it."

"You don't even know what it is," Reva said with a sigh. "How do you know you'll want it after you've got it?"

CHAPTER 17

"Walk, Rags." Scotty's voice fanned the dog's enthusiasm, which was already at fever pitch from hearing her favorite word. Rags began to yip and run in circles.

"Okay." Elaine dug into a canvas bag and handed around flashlights. "It'll have to be short." She pulled out the last one and switched it on. "Scotty and I will share."

Rags raced back and forth as they strolled to the water's edge, her frenzy taking her near Reva. The woman kicked out, barely missing the furry bottom. When they got to the water, Rags quieted and began to trot along, sniffing the sand as the flashlight beams swept its surface.

"Looky at them alligator eyeballs a-shinin' red in the light." Scotty nudged Elaine.

"They look like running lights on a boat, don't they?" she whispered.

The adults stood bunched together, and in the darkness, Elaine felt Reva shudder. "I never want to see another alligator as long as I live!"

"Nothing's going to hurt you," Elaine beamed her flashlight to illuminate the other woman's face and moved it quickly to her waist, yep, as she expected, encircled by Hank's arm. She jerked the light away. "Come on, then. Stoop down so you can get under this spider web."

Ira pointed his flashlight at the silken barrier stretched across the trail. In its center sat a golden orb with eight spindly legs radiating from her body. Black fuzz on each joint resembled a leg warmer. With the circumference of the legs, she looked as big as a saucer.

"Wow, she's huge." Scotty whispered, craning his neck. "Is that little bitty brown spider her husband or her supper?" He thought a minute, then said, "Both, I bet." When the female moved, Scotty jumped back. "They're cool," he said.

"I'm not about to crawl under that web thing." Reva turned away.

"No, wait!" Scotty grabbed her arm. "Give me the flashlight, Laney. Wait!" They all watched as a shiny brown June bug was caught in the web. Its struggles, rather than setting it free, caused the sticky threads to entangle it more. The mistress of the house ran down the web, grabbed the bug, and started to wrap it, rotating it with her back legs into a cocoon-like mass. Soon all that was left of the bumbling creature was a tiny, slowly pulsating ball.

"When she gets hungry, she'll suck the juice out of it," Scotty notified Reva, who made a low sound of disgust.

"I can't bear this." Reva moved away from the group muttering, "Alligators, spiders...don't you people do anything civilized?"

"Civilized?" Elaine asked, annoyed at the condescending tone.

"Well--plays, art exhibits, estate auctions," Reva spluttered.

"She likes kick-boxing, too," said Hank, "and bullfights."

"Bullfights?" Scotty asked. "Can I go, Miss Reva?"

"No!" she said without hesitation.

"My friend's dad fights roosters," Scotty said, but Elaine covered his mouth before he could start negotiating for an exchange: I'll take you to the rooster fights if you'll take me to the bullfights.

Tired of all the talk and ready to move on, Scotty ducked under the spider web. He swept his flashlight across the path. "Hear that noise? It's over there somewhere," he whispered.

"Come on, Reva," Hank encouraged her, "the web is at least four feet off the ground, and you'd hardly have to bend over."

Reva waited to see if he would change his mind, but when he didn't, she deliberately walked through the web, destroying hours of the spider's work. Suddenly, she began to scream and flap her hands around her head and shoulders. "Get it off!" she cried.

"It's not on you," Elaine said, taking Reva's shoulder and giving it a shake. "Look. It's dangling from what's left of the web."

"There it is!" Scotty cried and Reva's problems were forgotten. His light focused on an animal with a long pointed snout and layers of leather-like jointed armor. The creature's ears were pink and pointed, and it had long sharp claws with which it scrabbled at a deepening hole at the side of the trail.

"You brought me out here to look at a stupid armadillo?" Reva squawked.

"They can't help it 'cause they're stupid," Scotty said. He looked at Reva as though he might change his mind about liking her so much. The animal stopped digging and rose on its back legs, his pink nose smelling the air because he couldn't see well enough to know who and what was there.

Elaine knew that Scotty and Reva were both right about its intelligence, but it had no natural enemies, and its thick, rubbery exoskeleton protected it from predators, except for bobcats and big dogs.

"Skitchem, Rags!" Scotty yelled, showing off. The dog was smaller than the armadillo, but game for anything.

"Be quiet. Let us look at him." Elaine poked Scotty in the back, but it was too late; Rags had gone right up behind the armadillo and was barking a high-pitched racket that resonated through the woods. Becoming alarmed, the animal sprang away, crashing through the undergrowth with Rags in pursuit.

"You liked him, didn't you, Miss Reva?" Scotty asked, eagerly tilting his face toward hers. "Do you want me to find another one and catch it for you? It's easy, all you got to do is grab 'em by the tail."

"Absolutely not." Reva wrapped her arms around herself, and Elaine began to wonder if she might be genuinely distressed. "I want to go home. Can we at least go back to camp?" Her voice caught with tears.

"Well sure, Miss Reva," said Ira, obviously still in thrall. "Let's take her back. Us gents will sleep out under the stars," he said, "and you ladies can have the tent." He patted Reva's narrow back, and she looked archly over her shoulder at Elaine with a small, satisfied smile.

Ha! Elaine thought, she's about as helpless as a civet.

A few coals still glowed in the campfire as Elaine and Reva passed it to enter the tent. Elaine put on an oversized tee shirt with a UCF logo on the front.

"I went to Smith," Reva said in a haughty voice, as if everyone knew Smith was superior to any school on the planet. Elaine managed to keep her mouth shut.

"Where's my air mattress?" Reva demanded.

"I'm sorry; they take up too much room." Elaine rolled over on her side with her back to Reva.

"You people don't know anything about comfort, do you?" Reva said. She got under the sheet fully dressed as if ready for more trauma and disaster in the night.

"I'm comfortable." Elaine turned her head and saw that the back of Reva's hand rested on her forehead in the pose of a damsel in distress. When she sighed her last frustrated sigh and was quiet, Elaine lay staring into the darkness. Hank is right out there on the other side of the thin piece of fabric, she thought.

"What a great day we've had!" Hank said. As Elaine startled awake, she thought he was in the tent. She found herself wishing he was.

"Yep," agreed Ira. "I like being around you young people, but now it's time to sleep." He sounded weary. "Can you put that fire out, son? Get her out good. We don't need any forest fires." Elaine imagined Hank walking down to the water with the empty coffee pot and bringing it back. *Shish*, the fire said.

"Granddad uses sand," Scotty piped up.

As the men quieted, Elaine closed her eyes again. Halfway between waking and sleeping, she heard Scotty whisper, "Boy, it was scary almost being eaten by an alligator. If he got me, I'd be dead, wouldn't I?" The little boy's voice quivered slightly.

"Yes, you would." Hank sounded tired, but patient. "I should never have let you and your sister get into the water."

"But she did it all the time when she was my age." Listening from her sleeping bag, Elaine grinned.

"Times change," Hank answered drowsily.

"Hank," Scotty asked, "Do you ever pray?"

"Sure do," the man's deeper tone answered. "I couldn't get through a day without it. How about you?"

"Granddad teaches me, don't you, Granddad?" The answer was a gentle snore.

"He's asleep," Scotty reported.

"Well, we'd best get some sleep, too," Hank said. But Scotty was not to be put off.

"Who do you pray to, God or Jesus?"

Elaine's brother was into one of his philosophical discussions. As she lay in the tent listening, she was glad Hank had to answer instead of her.

"I'd say I pray to God," Hank replied, "but I really don't know whether it makes any difference or not. God, Jesus, and the Holy Spirit are all the same person, you know."

"Why don't you pray to Jesus? I like him."

"That's fine," Hank said.

"I like Jesus, though," insisted Scotty. "He's more like my friend."

"He does love you."

"You mean Granddad?"

"Yes, your grandfather loves you, but so does God." Hank cleared his throat. Elaine waited, and he cleared it again, then went on. "He created you because he wants you to be his friend and companion. He made every one different from every other person. No one else can take your special place in God's heart or in the world."

"I don't understand all that. I wish I'd hurry and grow up."

More silence. Elaine knew Scotty lay on his blanket, thinking deep thoughts. She wondered if everyone was as special to God as Hank said. She had to admire the certainty in his voice. He believed it, anyway.

"Hank?" Scotty's voice came again, jolting Elaine awake—probably Hank, too.

"Yeah?"

"What does God want me to do?"

"He wants you to give him your life and then talk everything over with him so he can take care of you." She heard a rustle and imagined Hank turning toward the boy.

"I'd like that, but I don't know how."

"Um," Hank mused, "why do you want to?"

"Did you?"

"Yes."

"Then I want to." Scotty had developed a great admiration for Hank.

"That's not a good enough reason, ole buddy." Hank wasn't making anything easy for the boy.

"Maybe he doesn't want me," Scotty said. "I've been bad. I told lies, I disobeyed Laney and Granddad lots of times, and sometimes my friend, Harold, and I swore."

"The way I see it, sin is doing whatever we want to do or think we ought to do without getting to know God and praying about what he wants."

"But I did something else." Scotty's voice held a tremor of fear.

"What?"

"I stole something at the Crossroads."

"What did you steal?" Hank sounded serious, as if he knew the boy was searching his own heart, finding the sins of an eight-year-old, and suffering for them.

"Bubble gum one time when Laney wasn't looking." His voice quivered with emotion as he spoke softly and reluctantly. Elaine could hardly hear him. She wondered if she should even be listening, but couldn't see any way to avoid it, even if she wanted to.

"Maybe you should go down and tell Mrs. Cumberly and pay for it. But you can still ask Jesus into your heart because he knows all about everything you've ever done; and loves you anyway. Someday we'll talk some more about these things. You see, Scotty, here's another thing that's hard to understand, but if you work on it and ask him to help, you may come to understand some of what it means. When Jesus died on the cross, he was the sacrifice for our sins, mistakes, failings, and shortcomings. He traded his brilliance for our dullness and now he wants us to let that brilliance shine." He paused. "Look, buddy, try praying something like this." Hank was silent as if trying to choose the perfect words for such an important occasion.

Elaine listened with body, heart, and soul.

"Lord Jesus," Hank prayed.

"Don't I close my eyes?" asked Scotty.

"If you want to."

"Okay. They're closed."

"Lord Jesus," Hank began again.

"Lord Jesus," Scotty repeated.

"I open my heart and my life to you."

Scotty repeated everything Hank said, his voice telling Elaine he meant it from the depths of his being. Elaine found herself praying along, wanting what they were talking about. Suddenly, Scotty's voice cracked, and Elaine, too, began weeping without really knowing why. "You okay, buddy?" Hank asked.

"Yeah. I know big boys shouldn't cry, but I can't help it."

"It's all right," Hank reassured him. "Sometimes when we sense God is near and that he really does love us, we cry. Even big boys, even me." Hank's voice had a catch in it too. "It's partly because we've needed to know these things for such a long time."

Elaine wondered about what Hank said. As a biologist, she knew tears relieved stress. However, these tears felt different. They came accompanied by the warmest, most loved feeling she'd ever had, one that transcended the melancholy she'd experienced while Hank was playing his harmonica. But why cry when you're so happy, you're almost hearing heavenly choirs? Love is complicated. God loves us; Granddad loves us; Annie loves us; Hank loves everybody, including Reva. She felt her limbs go numb with fatigue. Moreover, I love Hank, even if I can't have him. I know that now. She pulled the band from her hair and spread the still-damp strands over her pillow.

Scent and sounds of the nighttime swamp receded as Elaine floated on the incoming tide of sleep. She drifted in her dreams, swirled by troubled currents of longing and despair, reaching out for Hank. Even as his arms enfolded her, foreboding stole her happiness. The gentle, supporting flow turned vicious, pulling, dragging them toward a thundering vortex. Elaine's eyes flew open. The thunder was real! Streaks of lightning lit the inside of the tent.

CHAPTER 18

"It's starting to rain; come inside before you get soaked." Raindrops pelted Elaine's shirt as she knelt beside Ira. She shook him. He half turned and groaned, still asleep.

When she saw that he was awake, she roused Hank, then Scotty, and hustled them into the tent. Hank stood blinking in the yellow glow of the flashlight. He looked so sleepy and tousled that Elaine wanted to tuck him in and kiss him good night. But, she thought, I must tuck everybody in, not just Hank. The light also revealed Reva with her arms and legs sprawled, taking up the center of the tent.

"We'll have to move her," Hank said taking charge. He bent to pick her up.

"What are you doing?" Elaine hissed.

"She's taking up too much room." Completely at ease with the situation, he held Reva lightly, with her head lolling against his chest.

"Put her over there by the wall," Elaine said. "How come she doesn't wake up?"

"She takes sleeping pills, and they really knock her out. I think she's addicted, but I don't know how to help her."

"You know a lot about her sleeping habits," Elaine said tersely. She squeezed her lips together immediately.

"Common family knowledge," Hank answered, stepping to the far side of the tent.

Elaine hurried over with a blanket for his unconscious burden. She hesitated. "I'll sleep next to her. Scotty, you can sleep in the middle, then Granddad, then you, Hank." Ira awkwardly lowered himself to the ground.

"Your arthritis?" she asked.

"I'm fine, honey. You get some sleep."

Contrary to Ira's directive, she lay wondering about the relationship between Hank and Reva. They'd known each other all their lives, but they didn't act like old friends, brother and sister, or girl friend and boyfriend. She wondered what besides business kept them together. *I wonder why he treats her as if she were a child that needs looking after, and why she's so possessive and controlling.*

Elaine turned her attention to the soft rhythms of thrumming cicadas. In a short time, she felt sleep creeping into her limbs. She took a deep breath and, lulled by the pattering rain, let go of the day's problems and fell asleep. From time to time, she woke, hearing drum rolls of faraway thunder, but for most of the night, she slept as if she, too, were drugged.

The sharply repeated chirp of a cardinal woke her. In her mind's eye, she saw his perky red crest, shoe-button eyes, and stout orange bill. She heard his mate answer and smiled to herself at the way cardinals seemed to share their lives by giving each other seeds beak to beak as gifts.

Surfeited with sleep, Elaine opened her eyes and saw sunshine filtering through the nylon, turning the tent into a glowing green shell. Hank's long body lay next to her, his thigh welded to hers. She tried to figure out how he got there as the nerves in her spine realigned themselves. Rags lay so close to Scotty's nose she wondered how her brother could breathe. She rolled over to see Reva right where Hank put her the night before as if she hadn't moved once.

Knowing she'd never get past Hank without waking him, she decided to stay where she was. Last night she had eavesdropped, and now she spied on him in his sleep and enjoyed his nearness without his consent. I'm a woman without pride or principle, at least where he's concerned, she thought.

She gazed on the face that became dearer to her every day. Laugh lines etched around his eyes and mouth revealed that he was a man who smiled easily and often and that he lived with gusto and warmth. He sighed, settled closer to her, and flung his arm across her throat. She coughed quietly, hoping to disturb him enough to make him shift without waking him. He didn't stir. His arm pressed heavily, and the sun was beginning to heat up the tent. She couldn't breathe. Was it merely because his arm blocked her airway, or was it the excitement of being so close to him? She moved, watching his face, and stopped trembling when his eyelids lifted to reveal an amused gleam.

"Good morning," he whispered. "Where are you going?" He stretched. "Um, that feels good."

"Shh," she hissed.

"Elaine." He wanted to say her name. How wonderful she looked with her hair the color of sunlight, blue eyes open, honest, trusting-- and so serious.

He watched entranced as a small frown gathered on her brow. Her soft lips teased, making him want to take her in his arms. He couldn't help grinning when she shook her head as if she had read his thoughts in his eyes. "Come here." He slid his hand under the back of her neck and tugged. "Or I'll wake them up."

"Don't." Against her better judgment, she made her body go in the direction her heart had already gone. Now, instead of butterflies, hard-winged dragonflies bounced off the walls of her stomach.

"What were you dreaming about last night?" Hank asked quietly. "I woke up and you were breathing on my shoulder."

"How would I know? I was asleep," she said. "Don't you think we should wake them, so we can get an early start?" She squirmed away a few inches.

"Not yet. Come back so they can't hear us." His hand moved down to her shoulder and pulled her forward. "I dreamed about you," he said. "I dreamed this..." His warm lips touched hers for the space of two rapturous blinks as she felt a feathery brush of happiness.

"Are you cozy, Laney?" Scotty snickered. Elaine drew back sharply, heart thudding like a well digger's rig.

"It's beastly in here," Reva complained.

"Good morning, everybody," Hank said heartily, ignoring Reva. A dimple creased his cheek, and his eyes sparkled.

"Good morning," Elaine responded, hoping it would seem they had just awakened.

Would Scotty keep the kiss a secret? Maybe she should bribe him, but wouldn't that open her to blackmail?

"What's for breakfast?" Scotty said seemingly in complete innocence, but Elaine knew she'd have to be careful with him if she didn't want the whole world to know her business.

"Pancakes," she answered quickly. Rags thumped her tail; she liked pancakes too.

Ira moaned, rolled over, sat up, and rubbed his eyes like a child.

They built a fire and Elaine mixed water into the pancake mix. When they'd finished, everyone except Reva helped pack up. They had a few hours before they got to the landing where Ira's friend, Joe, owned the filling station. He was to take them home in his truck, hauling the canoes on a trailer with slots for boats.

"Granddad," Elaine invited, "please get in the canoe with me." She felt an overwhelming need to be near him in order to get her balance back after the emotional shock of finding herself in that compromising situation with Hank.

"Sure. You want to steer, Scotty?" The boy happily took the stern, with Rags settling at his feet. Hank pushed the other boat off the bank and stepped in. The stream flowed swiftly now, so they used their paddles only to navigate curves or steer around overhanging branches. When they'd been on the water for about an hour, Elaine estimated they had another hour left before the landing. Filled with euphoria as they floated swiftly on a wide, smooth stretch, she rested her paddle across her knees.

She looked at the canoe ahead of them and with surprise, saw that

Ira was leaning to the right, strangely immobile and making the boat list. She released her paddle into the canoe and tried to reach him. "Don't tip the…!" Granddad, Hank, and Reva all plunged into the icy water. "Get out, Scotty," she said rolling from their canoe and seeing him do the same. She fought her way to the surface, frantic to find Ira before it was too late.

CHAPTER 19

After surfacing, Elaine took a few precious seconds to tread water, fighting the current while she tried to place everyone.

Scotty's thatch of brown hair bobbed away as he swept along ahead of her. As he caught hold of a protruding branch, she knew he'd be fine.

Hank caught an overhanging palm frond, and Reva hung onto Hank as their canoe went on downstream without them, but where was Granddad?

Elaine's heart pounded as she frantically searched the jungle on shore. Below in the transparent water, the yellow backpack and the red cooler bumped along the bottom like bright tropical fish. Her canoe was moving downstream. They could retrieve it later. Time was passing. She glanced from one green bank to the other, knowing she'd have to find him soon.

There! She caught sight of a bundle of blue rags hooked on a limb a few yards away. The canoes had come up against it and stuck there. In three crawl strokes, she was tugging at the overall strap that had caught on a partially submerged limb and kept Ira from floating away. She couldn't tell whether he was breathing or not.

She held his head above the water and suddenly Hank was in the water with her supporting Granddad's body. They'd have to get him into a canoe somehow so they could take him downstream and get him to a hospital. The stream was too narrow for an airboat to come and rescue them.

Scotty had caught up with the canoes and was waiting. "Is he going to be okay?" he shouted.

"Yes," Hank answered. "Can you hold on?" His quiet confidence stirred deep gratitude in Elaine. "Ready?" he asked. "We'll hold him between us. It won't take a minute to float down to the canoe. I'll empty it and we can get him out of here."

Though the old man didn't weigh much, it was an awkward lift as Hank got on the bank and pulled. Elaine helped from the water. Hank's strength amazed her as he pulled Ira onto the shore. What would she ever have done without him?

"My arms are getting tired," whined Reva, who was holding on to a branch.

"Get out of the water then," Hank said, encouraging her. He straightened Ira on the sand and turned his head to the side so that water drained from his nose and mouth.

Elaine prayed as Hank put his mouth over Ira's and pinched his nose to begin pouring air into Granddad's lungs. Elaine's heart faltered when Hank frowned and shook his head. After four breaths, he stopped for a moment.

Hanks fingers flew to his own throat where signs of pounding life were clearly visible; he then gently touched the same spot on Ira's neck. Granddad began to choke and cough and Hank raised him into a sitting position so the rest of the water could spew out.

As he nodded to Elaine, she sighed and tears of relief pooled in her eyes. "Oh, thank you! I'll get the canoe." She set off to swim downstream and to bring back the larger canoe.

A piercing scream made goose bumps run up the back of Elaine neck. She did wish Reva could find another method of communicating her panic. However, when she saw the three-inch palmetto bug crawling up Reva's arm, she shuddered with empathy.

The woman leaped into the shallows and managed to dislodge the cockroach relative, which then sailed onto Elaine's head and began to slide prickly-footed down her neck. She slapped at it, but the creature was already in the water, drifting away like a flat, dry leaf. She shuddered.

"Oh, shut up, it's gone," she shouted over Reva's protesting shrieks.

"Ugh, I hate those things!" Reva's eyes flashed with anger and fear.

"You're all right." Hank's voice was calm. With this simple reassurance, the wild look left Reva's eyes and she calmed down.

"Let's go find help," Hank said. They lifted Granddad into the canoe and Hank held him in a sitting position until Elaine could move onto the to the end deck of the stern and support his weight, holding him between her knees as if he were a child on her lap.

"What happened? Was it another stroke? Will he live? He has to. He and Scotty are all the family I've got." Her nervous chatter stopped only when Hank broke in.

"Reva, you and Scotty get out of the water and stay here," he instructed.

"No! I can't. Please take me with you." Her face blanched in dread.

"You know I'll come back for you." Hank's resigned manner showed he had dealt with hysteria many times. Elaine's respect for his patience grew steadily.

"Don't worry, Miss Reva," Scotty said. "Rags and I will take care of you."

"You? You're only a kid!" she sneered.

"Scotty is a skilled woodsman." Elaine couldn't help defending her little brother. He's growing up, she thought....and starting to take care of poor little Reva, just like Hank and Granddad.

"Can't we all go?" Reva's voice was so plaintive and her misery so deep that for a moment even Elaine wondered if they might find a way to take her.

No, she decided; there's simply no room and although she trusted Scotty to stay, she didn't think he and Reva could manage the canoe alone. Wrestling with a gator, a bad storm, and sleeping on the damp ground were all too much for Granddad. For a moment, she found herself racked with conflict.

"You can find a dry spot farther up." Elaine leaned back, reaching for a plastic bottle of insect repellent, which she tossed to Reva. "Use that so the bugs won't eat you--and stay in the shade."

"I don't want that stuff on my skin," Reva shrilled. She threw it into in the water and it, too, floated away. "Take me with you!"

"I'll be back as soon as I can." Hank waved from the back of the canoe, took up his paddle, and worked the vessel into the middle of the broadening stream where the current flowed swiftly.

"It's a good thing this canoe has a broad draft and no seat in the middle," she told Hank.

"He's alive, and he's going to stay that way. Didn't you say he already survived one stroke?"

Elaine nodded, filled with new hope and strength. For the first time since Granddad fell from the boat, she began to experience a moment of tranquility.

The water ran smooth and deep, reflecting the great white clouds billowed in the sky above. She heard a pileated woodpecker, a peeping frog, and the omnipresent *churr* of cicadas echoing from the deep forest. "We'll take him to the hospital in Orlando and--then what?" A parasitic worm of dread crawled through her mind.

"Remember, whatever happens, you and I are friends." Hank's deep voice brought the return of reason as nothing else could--except maybe seeing Ira sit up and talk. It helped her to start thinking rationally again.

"We'll call Nick at the Fish and Wildlife office," Elaine said. "You and he can go back up and help Reva and Scotty. I'll go to the hospital with Granddad. We must call Annie. She'll want to know, she..." Elaine paused. No, she decided, I won't tell Hank about her love for Granddad. That's her secret.

"I want you to call my sister and let her pick you up at the hospital if you find you can leave," Hank said.

Elaine marveled at the oneness she felt with him as they made their plans. Together we can solve any problem, she thought. Well, mostly they're my problems.

They paddled under the high bridge that was their destination and beached the canoe. Elaine stayed with Ira while Hank went into the station to call the ambulance and Elaine's cousin.

"The Crossroads Emergency Vehicle is on its way," Hank said, coming out. He gave her a bottle of water and a candy bar. Keep your blood sugar up," he said. "Your cousin's coming with the airboat, but I couldn't get in touch with Annie. Doesn't she have an answering machine?"

"No, she says they make her nervous." Elaine hesitated. "Will I see you in town later?" Immediately, she wished she hadn't asked. While it was true that she wanted Hank around, he mustn't think she was as helpless or as demanding as Reva.

"Yes, certainly. I'll bring Scotty in. I called; and my sister will be waiting for you. Take a taxi. She'll pay for it when you get there. She's at home with her little girl and this will be easier for her. It's okay; let's don't talk about it now." He held up his hand when she tried to thank him again.

She looked into the green eyes glowing with compassion and concern. Her gaze traveled to his mouth and lingered. She saw a sweetness that she knew would always linger in her memory. She shook her head. Stop it; he doesn't belong to you.

He took her face between his hands. "Any time you need me, I'm here." With her cheek against the warmth of his big palms, she allowed a soft quilting of comfort to descend upon her and leaned into him. He held her for a moment.

Euphoria filled Hank when he felt Elaine drop her guard. To look at her...to touch her...to know she needed him made him want to carry her away where nothing could ever trouble her again. Why doesn't she fully trust me, he wondered. Is it because she's so strong, has such vitality and resilience that she thinks she doesn't need anybody?

Fearing the lovely woman beside him might sense his overwhelming feelings of tenderness and be alarmed, he moved away. "Everything will be all right, Elaine, you'll see," he said gruffly.

Their brief intimacy shattered as an airboat roared around the bend and slid onto the grassy bank. The uniformed officer who stepped out was as tall as Hank and about the same age. He wore a summer park ranger's hat and had a closely cropped beard to help shield his already tanned face from the tropical sun. He smelled of woods, water, and skin bracer as he put his arm around Elaine's shoulders. She rested against him.

"Nicolaides," he said by way of introduction, offering his hand to Hank.

"Nick," Elaine amended. "My best cousin; he's Ira's grandchild, too."

"How is he?" Nick said, kneeling down next to the unconscious Ira.

"He's breathing," Elaine answered. "We called the ambulance and Hank's girlfriend is waiting to be rescued." She heard Hank's quick intake of breath. Had she said something wrong? In this case, she hoped she had.

Short blasts of a siren announced that paramedic's vehicle had arrived. The driver got out and helped lay Ira on a stretcher. "There's room in the van if you want to go along, Elaine," he said. Without hesitation, she climbed in beside the pathetic, supine form and sank onto the narrow seat.

Hank leaned in the back door. "Don't worry; I'll find you." He stepped back and gently closed the door.

Elaine picked up Ira's dangling hand and held it tightly as the siren resumed its wail, speeding them toward town and more help.

CHAPTER 20

At the hospital, the driver directed Elaine to the emergency waiting room and then began helping unload Ira's gurney. While she waited inside, she called Annie again. After an endless forty-five minutes, Annie walked in and enfolded her in her arms. The two of them sat holding hands while Elaine told the story of Ira's mishap.

"You mustn't lose hope, dear," Annie said. Elaine shook her head, unable to speak past the tightness in her throat.

Elaine held her breath when she saw Dr. Potter round a corner on his way to talk to her. He and Ira had been friends since they were boys, and many a time Elaine had fallen asleep to the murmur of their voices as they played chess and talked far into the night. "Well, now, I'm sure you want to know what to expect," Dr. Potter said. "Let's walk down to the cafeteria, and I'll tell you what I know."

"When can we see him?" Elaine asked.

"After he's had further tests, I can tell you more," the doctor said, looking at her over his glasses. "I believe he's had another stroke, but he's a tough old bird." He touched Elaine's shoulder. "Studies show that people in comas can hear and sometimes understand what's said--it depends on how much brain damage..." Seeing the expression of alarm on her face, he changed the subject. "I want you out of here at night. Hospitals aren't restful for patients or anybody else. Think you can do that?" They both nodded.

"I'll see to the campground," Annie said. "Are the Braithwaites still there?"

"Good friends," the words tasted sweet, "have invited Scotty and me to stay with them."

When Dr. Potter had excused himself, Elaine and Annie went upstairs to a desk where two scrubs-clad nurses with stethoscopes ornamenting their necks stood talking. Elaine was aware that she must smell of wood smoke, insect repellent, and unfortunately, sweat. She jerked on the bottom of her wrinkled shorts, trying to smooth them down. The nurses finished talking and one of them came over. "May I help you?"

"Could you tell us where Critical Care is, please?"

"Through those double doors." The nurse smiled. "You're Miss Donovan? They'll see you in admissions after your visit," she said. "We'll let you both go in this time, but you can only stay five minutes out of every hour."

In a glass box of a room, another nurse sat before a screen, monitoring the progress of patients in four beds. Ira's was in the far corner. The beeping, flashing machines near each patient seemed more alive than the man who lay there unmoving, shrunken since she last saw him an hour ago. She and Annie stood next to the bed on either side.

"Can you hear me?" Elaine asked. Suddenly wrenching sobs overcame her self-control. She leaned forward, laid her head on his chest, and wept a puddle into the sheet. Annie came to stand beside her, patting her back.

She raised her head and looked at Ira. The skin around his mouth and eyes reminded her of a papery old snakeskin she had picked up one day when cleaning the park. A puff of wind had plucked it from the palm of her hand and wafted it heavenward. Was Ira now about to float away in the same direction? The thought of losing him sent a chill through her body.

"Granddad?" She gave his hospital gown a gentle tug. He did not respond, not even by the twitch of an eyelid. "You can make it. You have a lot to live for. We need you," she said. His chest barely rose and fell as he lay breathing shallowly. She willed him to suck in air, open his eyes, speak words of reassurance, but he remained as still as a rag doll.

"I'm sorry, your time is up." Elaine rose reluctantly when the nurse signaled. "I must ask you to leave now."

"I'll call you if there are any changes." Annie wanted to stay for the next visit and urged Elaine to rest for whatever would happen the next day. Elaine doubted if she could rest, but agreed and gave Jean's number to Annie. Elaine then found a restroom where a large woman in a pale blue uniform polished the already-shining chrome fixtures humming "In the Garden" to herself.

"Could I ask you a question?" Elaine said.

"Why sure, honey, seems like you already did." The woman's white teeth flashed, enabling Elaine to smile back.

"Here's another question then; is there any place around here where I can sit by myself and think for a while?"

"Yes'm, try the chapel. It's just down the hall."

"Thank you." Elaine drew two paper towels from the dispenser, dampened them under the hot water faucet, and lifted them to her face. They were coarse, but their soothing heat penetrated her face muscles and helped her relax.

Aside from containing a cushioned kneeler, the chapel didn't look like Elaine's idea of a place to pray. She sat down on a hard couch facing two easy chairs with a coffee table in between. Her mind whirled as thoughts tumbled in a kaleidoscope of anxiety.

What would Granddad do if he were in her situation and somebody he loved lay at death's door. Of course, he would pray. She leaned forward and clasped her hands together. "We'll take good care of him, if you'll let him live," she pleaded. "Oh, and God, I don't know how I'm going to pay the hospital bills."

The door squeaked and she sat up quickly as a woman in a mauve dress and low-heeled pumps stepped into the room. "Are you Miss Donovan?" she inquired politely.

"Yes, I am." Elaine stood up.

"I'm Mrs. Strickland, admissions. I'm sorry to bother you, but you see, we have some papers for you to sign. Will you come to the office when you're finished here?"

"I'll come now," Elaine said, rising to follow her.

"That gives the hospital permission to treat Mr. Thompson and promises you will pay," Mrs. Strickland said, riffling through forms and laying several in front of Elaine. "You should have signed them when he first came in. Dr. Potter probably had something to do with that little oversight."

Mrs. Strickland shook her head and clicked her tongue against the roof of her mouth, deploring the unruliness of doctors. Elaine skimmed the papers and signed several copies. She left the office with an anxious dread in the pit of her stomach. She had promised to pay; now how was she going to do it?

When she called her mother, Monica said she'd fly down and offered a few suggestions about the future. Elaine then called Jean about visiting her at Casa Del Sol. It seemed a big favor to ask of a stranger, but Hank had made it sound as if she'd be doing Jean a favor to visit her.

"My brother has already called," Jean answered cheerfully. We'll be happy to have you. Are you ready for me to come and get you now?" Even though Elaine had thought she'd take a taxi, Jean assured her that she and her little daughter needed to get out for a while and they'd be there in half an hour.

Elaine saw Dr. Potter coming along the hallway and stopped him. He put an arm around her and it was almost like being hugged by Ira, except that Dr. Potter was shorter and had a paunch.

"You look tired," he said. "Did you get a place to stay?" She nodded. "Go rest. It's likely to be a long haul. Annie insists she doesn't need much sleep, so I'll let her stay tonight. I think she has a soft spot for him in that big heart of hers. Huh! Now that I think of it, they were thick as thieves when we were kids and Annie actually thought she'd marry Ira when we grew up."

Astonished, Elaine realized someone else had known the secret all along. She didn't want to talk about it, though, so she asked Dr. Potter to tell her what he thought about Ira's condition.

"All I can tell you right now is that I believe in miracles," he said, checking his watch and then patting her on the shoulder. Realizing he had many people to look after, she thanked him and got into the elevator, where she stood rigid and tense, as the walls seemed to close around her, giving her a sense of claustrophobia as if she were enclosed in an ancient torture chamber that slowly grew smaller until it crushed the victim.

Although tiredness permeated every cell of her body, she decided to take a walk and come back to the front of the hospital in time to meet Jean. As the heavy glass doors opened, she encountered a blast of heat and humidity that instantly drew perspiration from every pore.

City heat is so much worse than country heat, she thought. We have trees, water, and fresh breezes. All they have is cement and asphalt. A melancholy longing for her beloved wilderness suddenly touched her soul.

She strolled along, beginning to unwind. She passed century-old buildings with modern facades; here was a restaurant broadcasting the smell of fresh coffee accented by the clink of cutlery. Elaine remembered she hadn't eaten since breakfast except for Hank's candy bar, but she didn't care.

In a jewelry store window, gold and crystal figurines sparkled on a rotating stand under brilliant light. In the window of a beauty salon, she saw photographs of well-coiffed women whose sleek perfection reminded her of Reva. Her own hair now felt like a fur collar and she wished she had a clip to get it up off her neck and shoulders.

In the next block, she paused before the double doors of an ancient church. A gleaming brass plaque stated that this Episcopal Church was now on the National Register of Historic Places. Standing hesitantly on the bottom step, she thought, I'd like to go in; it must be cool and peaceful, and maybe I can get a sense of peace in here. She started forward, but a loud wolf whistle halted her in midstride.

She looked around to see a man waving from a low-slung convertible. She turned away in disgust. On top of everything, she was beginning to feel nauseated by foul exhaust fumes from passing busses. Suddenly, she heard her name called and pleasure sprang up from a well of joy. She waited with uncontrolled impatience for the light to change. Scotty jumped from Hank's old pickup and held the door so she could slide in. Their reunion was complete when Rags jumped into her lap and reached up to lick her cheek. "How did you find me?" she asked.

"We described you at the information desk, and they told us which way you were headed." Hank's long- fingered hands gripped the wheel as he carefully moved out into traffic; she couldn't help comparing their vitality with the pale hands of the man she'd just left. He stopped at a traffic light and glanced over at her. His face was drawn and tired and she could see he felt as exhausted as she did. "Jean was going to come get you, but we were closer, so I said we'd pick you up."

"I don't want to be a bother," Elaine answered.

"How about Granddad?" Scotty leaned against her as he always did when they got into a vehicle. Sometimes she had to push him away because the heat from his young body stifled her, but today it was a pleasure to have him there.

"He's stabilized," she said, putting her arm around him.

"What's 'stabilized'?" His freckles had burned darker from the sun; his mouth had a grown-up grimness about it.

"It means he's not getting worse. Dr. Potter says he believes in miracles." It was the best she could give the small boy whose life revolved around Ira and her. "How did you get rescued?" she asked to distract him.

"We waited a long time for the airboat, and Miss Reva was real upset and kinda scared. I looked after her the best I could, but there wasn't much for me to do," he said. "We didn't see any snakes or anything, so I kept telling her everything was okay; and I made her sit on a towel so she wouldn't get chiggers, but I think she got some anyhow, 'cause she was itching her bottom when she thought I wasn't looking."

"Scratching," Elaine, corrected, embarrassed by Scotty talking so plainly in front of Hank.

"Your cousin's a great guy; I like him," Hank said. Elaine nodded, certain that Nick must feel the same about Hank. Each of them operated from a position of quiet strength. "I'll leave you and Scotty at Jean's," Hank continued, "then I'll go back to my camper on the building site. Tomorrow is Nick's day off, and we'll need to get an early start to see if we can bail out that canoe and take it to the campground."

"You don't have to do that."

"We would have done it today, but Reva wanted to get back to town." He shot her a mischievous grin, and she nodded, acknowledging Reva's frame of mind.

The gates that led into Casa Del Sol were similar to those at the campground and was probably installed in the same era, but where the iron barrier at the campground gaped from one hinge like a bird with a broken wing, the shiny black gates of Casa Del Sol stood sturdy, straight, and well cared for.

"Here we are, House of the Sun," Hank said. He was glad to take Elaine and Scotty to his home and let them meet Jean and her little girl, Missy.

"It's beautiful," Elaine peered through the window at the large Spanish-style house. "It's the same style as the lodge on the property. I like those red-tile roofs."

"Me too," Hank answered, parking in the circular drive, "but they're a bear to replace because the tiles are expensive and a lot of them break when you're trying to install them. Anyhow, welcome."

CHAPTER 21

"*L*ook at the size of those banana plants," Scotty said. He craned his neck to peer up into the green canopy overhead. "See up there under that red pod. Can I have one of them little bitty bananas?"

"May I have one?" she corrected automatically. "No, you may not." In spite of her bleak mood, Elaine laughed. "Don't be silly. Green bananas will make you sick."

"I ate them before and they didn't. You ought to try one."

"I did when I was a kid like you; no thanks." Sometimes Scotty's nonsense annoyed her, but today it cheered her.

Nile lilies, society garlic with tiny lavender flowers on long stems, and liriope lined the brick walk that wound from the driveway to the heavily carved door. Hank pressed buttons on a keypad and the door swung open. "Jean, Missy, we're here!" he called out.

A young woman with short auburn hair, wearing jeans and a plaid shirt, and carrying a small child, appeared. The toddler pushed against the woman's chest. "Down," she said. When her mother set her on her feet, she threw her arms around one of Hank's legs and squeezed until her strawberry curls trembled. "Unca Hank," she said.

"Hi, sweetheart," Hank said, with a chuckle in his voice. He lifted the child and held her close.

"Where you been?" Her eyes glowed with adoration.

"I've been working," Hank said.

Working? Elaine thought. We've been camping. Was that all it was to him, part of his workload?

"Welcome," said Jean. "I've been looking forward to meeting you." She extended a slim right hand and Elaine noticed that she had no wedding ring on her left one.

Missy looked down at Rags, who was busy investigating the bushes. "Doggy!" she shrieked.

"She's crazy about dogs." Jean playfully punched Hank on the arm. "It's that picture book you gave her. You have such an influence on my daughter!"

"You better watch it, sis, or I'll bring her a real puppy." Hank's eyes twinkled. "What kind of puppy do you want, sweetie pie?" He looked into the little girl's happy face. "Would you like a Chihuahua to scare burglars away or a Great Dane to sit in your lap?"

"Oh you," Jean reproved him. Linking arms with Elaine, she led her away. "Just ignore him and come on in. Mrs. McGregor's been bustling around the kitchen ever since she heard you were coming."

"May I stay outside for a while?" Scotty requested ultra politely, hoping for an affirmative answer. "Me and Rags need to case the joint."

Blushing with embarrassment at Scotty's choice of words and the grammatical errors that had waylaid him, Elaine glanced at Hank, who nodded, giving permission.

Inside, they walked down a long hall lined with wildly colored toddler paintings in fine metal frames. It was a veritable art gallery in itself. She caught her breath at the size of the living room that opened before them. A wall of glass made the room one with the garden and the shimmering gold-and-blue-tiled swimming pool beyond. A sense of comfort and spaciousness filled the clean, elegant room with its perfect harmony of line and color.

Hank, delighted with Elaine's obvious enjoyment, said, "Jean raises hybrid hibiscus." He pointed to the backdrop of flame-tipped greenery.

"Please sit down." Jean's smile warmed her heart. The small glass table next to the couch held a cut-crystal bowl with a single white gardenia that fragranced the room.

"Mrs. McGregor can't wait to see you. I'm supposed to tell her right away when 'our Mr. Henry' and his friends arrive so she can serve tea.'"

"Our Mr. Henry," Elaine repeated, delighted with the phrase.

"Henry is my real name," Hank said, grinning. "I could use a glass of tea and a sandwich." As he placed Missy in Elaine's lap, their eyes met and held. When Missy wrapped her arms around Elaine's neck, hearts melted. Satisfied, Missy slid onto the floor, where she sat plucking at the embossed carpet.

"She's been trying to get that flower off the carpet for days," Jean explained. "She has Hank's perseverance."

"Yes," Elaine answered. "He is persistent." Thinking of the campground, an involuntary shudder passed over her.

"Are you cold?" Jean asked. "Would you like me to turn the AC off?"

"No, I'm fine." Elaine shook her head. "It feels good; it's been awfully hot today."

"Tea is served," Hank announced. "Let us go into the kitchen. Scotty's already there. Mrs. McGregor made him leave Rags outside, but she'll be fine in the back yard…lots to explore." He scooped Missy up and lifted her to his shoulder where he held her carefully balanced.

"Mrs. McGregor," Hank said after he introduced everyone, "has kept us going by cooking for us all our lives." A gaunt woman with graying hair pulled into a bun turned from the stove to greet them.

"Now, laddie, I only cooked it. You're the ones who shoveled it in." A soft Scottish burr polished her words as they tumbled out of her mouth.

"Join us, Mrs. Mac," Hank invited.

"No, thank you, sir. I've got my taters to peel." Elaine caught a wavy glimpse of herself in the steel refrigerator door and pushed her hair back. While they ate, Hank told stories about the house and their childhood, and Elaine watched Mrs. McGregor, working with her back to them, shake with laughter and nod when she agreed with something. Elaine realized that Mrs. Mac loved Jean, Hank, and Missy as if they were her own.

After the snack, Hank settled Scotty with some video games and led Elaine upstairs to a bedroom of elegant femininity. "This is Mom's room." His voice broke.

She wanted to put her arms around him, to comfort him. "Your mother must have been a lovely woman," was all she said.

"You need clean clothes, don't you?" Hank asked. "Mother would be thrilled to lend you some of hers if she were here. Would you consider picking something out?"

"No, no, I couldn't." The conversation seemed too personal and the setting embarrassingly intimate.

"Please. If you'd only known Mother….She would love to share her things."

"Well, maybe," said Elaine, her resistance softening. "I hate to think about getting back into dirty clothes after a shower, but would you find something? I feel as if I'd be prying if I were to rummage around in your mother's closet."

"Sure." He scooted the hangers along the rack stopping at a pair of royal blue jersey patio pants and a matching top. "Help yourself to whatever you need. I think you'll find other...umm, things in the dresser over there against the wall." He took a pair of rose-and blue patterned espadrilles with crisscross straps over the toes from a many-layered shoe organizer on a shelf. "Do these go with the outfit?"

"Yes, they do," Elaine said. "They're lovely. Thank you."

After he walked out, she closed the door after removing a stone dove propped against it to keep it open. She found the rest of the clothing she needed, and when she had showered and dressed, she spun around on her bare feet to enjoy the silkiness of the full pant legs next to her skin.

"Where is everybody?" she asked Jean at the pool.

"Hank and Scotty went to the property for the night and Missy's in bed." Jean stepped forward to meet her. "It's just us, I'm afraid."

"Gone?" Elaine remembered now that Hank had said he would go, but her spirits drooped, confirming what she hadn't admitted. She'd spent extra time and effort to look as nice as possible and it was all for him.

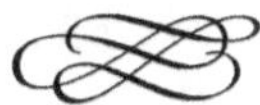

CHAPTER 22

"We sent Scotty in to ask you if he could go too." Jean seemed afraid Elaine would accuse her of wrongdoing. "And he said it was all right."

"I was in the shower. He probably yelled, but I didn't hear him. Oh well, he knew I'd say 'yes.' I hope Hank doesn't mind him tagging along."

"Oh, I'm sure he doesn't." The worried look left her face. "He enjoys kids." She gestured for Elaine to join her on the patio couch. "Mrs. McGregor left supper in the refrigerator; we'll warm it later. I put Missy down early so we could have some time to ourselves. I'm so glad you're here."

"I can use a friend right now," Elaine said, sinking into the cushions. "Where did you learn decorating? Your home is beautiful."

"I studied with a friend of Mother's after school and in the summers and planned to go into interior design; but I didn't make it to college. Someday I'd like to buy an old house and see what I could do with it." Green eyes exactly like Hank's lit with pleasure as Jean looked into the rotating circles of evening light in the pool.

"Not restoration as much as resurrection. We have too many beautiful and practical materials now to use the old woods and metals that take so much upkeep. Still I'd like it to end up looking as close to the original as possible and with as much of a Florida flavor as I could get."

"You have to see Sacred Spring. We have lots of history out there." Feeling as close to Jean as if she'd known her all her life, Elaine went on to describe the hanging tree and the Old Mill and to segue into a monologue about Granddad and Scotty. It made her realize how lonely she was and how she'd deprived herself of female company.

She became aware of dominating the conversation, so she asked a question to get the spotlight off herself and onto Jean. "Have you started looking yet?"

"Not too seriously. I check online every now and then. I suppose I'm waiting for the Spirit to move me, if you know what I mean."

Jean watched her guest as Elaine shook her head "no." That abundance of blond hair could use some styling, she thought, but other than that, she's a beauty. She reminds me of Mother; perhaps it's her gentleness. I can tell Hank likes her a lot; they'd be so good for each other.

"The doctor says he believes in miracles. I guess that means he thinks it'll take a miracle for Granddad to get back to normal." Not knowing what else to say, Elaine went back to her real concerns.

"Surely he'll be all right." Jean's brows drew together in empathy. "Would you like to hear about why I'm not married, yet I have a child?"

Elaine sensed that Jean was offering to share an important segment of her life in order to distract her from her worries. She curled one leg under the other and settled back to listen.

"You know how our parents and Reva's were killed in a plane crash?" Jean began.

Elaine nodded.

"It was three years ago that Richard came as tennis pro to the country club where I was working as a lifeguard. He was so good looking all the girls at the club fell for him. However, my parents, who usually respected everybody, didn't like him. He was a little too charming--too slick, my dad said. I obeyed my parents and avoided him, and that probably made me stand out from the rest of the girls who were infatuated with him.

"He showed up at the funeral. I was impressed and very lonely." She shrugged in a self-deprecating way. Elaine tried to put herself in Jean's place, and could understand her new friend's vulnerability.

"Mother and Daddy taught that God wanted me to keep myself for marriage. They said Christians should marry other Christians so they could have a common goal of loving God and serving him together. Richard didn't meet their most basic criteria.

"On his part, I didn't realize it at the time, but he was mocking my family and my faith in subtle ways. I dreamed about him and thought about him all the time. He was more adult, more of a man than the crowd I'd been with most of my life. He was there for me when I needed someone. I became obsessed with him--couldn't eat, couldn't sleep. I've never been so weak-willed in my life, and I hope I never will be again."

Elaine looked up, startled. She'd been feeling much of what Jean was describing. Was it wrong?

"What did you do?" she asked.

"When Richard asked me to go away with him, I went. He promised we'd get married." She leaned forward and put her face in her hands.

"It's difficult to talk about, isn't it?" Elaine reached forward and touched Jean's shoulder. The other woman leaned back again and looked at Elaine as she went on with her story.

"We lived in a cockroach-infested hotel in a run-down neighborhood. Ha," Jean said. "If I'd known I'd be the one paying all the bills, we would have moved to a better hotel."

"I guess you would have." Elaine smiled, appreciating the other woman's wry humor.

"A month later, I began feeling sick and asked Richard to get me a pregnancy test. When he brought it home, he bragged about how he'd talked the pharmacist into donating it to a worthy cause. He could talk anybody into anything, but that's no excuse for my behavior.

"I had choices and I made the wrong ones. Anyhow, the strip

turned pink." At Elaine's puzzled look, she explained, "I was pregnant. But I figured, so what? Richard would marry me, and we'd have a lovely little family. At this point, I desperately needed a family."

"What did he say when you told him?

"His exact words? 'You got to get rid of it. How do I know it's mine, anyhow?'"

"No!" Elaine felt heartsick.

"At first, I just stared with my mouth open, but when I got over the shock, I told him I wouldn't think of harming our child. I didn't see how he could either.

"'You get it done, or I'm out of here,' is what he said. 'You can afford it.' I refused and he said, 'Bye, Bye Bimbo.' He packed his bag and left."

"Just like that?" asked Elaine, with a snap of her fingers.

"I couldn't believe he wasn't coming back." Jean fingered her collar. "I lay on that lumpy bed and cried for days."

"How awful, but I admire you for refusing an abortion. That took courage."

"No, I think it would take more guts to go through something like that considering the physical, mental, emotional suffering. Besides, you have to be foolish to do something so horrifying that can't be undone. There may be cases when it's necessary, I really don't know, but I know several women who did it and not one of them has stopped feeling guilty and grieving to this day.

"At about two months, I had a sonogram, and the nurse could already see a tiny head, arms, and legs, mostly because she knew what she was looking for.

"Anyhow, I eventually got out of bed and went looking for Richard in hopes of changing his mind. You'd think I'd have more pride, wouldn't you?" Jean lowered her eyes.

"How did you know where to look?"

"He liked to hang out at this Cuban bar and restaurant, so I went there first. 'You mean that bad boy, Ricardo?' the owner said. 'He took off to Colombia with my daughter, Carmelita. Said he had business down there.' He looked me up and down, and I felt like a horse on the auction block. 'You got a job, *chica*? I could use a wholesome type like you.'"

"Did you take the job?"

"No, I called my brother and he came and got me. He was so glad I was all right. I never gave a thought to how he must be worrying. I'd left a note asking him to let me go and he wanted to give me some space, but it was hard for him not to hunt us down or to call the police.

"Hank was so kind and supportive. He even took some of the blame, which he didn't need to do. He said he was sorry for neglecting me after our parents died. I understood though, he was trying to hold the business together and he had his own grief, but it did make me feel better to know how much he cared."

"And now he loves Missy, with all his heart," said Elaine.

"Yes, and he's been so good with her."

Elaine was silent, deep in thought for a moment. "You're right about Hank. He's a truly good man."

"But?"

"Has he told you about his and Reva's plans to buy my campground?"

"Yes." Jean nodded. "I'm an equal partner, you know. I do most of the financial work here at the house."

"He wants to build a subdivision, but Reva has an industrial park in mind. I could almost go for a subdivision I suppose, but it would destroy me if they put in a lot of factories and warehouses. We have a beautiful, pristine spring. It's delicate, as all the springs are, and could easily be destroyed with too much building, and laying roads, and vibrations from the big machines and all that."

Jean listened with intense concentration as Elaine, relieved to be heard, explained, "Not only the spring, but more of the real Florida; the old Florida is being destroyed. A lot of plants and animals have come back from the brink of extinction, but only because people cared.

"When you come over, you'll see the big oak on the edge of the stream where over a hundred egrets roost every night. Even if the new owners don't cut it down, the birds won't stay during construction.

"Your brother seems to care deeply about people and home and family; I wish he cared as much about the wilderness." Elaine wondered if she'd gone too far when she saw Jean's frown again.

"He does care," her new friend answered. "He loves the out-of-doors. I think he's just been going along on automatic, doing the things he's always done. Reva keeps buying more property like some kind of mad Monopoly player, and he develops it however she wants."

Elaine turned her head to look out at the reddening sky. "When are they getting married?"

"When is who getting married?"

"She wears a big solitaire...and the way she acts..."

"Hank and Reva? Never!" Jean shook her head.

"You mean Hank's not in love with her?"

"She's been chasing him since they were two years old, but he's never been in love with her." Jean got up. "Come on in the kitchen. We need to talk about this over dinner."

Elaine followed, waiting impatiently to continue the conversation until Jean had put plates in the microwave and pressed all the correct numbers. "You're talking about the ring?" Elaine nodded. "Reva bought the ring herself," Jean said.

"I guess I am naive. Are women doing that kind of thing now?"

"You have to understand about men like Hank," Jean said, setting out glasses. "The worse a person treats him, the nicer he gets. It's part of his code of honor; it's how he lives out 'turn the other cheek.'

"Reva persuaded herself that his kindness is evidence of romantic interest. I've tried to tell him. My counselor says there's something called 'setting boundaries.' That means certain things you don't let people do to you, but Hank doesn't set many boundaries with Reva, because deep down he doesn't want to admit he doesn't like her. It seems to me, though, that knowing you is giving him a different perspective."

Elaine's heart leaped. Hank liked her enough to let it influence his life. It was a heady feeling. "Well," she said, hoping to distract Jean from romantic notions that might or might not be true. "We need to keep all this strictly business. I have absolutely no desire to get between Hank and Reva."

Jean shot her a look. "Ha! If that's what you really think, you're kidding yourself."

Elaine had to grin back; apparently, Jean had learned a few lessons about honesty in her counseling sessions.

After dinner, Jean showed her the rest of the house. In another wing, Jean opened the door to a suite containing an office, complete with computer, a sitting room with a small fireplace, and a bedroom. Hunter green and ivory, with touches of burnt sienna throughout, gave the room a rich, masculine look.

"This is Hank's suite," said Jean. "Mine is on the other side of the house."

"How many bedrooms do you have?" Elaine asked, unable to keep count of the rooms Jean had shown her.

"Ten. It's too big for Missy and me, and Hank is usually in his trailer on site. We're thinking about selling it. The memories can be sad sometimes, because the folks are gone. Walk down to the end of the drive with me. I need to make sure Hank locked the gate. I know it sounds paranoid, but we're careful around here since Richard tried to kidnap Missy."

"Why would he do that when he didn't even want her?" Elaine asked as they started down the drive.

"Probably ransom. I can't imagine him voluntarily taking on the care of a child, even his own."

"I knew a girl in school who wanted to be a social worker. She was talking about it one day and said sometimes the people least able to care for kids are the ones who most want to keep them. She thinks they like to have someone to control that can't fight back." Elaine offered the explanation not knowing if it was on target.

She slapped at a sting on her ankle and saw a cloud of mosquitoes coming in for the kill. "How did you stop him?" she asked.

"Hank was working late in here and hadn't locked up yet. I'd gone to bed, but I've slept lightly since Missy was born. I heard a noise and went into her room.

"Richard was standing over the crib. My first impulse was to put my arms around him--I needed more counseling, obviously--but I didn't. He was belligerent and claimed he had a right to her.

"The more I tried to talk him out of it, the more determined he got. When he picked her up, I started yelling for Hank. Missy woke and started screaming, so between us we made quite a ruckus.

"Richard was telling us both to shut up. He let go of Missy when Hank rushed in. It was a good thing I had hold of her. I caught her by her heel, or she would have hit her head.

"Hank wanted to talk, but Richard took a swing, so Hank grabbed him and held him in a half nelson while I phoned the police. They called it a domestic disturbance, took him down to the station, and after a while they let him go. That's what they told Hank when he checked the next day. I live in terror of his return." They found the gate locked and strolled back up to the house.

"Missy's next to you and I'm down at the end of the hall," Jean said at Elaine's door. "Good night, sleep tight."

Elaine slipped into the white satin nightgown she found in the drawer and got in between crisp, fragrant sheets. Stretching out, she let tension drain from her body.

Behind closed lids, pictures and feelings played through her fading consciousness. She again saw the green lantern tent and heard the cardinal calling to its mate. She savored the languid feeling of heat and languor caused by proximity in the early morning tent. She thought of Ira, sirens, and beeping machines. Sleepily, she wondered about Richard, a man who would break into a house to steal a baby.

CHAPTER 23

Sitting up in bed, Elaine woke; heart racing, mind befuddled. As she listened, a tiny click came from the direction of Missy's room.

With certainty born of panic, Elaine knew the kidnapper was back. Well, if he thought he could creep into this house and snatch that sweet little girl, he'd better think again! She took a deep breath. I'll need a weapon to hold him off until somebody can call the police.

She picked up the stone dove, tiptoed into the moonlit hallway, and ran silently along the carpet in her bare feet. A split second before she could warn the dark figure coming out of Missy's room that if he didn't surrender she was going to bash him, he whirled and pinned the arm holding the weight behind her. She screamed. He suddenly let go of her arm and clamped his hand over her mouth.

"It's me!" He shook her gently, and it was the kindness in him more than the voice that penetrated the fog of fear in her brain. She sagged in his arms, hardly able to believe it was really Hank. As soon as she stopped fighting, he took his hand away.

"I thought you were Richard," she gasped, breathing hard, her heart trying to pound its way out of her chest.

"And you were going to brain him with a dove?" Hank let a laugh escape while he continued to hold her. He reached up for the dove. The movement sent the feel of his body through the thin fabric of her nightgown. Shivers of pleasure rippled from her shoulders to her feet as she inhaled the spicy fragrance of pine-scented night that clung to his clothes. All the fear left her. Almost of their own volition, her arms crept around him.

"You're so funny." His voice held laughter to keep a more powerful emotion at bay.

"Missy's father did try to kidnap her, or have you forgotten?" she said becoming more lethargic by the moment. Though his arm tightened slightly, she dreaded the moment of awareness that would force him to release her. They were so close, she wasn't sure which of them was trembling.

Hank knew though, that he was the one who quivered uncontrollably. Let go of her, he told himself. It's not decent to stand out here in the dead of night holding her this way. He looked deep into her eyes and kissed her with a longing that closed his mind to rational thought.

Elaine couldn't get enough of his warm, demanding kisses. He could do whatever he wanted with her. Nothing mattered but the two of them finally holding each other.

In his mind's eye, Hank saw the bedroom she had come from, his mother's bedroom with the Bible next to the bed. No, he couldn't. That wasn't the way...wasn't God's best plan for her, or for him. Hank let go of her so quickly that she stepped back against the wall. She stared in confusion.

"What am I thinking?" He shook his head like a bear tormented by a swarm of bees. "I'm sorry, Elaine. Did I hurt you?"

"Hurt me?" Dazed, she fought to regain physical and emotional poise. "No, I'm not hurt...but..." She took a step toward him. "Why...?"

His body language told her all she needed to know as he turned his face away. "You go get some clothes on," he said and to her ears, it sounded harsh. So that was it. She'd shocked him. She felt a blush crawling up her neck.

"Excuse me," she said primly. "I was only trying to save your niece from being kidnapped." Then she remembered Scotty. "Where's my brother?"

"He was so worried about his grandfather he couldn't sleep in the camper, but he fell asleep on the way home and I carried him to my childhood room." Hank looked at the ceiling, the floor, anywhere but at her.

For a second, she allowed herself the indulgence of wishing he would take her in his arms again, but she shook her head and said, "It was a lot of trouble for you."

"Here I am innocently checking on my niece, when all of a sudden an avenging angel comes at me with a deadly weapon" A ripple of good humor invaded his voice. He held up the figurine. "I thought a dove was supposed to be the symbol of peace." Elaine chimed in with a giggle.

"Shh," she hissed.

"Shh yourself," he answered and in the moonlight, his gaze wandered across her bare shoulders and came to rest on the rounded bodice of her gown. He looked away again, nervously clearing his throat. "Did you call your mother?"

"She's flying in tomorrow with Scotty's dad. Jim's thinking about buying my property." She delivered the news in a soft voice, not wanting to sound eager, hoping not to hurt his feelings.

"He says he'd keep it a campground." She hurried to get it over with. "It's to be a membership campground, and he'll let me stay on as manager. The habitat would be protected, and we'll have our home." Her voice froze in her throat as she saw shock fly across his face and turn to stoic coolness.

"I know it's late, but if you want to get dressed, I'll make us a cup of hot chocolate." He spoke coolly into the distance between them, and she was suddenly bereft. Well, they had to get things settled. Cocoa would mean a little more time together. Her stomach rumbled. I'm hungry, she thought in surprise.

"Can you make toast?" she asked.

"Can I make toast? Can birds fly? Yes, ma'am. I'm probably the best toast maker in town, besides; I've got a champion toaster."

While she slid her feet into the espadrilles and donned the patio pants outfit again, she read the clock beside the bed. Two a. m. She stroked the satin luxury of the nightgown as she folded it and put it under the pillow. She closed her eyes to let her body relive the warmth of Hank's embrace. She quickly pulled a hairbrush through her hair, applied some soft pink lipstick, and was on her way.

Hank looked up from measuring powdered cocoa into mugs and smiled. "You look good. Mother would be pleased." Seated at the table, they began to talk, Hank's eyes riveted on hers with fine-tuned interest. Elaine told him as much as she could about her mother. "She wants us to move to New York and live with her. She says she can get me a job as a model. I thought I was too old to start something like that, but Mother says not."

"I wouldn't like to see you move so far away," Hank said wistfully. "What about your grandfather?"

"Mother wants to put him in assisted living up there. She says they have some excellent ones and he'd be happy and well looked after. She assures me we'll visit often. I'm not too happy about that, though. She doesn't understand about family. Never has."

"Ira doesn't seem the type to be stuck in a nursing home. I don't know about you, but I'd be a real grouch if I didn't get my daily quota of fresh air. Did you enjoy the camping trip? I did."

"Yes," she said, smiling. Now I understand how Annie felt, she thought. As long as I keep my distance, he'll talk to me. I couldn't bear being excluded from his life. If he knew the depth of my feelings for him, he would certainly avoid me.

"Look, I care about the future of Florida," he said. "I'm always looking for ways to save the environment. I follow the regulations even when red tape holds up construction and eats us up financially. Isn't it better for someone like me, who cares, to build than someone who tries to get by with a minimum of compliance?"

"I suppose." She nodded uncertainly, disciplining herself to keep her temper. "But I don't want my campground turned into a subdivision." She paused. "On the other hand, Granddad's hospital bill will be out of sight, and I still owe you for Scotty's. I know I have to sell," she sighed. Falling silent, she thought about Sacred Spring. "Can you honestly see the spring surrounded by houses, roads, sidewalks, and people?"

"I wish we could come up with another answer," Hank said. They talked until the dregs of chocolate had almost dried in the mugs. Hank believed in helping people, and Elaine believed in keeping the wilderness protected. They were on common ground because both believed strongly in the beauty and fragility of Florida and the joy of family ties.

Hank took the mugs to the sink and ran water in them. "Tell you what. You showed me your world, now let me show you mine. We've had a big crew in and done a lot of work lately."

Glancing at the clock, Elaine gasped. "We stayed up all night!"

"It was the company." He stuck the jam in the refrigerator. "Come on, I'll show you the dawn. Can you leave a note on that pad over there, please?"

While Hank checked the alarm at the entrance to the house, she got into the truck and leaned back, looking at the fading moon through the windshield.

A breeze ruffled her hair as she stretched, enjoying the coolness along her bare arms. The wonder of night turning to day was her last waking thought until the long driveway where Hank slowed down to wait for the gates to open.

She slept again and woke when the pickup slowed and turned. They entered a completed development through a coquina arch with cast-iron herons on either side.

"Good morning, sleepyhead. Are you feeling better after your nap?" He smiled across at her.

"I wanted to show you this finished community. People will be moving in soon. The guy who built it is a friend of mine who hired an environmental consultant and a community planner to keep it as habitat-friendly as possible."

They cruised past houses nestled among trees. Most of them looked finished. All were empty, waiting for mothers, fathers, and children to bring them to life.

"I didn't feel sleepy." She rubbed her eyes.

He'd like to look at her first thing in the morning for the rest of their lives. He could imagine her paddling a canoe, cooking over a campfire, walking down a long bamboo tunnel. He recalled her holding Missy on her lap. He looked at her and he loved her. He wanted her for always. He wished he could somehow make it possible.

"There's the dawn you promised. It's glorious!" she cried, experiencing a profound sense of happiness. All around them, midsummer spread her sensuous feast: a concert of birdsong, a host of plant fragrances, and the jungle thrum of cicadas.

If I stopped to kiss her again, he thought, she might think I was using the physical attraction between us to sway her decision. Even worse, if I touch her, I won't want to stop. He looked away, not daring to gaze upon the woman beside him: mysterious, eager, and tantalizing.

"See over there? Cedar wood paths, no sidewalks." Hank slowed, pointing out the wonders of his handiwork.

"Every few blocks there's a small park with a playground. We cleared trails into the woods; some go to the river where we have piers so folks can launch small boats and canoes, and to fish from.

"Every porch has a swing, and each backyard has space for a sandbox and a gazebo. See the smaller buildings over there? They're townhouses for people who don't want to take care of big yards, and we're going to put in a retirement complex down that way.

"The town center, a grocery, a library, a small church, and a community building that people can access on foot." He stopped the truck where the road became a sand track so they could walk back a ways.

"I don't suppose many builders are willing to spend money for this kind of thing if they don't have to," Elaine said. They passed a waterfall splashing into a pool.

"We'll stock the pond with small carp and put a footbridge over it," Hank said.

"What else will this paradise of yours have?" Elaine asked.

"We'll have woods running through to act as wildlife corridors," he hastened to reassure her. "We'll have plenty of space for birds to build their nests and for all the squirrels, possums, and raccoons anybody could want."

"Good," she said. "Raccoons get into people's garbage." Before he could react to that, she tossed her head saucily and went on, "It's all right, but I still wouldn't want to do this to my campground."

"I'd like to see it stay wild too, but how will you survive, you and Scotty and Ira? If you'll sell to me, I can start getting my permits before the environmental rules get even more stringent than they already are. I've got some property I can offer in mitigation." He nodded.

"Mitigation!" She almost spat the word. "Mitigation is one of the craziest things I've ever heard of. You take a perfectly natural wetland like my spring and the marshes around it, and you drain it and fill it.

"Tadpoles and snails die--they're the lower part of the food chain-- and the birds don't have anything to eat. As things dry up, there isn't any water for the other creatures. Then you start in on high, dry land with its own ecological balance.

"Aren't you exaggerating just a mite? We figure once you've made the wetland available, the right kind of plants and animals will move in. We plant things, too, you know."

"Oh, the whole thing is just too ridiculous to even discuss," she said, angry that he was so bullheaded.

"But if you don't sell to us, how will you..."

"I'll sell to Scotty's dad." She bent to pick up a leaf and finger its serrated edge. As they skirted a puddle in the unpaved road, their shoulders touched and she jerked away as if she'd been burned. "I told you that!"

"Let's go back to the truck," he said abruptly. "I want to show you something."

They left the development and drove onto the two-lane highway where tall grasses grew wild along the shoulders, and beyond them bushes hid the bases of large oak trees and palms. In a few miles, they came to a gate with a sign that said "Pine World."

"Isn't it enough that we already have Disneyworld, Sea World, and

Flea Market World, and every other kind of world you can think of?" she said testily.

A young man with spiked hair, wearing a chartreuse tee shirt stepped from a guardhouse, bent over, and looked in the car window. "Morning, sir--ma'am." He nodded. "Do you have an appointment with one of our salespeople?"

"No, but is it all right if we drive in and have a look around?" Hank asked.

Elaine was already having a look. She saw a vast plain where acres of forest had been cleared and upon which fifth-wheelers and large coaches stood close together like cans on a grocery shelf, each one in a tiny space with no more than a few feet between.

Only three scraggly pines grew in the whole park, and they looked abandoned and forlorn trying to thrive next to an Olympic-size swimming pool filled with chlorinated water, which Elaine knew was poison to people and animals. Elaine could smell it through the open car window. A large structure to the left proclaimed itself the Recreation Building. "Hank, I don't want to."

The guard interrupted, "Sorry, you can't go in, but I'll be happy to make you an appointment with a salesperson. Would you like me to set you up for a complimentary weekend of camping, sir?"

Hank clenched his jaw. "You mean we can't drive in and turn around and drive back out?"

"No, sir!" He answered smartly, straightening his weight lifter's shoulders. "We have tight security here. No one goes in unless they live here, are guests, or get shown around by a salesperson."

"I've already seen all I need to," Elaine said, feeling Hank's irritation at the man.

Hank nodded curtly, threw the truck in reverse, and backed out. "He practically accused me of being a criminal," Hank said. Used to being honest and experiencing the resultant trust from everyone he knew, he was insulted by the near accusation that he would vandalize the campers or steal something if allowed into the camp. "How can people do business that way?"

"I guess he was just doing his job. He didn't mean anything

personal. He doesn't even know you. If he did, he'd know you're a good man." She spoke softly to soothe him

"Yeah!" he grinned, good humor restored. Elaine was amazed at how little it had taken to pacify him. She could not know that her trust was something Hank wanted more than anything, and that her expression of respect had made him a happy man.

"You weren't the most exciting company on the way home, but I'm glad you got some shut eye," Hank teased her when they got back to Casa Del Sol.

He looked into her eyes with an intense, emerald gaze. "I hate to leave you, but you might want to get a bit more sleep before you go down to see Ira, and I've got some work."

He bent to kiss her cheek, but a sudden impulse caused her to move her head so that the kiss landed on her slightly open lips. She was immediately abashed; but then he was gone.

The morning was young and the household had not yet begun to stir when she went to her room to lie across the unmade bed. I'll rest a minute before anybody knows I'm here, she thought before falling into a deep and dreamless sleep.

CHAPTER 24

*S*everal hours later, a high-pitched voice cut through Elaine's fog of sleep. She tried to open her eyes, but managed no more than slits that invited shards of light to cut into her brain. She shaded her eyes with her hand and focused on freckles, a cowlick, and a cocky grin.

"Mother wants you on the phone," Scotty said.

"What time is it?"

"Ten o'clock. Are you going to sleep all day? Here, Rags, come wake Laney up." He set Rags on the bed and she started trying to lick Elaine's face.

"Tell Mother I'll call her back," she said, pushing the dog away.

"Early to bed, early to rise, makes a man healthy, wealthy, and wise," the boy chanted.

"Leave me alone!" Deeply regretting the times she had awakened him ungraciously and without concern for his slumberous state, she pulled the pillow lightly over her face.

"What? I can't hear you. Get out of that bed or I'll throw cold water on you," he said.

Next time I have to wake him, she thought, maybe I'll just carry him down to the spring and throw him in. Wait, what was that?

Silence. She felt for the sheet and pulled it up over her shoulder, congratulating herself on ousting him so easily. She heard water running somewhere in the house, but she ignored it and drifted off again, for a moment.

The sheet flew off, and a million cold spatters hit her face. She looked up in time to see Scotty dip his hand in a glass of water.

"You're going to be sorry!" She lunged for him but instead of running, he picked the phone up off the bed where he'd left it and stopped her with it.

"Phone!" he said.

Elaine groaned and took it from him. He sat down on the end of the bed Indian style to listen to her side of the conversation. She motioned for him to leave, but he crossed his arms and shook his head "no."

"Hello?" she said. No answer. She opened her eyes and looked at Scotty. "She hung up."

"The phone's upside down." He smirked.

"Hello, Mother," she said, twirling the instrument around.

"Hello, dear; are you all right?"

"I was asleep," Elaine grumbled.

"Is your granddad worse?" Elaine heard the anxiety in Monica's voice.

"No, he's the same. I'm heading up there soon."

"I'm glad to hear that. Now what are you going to do about the campground?" Monica asked. "Are you going to sell it?"

"I don't know."

"Well, dear, I called to give you our flight information. We're arriving at noon today. Go ahead and park in the garage, we'll pay for it. I'm bringing Jim."

After lending her a melon-colored tee shirt and khakis, Jean offered to let Elaine leave Scotty at Casa Del Sol and borrow her car for a trip to the hospital. Elaine decided to take her up on the offer and thanked her profusely. Although she loved Scotty to distraction, she had to admit that sometimes things went more smoothly without his freckled energy bouncing around.

The nurse on Ira's floor said admissions wanted her right away. Fighting panic, she went to the office. If they would only wait until she'd sold the campground, she'd have plenty of money. She put her hand to her forehead, the spot where headaches began. By the time the elevator stopped, she could hardly force herself to get off.

Maybe this is how Jean's panic disorder feels, she thought in a moment of empathy. Inside *Admissions*, she stood irresolute until a middle-aged man came out of one of the cubicles.

"You must be Elaine Donovan," he said. "I am Tarkington P. Adams. How do you do?" The small man with big eyes offered his hand and she shook it.

"Sit down," he said, leading her back into his office. "Dr. Potter persuaded us to admit your grandfather before we had the papers filled out."

Mr. Adams rattled on about hospital policy while she burned with shame under his chastising tone, trying not to inhale the scent of his musky aftershave. "We did get them, but I have a few questions about how you plan to pay and when. Do you have access to Medicare, Medicaid, Catastrophic coverage, anything?" he said.

"I don't know. You see, Granddad handled all the bills." She felt a stricture in her chest. "I should have paid more attention." She paused, then decided to be perfectly honest with herself and with him. "No, I'm sure there's nothing."

"Indeed." Tarkington P. Adams frowned and tented his fingers. "I am going to give you some time to work things out. Talk to the hospital social worker. See what government programs are available, and try to find out if there is insurance of any kind."

Elaine knew Granddad hated welfare, but she also knew the money had to come from somewhere, and soon.

"Don't hesitate to use government help; after all, your taxes paid for it." He walked her to the door, and she headed for Ira's room, thankful for a reprieve. Ira, now in a semi-private room, lay next to the window.

Elaine walked up to the bed and took his hand. "Granddad, please come back. We need you." Would he ever smile at her again?

A nurse came in and looked him over. "It's a good idea to talk to him," she said.

"I'm trying, but I don't know what to say; he's so still." Elaine heard the catch in her own voice. Reaching into the drawer of the night-stand, the nurse pulled out a Bible and laid it gently in Elaine's lap. "You could read to him."

Elaine opened the book in the middle and sampled a few pages until she came to something that felt right: the ninety-first Psalm. She remembered Granddad reading it aloud to her and Scotty.

Her throat was tight as she started. "I will say of the Lord, he is my refuge and my fortress: my God; in him will I trust."

The words echoed in the room and in her heart. I want to trust God more, she thought. She began telling Ira everything that bothered her. He'd hear and understand, even if he couldn't reply. "I'll bring Mother back with me this afternoon," she said when the nurse signaled her to leave.

"Hurry," Jean said, undeterred by Missy's weight on her hip, "or we'll miss them."

Scotty took Elaine's hand and she wondered if he was a bit nervous about seeing his mother and meeting his dad for the first time. They arrived in time to see passengers pouring from the gate exit. Elaine spotted Monica in the long line of people, and got her first sighting of Scotty's father, Jim.

"Let me look at you." Monica first enveloped Elaine in a cloud of perfume that would cling until washed off, and then held her at arm's length. "You look more like me every time I see you," she remarked. "How delightful."

Elaine stepped back and examined Monica. Yes, it was like staring into a magic looking glass, seeing herself a few years older and a lot more glamorous--flowing hair (she'd have to have hers straightened to manage that), flawless makeup, and eyes like sapphires. Monica's shoulder-duster earrings swayed and bounced, constantly buffeted by restless energy. A peasant dress similar to the ones she had sent Elaine from various countries completed her outfit.

The quarterback-sized man beside her made a low sound in his throat to call attention to himself. Elaine gave a quick appraisal that took in brown eyes and hair that reminded her of Scotty's. In no other way, however, did he seem familiar.

"These beautiful people are my children, Elaine and Scotty," Monica said.

Smiling down from his great height, Jim held out his beefy hand. "It's good to meet you, son. We'll have to get to know each other," he boomed.

"You're my dad, huh?" Before Jim's hand could clasp Scotty's, Monica moved between them, smothering the boy in a hug.

Elaine watched, thinking Scotty would explode from his mother's embrace with a remark about mushy stuff. Instead, he sighed and leaned against her. When she let go, he reached for her carry-on bag. "May I take this for you, Mother?"

"Thank you, dear." Monica handed him the bag. "Who are these charming people?" she asked, looking at Jean and Missy.

"Jean and Missy," Elaine said. "We're staying with them while Granddad's in the hospital, and they've invited you to stay as well."

"The boy and I will get the rest of the bags, and the rental car," Jim said. "You ladies can take your time. Just tell us where you're parked and we'll swing by for you when we're ready to go." When she told him, he said, "We'll find you."

"I wish I'd come to see him before this happened," Monica said when Elaine had finished describing Ira's stroke and his recovery so far.

"I know how you feel." Jean spoke over Missy's shoulder. "There are things I wish I had done and things I wish I hadn't done. Why don't you tell us about Jim?"

"He owns the modeling agency I work for and several other successful businesses. We married ten years ago, but after Scotty was born, we decided we'd be better off as friends. Sometimes I think the divorce was a big mistake.

"I sent Scotty home to Elaine and my father because Jim and I both had to work--often out of town. It would have been no life for a toddler, going from one baby sitter to another in a big city."

"He's a blessing, and we love him," Elaine said. She spoke a truth she had never really stopped to think about. Her life wouldn't have been as much fun or as happy without Scotty. Maybe she wouldn't throw him in the pool the first chance she got, after all.

"Jim wants to get to know him now." Monica linked her arm through Elaine's. "He's starting to realize that he's going to die someday and that he'd like to leave something behind besides money."

"Would Jim move down here if he bought the campground?" Elaine stopped in her tracks as a chill raced up her spine, for in spite of Monica's wandering commentary, a central idea came to the forefront of her mind and stood waiting for attention. Jim wanted Scotty. The others paused, waiting for her.

"He could never leave New York." Monica looked from Elaine to Jean but got no response. "Jim also owns a film company. He says he might like to use the wilderness for a remake of some of the Tarzan movies. By the way, do you know a good place for dinner? He wants to take us out."

"Please come and have dinner with at the house," urged Jean. "Mrs. McGregor's been cooking all day. You can be comfortable and talk business afterwards."

"Jim would be tickled. He adores home cooking and complains about how infrequently he gets it. However, you have to promise you'll let him take you out another time. Jim, like Ira, hates to owe anybody."

It seemed strange to Elaine that Monica knew that about Ira, but after all, Elaine thought, she is his daughter, why wouldn't she? She realized decades of relating had gone on between Monica and Ira before she was even born.

They settled Missy in her car seat and waited with the doors open in the parking garage. Suddenly Scotty appeared at the driver's door. "We got the suitcases and the rental car and now we're waiting for a taxi. Jim says there isn't enough room in any one car for the luggage.

Can I ride in the taxi, Laney? Why did you bring so much stuff, Mother?"

"I'm going to Europe for a month after I leave here." She smiled fondly at the little boy whose fast-paced manner of speaking matched hers.

CHAPTER 25

Jean let Elaine and Monica out off at the hospital, and they found Annie in the waiting room down the hall from his room. The warmth of belonging stole over Elaine as she watched the two women hug each other.

Annie showed Monica where Ira's room was. "Go and talk to him," she said. "Maybe someplace deep inside he'll recognize your voice." Monica was back within two minutes, stark fear glittering in her eyes.

"He's so thin and pale; I had no idea he had aged that much."

Elaine sensed the pull of the guilt attacking her mother and felt sorry for her. Annie took yarn and needles from her commodious purse and started to knit, drawing mother and daughter together with strands of conversation. In spite of her efforts, Elaine had a hard time concentrating.

"There's nothing you can do here now," Annie said, at last. "Why don't the two of you go off and spend some time together?"

"I could use a shampoo and a facial," Monica announced.

"Jean goes to the salon right down the street," Elaine said. "We'll call and you can tell them what you want."

"Oh, no, my little one. It's not just what I want; it's what we're both going to have." Monica linked arms with Elaine, and they headed for the phone.

"Mother, I can't afford..."

"My treat," Monica said.

Monica hadn't been to visit since she brought Scotty to stay, but that time she had taken Elaine for a haircut, so she recognized the pungent scent: the mixture of permanent wave solution, hair spray, and incense, which were daily sacrifices to the gods of beauty.

Inside, blow dryers blasted hot air while at the receptionist's desk cold wind from the air conditioner blew down the backs of their necks. A young woman in a turban and diaphanous Turkish pajamas looked up inquiringly. A smile of awe spread across her face as she recognized Monica.

"Miss Marlette!" she said reverently. "I just saw your picture in that fashion magazine over there. Here, I can show you."

"No, no, that's all right; I've seen it." Monica waved her hand to dispel the aura of fame and success her presence obviously brought to the society of stylists.

"This must be your sister." The hairdresser refused to become distracted from her hero worship. "She looks just like you." Sensing the girl was enjoying herself, Elaine put on her most brilliant smile to please her.

"Shall we have styling, facials, manicures, and pedicures? And when you're finished, you can go into the boutique and get new outfits."

"You've come at a good time; we're running several specials." She reached under the desk and brought out red and white checked cotton robes. "Please put these on." She pushed at a curtain of multi-colored glass beads and called, "Zarriya!" then directed them, "through here and to the right."

"Come on, darling," urged Monica as Elaine hung back. Laughing, she tugged on her daughter's arm. "I'll protect you, I promise."

"I've wanted to have a heart-to-heart talk with you for a long time, but I don't know where to begin," Monica said as a gorgeous African-American girl that Elaine could imagine racing across an African desert on a sleek Arabian horse showed them to a dressing room. Monica removed her earrings and dropped them in her purse. "I guess I could start by asking if you're hurt that I wasn't here to watch you grow up."

Elaine wasn't sure she'd heard right. How could her mother even ask such a thing? Of course, she was hurt. Every day had started and ended with the pain of not having a mother like all the other girls, pain caused by knowing her mother didn't love her enough to want to be with her.

Elaine studied the youthful face with the innocent blue eyes. Was she looking for reassurance? Elaine knew she had to be truthful. "I always wondered if there was something wrong with me because you didn't want me."

Elaine heard the agony in her own voice as she slipped her arms into the robe. She despised herself for being so blunt and self-pitying.

Monica put her hand over her eyes as if she too were suffering. She sank onto a low bench. "You were a colicky baby and cried all the time. When you were two years old you started saying 'no, no, no,' to whatever I wanted you to do. When you were four, you kept running away."

She looked up defiantly. "I finally tethered you to a tree by your arm you'd have to stick around, but you took off all your clothes in the front yard and I was embarrassed to death. On top of that, you sucked your thumb until you went to kindergarten and the kids made fun of you.

"I tried painting it with hot sauce but you licked it off. I bandaged it, but you unwrapped the bandage; I tied your hand to a bar of the crib, but you worked it loose." She shook her head. "I thought there was something wrong with me, not with you."

"I remember being tied to that tree." Elaine had to chuckle. "I took off my clothes because I thought it would get my arm out of that rope."

She then fell sober. "Mother, did you never like me?"

Her mother blinked, as if the truth, thus stated, shocked her; but Elaine pressed on. "I find it hard to believe that a mother who loved her children would give them to somebody else to bring up." Her voice quavered. Would Zarriya be pacing outside the dressing room, waiting for them to come out? Elaine realized she didn't possess the willpower to break away from this tortuous conversation.

"I had good reasons for what I did," Monica snapped. "Wait to judge me when you've had children of your own."

"I may not have any children. You'll have to explain it now." Elaine sat down on the bench next to her mother.

"We're ready for you, ma'am," said a voice through the curtain.

"Take someone else," Monica said with confident authority.

Apparently, she was queen bee wherever she went. By the time she looked at Elaine again, her eyes brimmed with tears.

"I was reared in a mechanic's garage in a small town on the wrong side of the tracks, the descendant of Florida crackers. My father adored my mother, and so did everyone else. The whole world could get along fine without me as long as it had them.

"When I was eighteen, I started running around with boys. Then I met Steven Donovan at a dance in the old grange. We liked each other a lot. He made me laugh. We danced all the dances, and the boy who took me was furious. He picked a fight, but when your dad knocked him down, he got up and left. Steven was gentle, but could be tough when he had to be." Her eyes brightened with amusement. "Because I'd had the example of a good father, it followed that I would marry a fine man like Steven."

"But he died." Elaine took the still-folded robe from her mother's lap and held it out to her. Monica took it absentmindedly.

"Yes." Monica lowered her gaze. "He died."

"How?"

"That's too complicated." Monica drew her lips together.

"Okay." Elaine shrugged. "It was you who said you wanted to talk." She got up and walked out, leaving her mother to come when she was ready.

Zarriya rushed over to her. "This way Miss Marlette," she said.

"Donovan," Elaine said in her mother's haughty voice.

"Is this your first time with us?" Leading the way, she chattered through a line of well-rehearsed subjects chosen to put patrons at ease. Monica hurried to catch up. In a well-lit room at the back of the salon, the attendant invited them to stretch out on a pair of sheet-covered couches and said she'd be right back.

"So you were the one that ran away in the end." She hated the harsh, bitter sound of her own voice, but she couldn't help it, she was boiling inside. "I could accept that you left me because you obviously never liked me, but what was your excuse for abandoning Scotty?" Her wild, injured feelings refused to be suppressed any longer.

"I'd watch my attitude if I were you. You owe me at least a little respect," Monica said.

"Do I? Were you playing at being mother when you sent fancy clothes instead of asking what I wanted or even needed? Do you care that I'm about to lose the campground?"

Part of Elaine was ashamed of this tirade, but part of her begged for reconciliation, for belated help and guidance from the older woman. "Granddad could be dying...my whole life is falling apart, and I can't see that you're doing anything about it--any more than you helped me with anything else in my life."

Conversation ceased abruptly as the cosmetician returned, taking a seat on a rolling stool at Monica's side. Another young woman who introduced herself as "Nia" approached. Hands moving briskly, she folded the robe down to get at Elaine's neck and bare shoulders and began massaging with fragrant oil. She squeezed, kneaded, and pinched the muscles.

Elaine winced, but the circular motion began to soothe her and ease the stiffness. "There now," said Nia. "A face is more beautiful when it's relaxed." She applied masque and left to allow it to set. Elaine wanted to continue talking to her mother, but when she tried, the thin shell on her face started to crack. Just like Humpty Dumpty, she thought ruefully. Will all the king's horses and all the king's men ever put me together again?

After washing off the masque and applying skin freshener and moisturizer, Nia moved Elaine to a shampoo bowl, then to a chair in front of a large mirror. With flashing razor and scissors, she feathered off clumps of red-blond hair. A hand-held drier blew the natural waves into a soft and feminine hairstyle around Elaine's face.

Monica sat a few feet away, getting the same treatment. Her laughter rang out like a bell, and Elaine marveled at what a good time she seemed to be having. She doesn't care, Elaine thought. She's used to having this done routinely and that's all that matters.

"A bit of blush." Feathery softness dusted Elaine's cheeks as Nia stroked with a long-handled brush. She pulled a mascara wand from its container and darkened Elaine's pale lashes to bring her eyes to sparkling life.

I look more like Monica every minute, Elaine thought, but I'm not like her inside. Not at all. I'm not. Putting down the mascara, the beautician stroked a small brush through pale rose lipstick and carefully painted Elaine's mouth.

"Now a touch of Prussian Pewter on the eyelids." Nia stepped back. "You are truly a work of art," she said. "It's a pleasure to have such a palette."

Elaine gasped as she looked at herself, barely recognizing the periwinkle blue eyes and the silky hair that moved and shimmered in the light as tossed her hair.

"How did you get it to do that?" she asked.

"It's all in the cut. You like it?" Nia's reflection addressed Elaine's image with pure satisfaction.

"Oh, yes," Elaine sighed. "It's the best I've ever looked." Nia turned the chair and whipped the cape off her shoulders.

Elaine stood and saw that Monica wasn't quite finished. "I'll repay you when I can," she said. She dashed to the changing room. Outside thunder rumbled from a storm-heavy sky, but as soon as she was dressed, Elaine ran out of the shop.

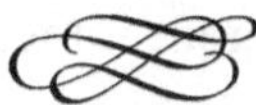

CHAPTER 26

*S*he came again to the old church she had wanted to enter before, and this time she indulged her urge and ran up its worn cement steps. As she gained the cool, dim interior of the narthex, rain began to pound on the roof. In the semidarkness, a stained glass window was suddenly backlit with lightning.

Jesus in a blood red robe glowed like a beacon. His hand lay lightly upon the shoulder of a travel-weary pilgrim who knelt at his feet; the shepherd's staff of one and the walking stick of the other were crossed and propped against a nearby boulder.

Elaine read the inscription *"Come unto me all ye who labor and are heavy laden, and I will give you rest to your souls."* Both the scene and the words should have been comforting. Instead, they tipped the brimming cup of bitterness to overflowing.

"Rest!" she said aloud. "I'm so tense and full of hurt these days, I don't even know how to rest."

As if in answer, thunder boomed and lightning flashed once again. The stained glass window glowed for a second time, before the atmosphere dimmed again.

"I have a poor opinion of the way you've handled things so far, sir," she said to the image in the robe, the red of which was the only color now visible.

Squeezing her eyes shut, she waited for lightning to strike her for talking to her maker in such a rude manner. She knew it would be quick, then all her troubles would be over, but a profound silence was her only answer. Her gaze fell on the inscription again.

"Come unto me..." Should she? Should she go to him and ask for his help? If she did, there was no guarantee he would help her. What had she ever done for him? Besides, wasn't she supposed to be a grown-up who could handle her own problems?

She waited quietly, sensing a presence. Then the thought came that God had managed to create the whole Earth and everything on it. Surely, her problems were small compared with an undertaking such as that. Maybe she didn't really want to ask him for help.

Ira once said, "God's ways aren't our ways and his thoughts aren't our thoughts. He has a better plan than we do."

What if that were true? Pulling out a kneeler, she pondered giving up her own ideas about what life should be like. If that happened it would mean that whatever God wanted her to do, she'd have to obey or else. Then reason counseled--what kind of a job are you doing running your own life?

You've worked yourself into a state of panic, yet you still don't have answers for any of your problems. Ira's health is out of your hands. People want to care for Scotty. Your mother will live her life as she pleases no matter what you do or how you feel. Don't you see that without me, you are powerless?

The window caught a flicker of emerging sun and gleamed with shafts of sapphire, topaz, and ruby. The storm was over. She tilted her head to study the image of Jesus with the weary supplicant at his knee. Her gaze rose to his face, which held an expression of deep tenderness. Looking again at the young man, she noted his utter trust and confident hope.

Waiting now in peace, she felt awareness begin to fill her mind, a profound knowing that someone cared about everything that happened to her now, then, and in the future. She recalled standing at the postal window at Crossroads Mercantile while Mrs. Cumberly delivered the latest gift from Monica.

"Somebody must love you an awful lot to send you all these packages," she had said. Granddad said much the same thing. "Your mother sends clothes to show her love because clothes are important to her."

Suddenly Elaine knew they were right. That's just what all the packages represented: an expression of love. I never thanked her, Elaine thought. She bowed her head and tears fell on the hands that gripped the pew in front of her. I didn't write, didn't call. I've wanted to hurt my own mother, when I could have tried to understand her better. She just had to be who she was, that's all anyone can do.

"Jesus," she whispered. "I'm sorry. I must have hurt her terribly...and I must have hurt you, too, because I closed my heart against her. Help me. I want to trust you; I have to trust you: I don't have any place else to turn."

Her spirit felt the comforting touch of Christ's hand, and faith to believe he would guide her came into her soul. She could put her life into the hands of someone wiser and infinitely more powerful. Pain gave way to a cleansing sense of forgiveness and profound peace.

She stayed until her knees complained of their trials on the hard bench, then she stood, and her spirit and heart soared. Granddad still lay in a hospital bed, his bills unpaid; the campground empty and run down; her mother probably hated her by now--yet Elaine was as happy as she had ever been in her life. She walked out of the church, heading for the beauty salon knowing that Monica would be waiting and worried. Monica's relief when she walked in was obvious.

"Please forgive me, Mother," Elaine said quietly. Suddenly they were in each other's arms, hugging fiercely.

"I knew you'd come back when you were ready," Monica said, a minute later. "I found some things for you." She held her hand out to Elaine, and picked up a large shopping bag. "We'll take a taxi."

Packages wrapped in Victorian paper and flowing silk ribbons lay scattered across Monica's bed. She smiled as she handed one to Elaine. "Start opening," she said. "There's a lot here."

Sitting on a corner of the bed, she continued to smile as Elaine obeyed. The largest box contained a chiffon dress shaded from light teal to deep turquoise with some spring green woven into it. It had a plunging back rimmed by a fluttering ruffle that went all the way around the neck.

"How lovely," Elaine said, truly meaning it, but wondering when and where she would ever wear such a creation. The second package held a bottle of Shalimar that must have cost a day's pay, even for a famous model.

Then came a soft, cream-colored slip along with other matching lingerie. There were sequined low-heeled sandals--everything to dress her in newness from head to toe. She forced words past the lump in her throat. "Mother, you've outdone yourself," she said, truly pleased. "Can you possibly forgive me for never thanking you for all the lovely things you sent? I didn't realize they were messages of love."

"Forgive you? But darling, I was never angry with you." Monica looked Elaine over and thought, If I look half as good as she does, I'm doing all right. She smiled at her daughter. "I love you, darling, and I always have."

"Maybe you had your own problems?" Elaine asked, ready now to talk.

"Yes, I had problems." Monica's head fell forward and her shoulders slumped.

"Can't you tell me?"

"No." Monica shook her head. "You couldn't understand; it would make things worse."

"Mother," Elaine slid across the bed, pushing the garments aside. "I love you and I want us to be close. We can't be close unless we're honest with each other."

Hesitating, Monica looked intently at Elaine. "I didn't think I was a fit mother. That's why I let someone else raise you and Scotty. I might have damaged you in some way. I was selfish and I knew it." She put both feet on the floor as if to brace herself.

"But whatever made you think that way?" Elaine frowned, concentrating on the nuances in her mother's voice.

"The accident," Monica said. Elaine waited while her mother took a deep breath before plunging into an explanation.

"Your daddy died when you were only three years old, and it was my fault. It wasn't an accident, really--it was my carelessness."

"If you tell me about it you'll feel better, and so will I." Elaine touched her mother's hand. "I'll still love you."

Slowly, reluctantly, Monica began. "By the time you were three, I had been so disagreeable so long that your dad had about fallen out of love with me. You see, I had sent my picture to a modeling agency and they wanted me to come to New York for an interview. Although he never said so, I knew he thought I was a bad wife because I wasn't content to stay and help run his beloved campground.

"I just knew he thought me vain and discontented because I wanted to go. As young as you were, the two of you had a wonderful time together. You wanted to know the names of the plants and animals, and nothing made you happier than going canoeing or swimming with him or hearing stories about the history of the place. When I compared myself with him as a parent, or even with you as a companion, I came up sadly lacking."

"Was he sick?"

"Oh no, he was young and healthy. He was six feet tall and wiry. He had hazel eyes with flecks of yellow in them and curly golden brown hair. He was the handsomest man I'd ever seen. He always wore tan work shirts with the sleeves rolled up; I loved the look of his strong arms. When he came home with them rolled down, I knew he'd been in the deep woods where the mosquitoes and the brambles were after him. I really did love him, or I wouldn't have stayed with him as long as I did."

"Go on," Elaine begged, leaning toward her mother. Monica looked up, and Elaine saw tears running down her cheeks.

"From the time I was little, I knew how selfish I was. I always wanted to be the center of attention, and I wanted things my folks couldn't afford. I didn't care about other people and their needs." She ran a finger beneath her eye, smearing mascara.

Scotty's head popped in the door. "Jean said dinner's in a half hour. She said tell you to dress--you look like you got clothes on to me."

Elaine willed Scotty to go away, but he sauntered into the room and wiggled across the bed to snuggle against Monica. She slipped her arm around him and continued. "Your dad--Steven," she said, her voice soft, "was the only person I ever wanted to please more than I wanted to please myself. That was at first; later, I got restless."

Elaine looked at Scotty, noting his serious expression as he listened with rapt attention.

"I'd always had a yearning for the big city, but he thought because I grew up in a small town, I could adjust to the campground. We had a small wedding--my folks couldn't afford much--and I moved out there and started helping him." A wistful smile lifted the corners of her mouth.

"We had a few good years," Monica said, "working together, making a game of it, swimming in the spring. We were best friends for a while; but things started to fall apart when I got pregnant and was sick and irritable. I started to feel trapped. We fought a lot.

"When you were three years old, one night we left you with your grandparents in town and went to a dance, and after drinking too much, I insisted on driving home. To this day, I don't know why he let me: it was foolish, but I guess he was in the habit of letting me have my way.

"On the way home, I told him I wanted to leave and we had a big fight. He made me stop the car so he could get out, and I drove on without him. Somebody came along later—we found out it was a carload of drunken kids drag racing on the country road--they didn't see him. He died three days later."

The trickle of tears sliding down Monica's cheeks had become a river. Elaine handed her tissues from the bedside table.

"Was he my dad?" Scotty asked.

Monica reached out and stroked his head with slender, tapered fingers. "Elaine's dad was Steven and yours is Jim, sugar. Your granddad raised you both because I wasn't a good mother."

"I think you're a good mother," Scotty said, kissing her elbow. "Please don't cry."

Straightening with a sigh, Monica rose and picked up the lovely dress, which had slid onto the carpet. "Will you wear this tonight? I'd like to see you in it. We won't be here long, but I promise I will come back often, and you will come to see me in New York."

"May I ask one more question?" Elaine inquired. "Did it bother you that Dad left the campground to me?

"No, I wanted to work as a model. Ira and Belle moved to Sacred Spring to look after it and you. They were happy there, until Grandma Belle died, and Grandpa did a good job of raising you children." Elaine sighed with relief; she'd always wondered if her mother resented not getting the property.

"I've got something for you, too, son," Monica said, steering Scotty out. "It's in your room."

Elaine found herself humming as she dressed. The foamy silk flowed around her like the swirling waters of the spring.

CHAPTER 27

$\mathcal{S}$cotty returned to his room, and when Elaine checked on
him, he was standing, brushing his hair in front of a big
mirror in Hank's bathroom. The dress pants and turquoise tee shirt
Monica had brought him fit perfectly.

Lying at his feet, Rags, too, looked clean and combed, and Elaine
wondered who had bathed her--probably the hard-working Mrs.
McGregor after Scotty had charmed her into letting Rags into the
house.

"Hey, I can't get this cowlick to stay down. Will you try?" He
handed her the brush, and she worked until it was temporarily
subdued, but she knew it would pop up again the minute he started
moving around.

"That's the best we can do. You look fine. How do you like your
new clothes?" she asked.

"They're okay, but do you want to see what she really bought me?"
He ran over to the dresser and handed her an electronic device. "See,
it's a Nintendo DS 3d!"

"You have to take good care of it," Elaine said. "It cost a lot of
money. Now leave it here and we'll go to dinner."

Jean placed Hank at the head of the table and seated the rest of the party around the table's wide expanse of starched white linen. A low bouquet of roses and carnations sat as a fragrant centerpiece on a round mirror with tiny gold and crystal swans surrounding it. Reva, present for the business talk, sat on Hank's left with Elaine on his right.

Hank and Jean took up the hands of the people next to them, so everyone else joined hands for the blessing as well. Mrs. McGregor brought salad and soon returned with plates of Cornish hen, a bubbling broccoli and cheese casserole, and a small bowl of macaroni and cheese.

"Umm," said Jim. "Nothing I like better than discussing business over good food." He twisted the leg off a piece of chicken and took a bite. The grease spot on the side of his mouth came off with a swipe of the snowy napkin.

"My compliments to the chef. Well, now, Elaine, I took the liberty of asking Jean to drive me out to the campground while you and your mother were getting beautiful this afternoon. Scotty showed us the way, didn't you, son?"

A warning sounded in Elaine's mind, something about the way Jim looked at Scotty and called him "son." She inched her plate away, knowing she could no longer get anything past the dread that paralyzed her throat.

"The campground is a mess, Elaine," Jim told her. "I'm sure it doesn't hurt your feelings for me to say what you already know."

Ah, but it did.

"We'll put in all new plumbing, clear out the underbrush, open up the spring and make a bigger, cement-lined pool of it. We'll have a lounge, rock band, video games for the kiddies, that is, if we decide to allow children.

"We'll bulldoze all those old buildings and fit in the maximum number of sites. It'll help if we cut down some of those big oaks; they're just in the way. Pass that casserole, please." He gestured with the half-eaten chicken leg.

"The oaks have been there since long before the Civil War," Elaine said.

"Well they've been there long enough, then," he said with a chuckle at his own cleverness. He looked around at Scotty and Hank who both watched Elaine's expressions with worried frowns. "You know we intend to keep it a campground, don't you?" Jim hurried to reassure her.

"Yes, but..."

"I've heard that Florida environmental laws are getting stricter. Will that make for problems?"

"I hope so," she said.

"What?" He emitted a booming laugh. "Oh, you're joking. I'll hire a consulting firm to take care of it. Have some of this, boy." He spooned a mountain of casserole onto Scotty's plate. "It's great."

He didn't see Scotty roll his eyes at Elaine, who knew how much he hated broccoli. She passed him the macaroni and cheese and he spooned some onto his plate.

"Exactly what do you have in mind?" Elaine asked.

"What do you know about time-shares?"

"That's where people pay for the use of a condominium a couple of weeks out of the year." There! Jim would know she was not a dummy to be taken advantage of. She sipped her iced tea and kept a wary eye on Scotty's father over the rim of her glass.

"Absolutely, our chain of campgrounds will be like that and as similar to each other as we can make them. People like familiar surroundings when they travel. Look at the burger joints if you don't believe me. We'll have nothing but the best and we can charge a mint, because only the people who can afford the big coaches are doing any camping these days."

Elaine gulped.

"We'll set up the electric so folks can run their air conditioners and of course, we'll have satellite for their TVs and wireless for their computers. If you think you can handle it, little lady, I'll give you a job managing this one. I can offer you a share of the profits on top of a good price for the property, plus your salary. Now how does that sound? Pretty good, I'd say."

"Very generous," said Monica, with a happy lilt in her voice. Her diamond earrings glittered in the light, and she seemed a different person from the mother who had earlier begun to bare her soul to her children. "I appreciate you taking such good care of my kids, Jim."

"You have to remember that one of them is mine too." He wagged his finger at her. "I'll get a run at doing right by him."

"A campground already exists like that," Elaine said quietly, not smiling. "It's not far from our place."

"Oh?" Jim's heavy dark eyebrows shot up. "Why didn't you show me that, son?" he asked Scotty, who looked up, startled. "Never mind. Anyhow, it's good the other one has already done the work. We can buy them out and incorporate them—more for us, eh?"

"We're a long way from all the attractions," Elaine added. Though her insides were jumping around with indecision and anxiety, she lowered her voice to make herself sound calm. This might be her only chance at reasoning with him.

"We'll have a shuttle service to Disney and maybe even to the Kennedy Space Center museums. We may have to spend a little money to let people know we're here and what we have to offer, but the advertising department will take care of all that. Maybe we'll eventually put in a monorail." Jim pulled out a ballpoint pen and drew the snowy linen napkin closer.

"Hold on a minute," said Jean. "I've got some paper." She rummaged in a drawer of the buffet. "I keep it handy because we never know when Hank's going to get an urge to explain something. He doesn't hesitate to use the tablecloth, napkins, anything handy, of course he's always sorry, but it's no use locking the barn door after the horse has been stolen." Elaine remembered joking about the scribbled-on chunk of wood on the seat of Hank's rattletrap truck--a long time ago.

"Okay, the RVs will be close together, but that way, we'll turn a profit in a short time." Jim started drawing.

"Didn't we offer to buy the property first, Hank?" Reva asked. Everyone ignored her.

"What about the bald eagles?" Hank asked, staring at Elaine. "Their nests are protected by law."

"No problem." Jim skimmed over the questions. "You have wild animals out there, too?"

"Well, sure, most of the property is wilderness," Elaine answered.

"We'll have to get rid of them."

"Isn't there any way you could save some habitat?" She was trying to open a dialogue—reason with Jim.

He put down the pen and picked up the body of his small hen stripping off the breast meat with his perfect teeth. Elaine looked at the bare bones on his plate and felt ill.

"Oh, yes indeed," he said. "We'll have a nature trail and we'll leave an area by the pool for sunbathing, and of course, we'll have the river for access to the lake so speedboats can run up there. Won't our guests have fun, though?"

"But the environmental people won't let you come in and clear everything, and because of the manatees, there's a limit on how fast boats can go."

"No problems we can't negotiate." He rubbed his thumb against the tips of his fingers. "We've got great lawyers, too. Don't be negative. I'm sure the word *campground* makes a good impression on local authorities." Jim's teeth shone in the light from overhead.

"Can you give me some time to think about all this?" Elaine got up from the table.

"We're having homemade French vanilla ice cream and chocolate cake," said Jean. "Don't you want some?

"I ate all my dinner so I can have it," Scotty said. "Are you going to eat your chicken, Laney?"

"I'm not very hungry tonight. I guess I need some fresh air." She picked up her barely touched plate, set it over his empty one, and scooted his broccoli out of the way.

CHAPTER 28

"I first met him at a dance in the old grange. We liked each other a lot. He made me laugh. We danced all the dances, and the boy who took me to the dance was furious. He picked a fight, but when your dad knocked him down, he got up and left. Steven was gentle, but could be tough when he had to be." Her eyes brightened with amusement.

The minute Elaine got out the door, she started running down the driveway. She wanted to get away from all those people and the desires and expectations they placed on her shoulders. Suddenly she fell onto the sun-warmed asphalt.

The shadows along the drive seemed to be creeping toward her. Her mother always feared muggers, and here she sat, a woman injured and alone in the growing darkness. Perhaps she was foolish to run off this way. At least she hadn't come far. She got up and hobbled back toward the house. I have to make a decision, she thought, right or wrong.

As she approached, she felt the romance of the house's floodlit Spanish lines. Hank and Jean are fortunate to live in such a beautiful place and to have plenty of money, she thought. Money can buy so many things people need.

It can pay bills, help bring good health, educate people; in the end, it can free them from a lot of worry. I can manage to live on a small budget, but I need to care for Granddad and Scotty. Granddad. The thought of losing Scotty was almost more than she could bear.

Hank rushed out the door and to her side.

"What happened?" he asked, putting his arm around her waist and taking some of her weight.

"I just took a tumble," she said.

"Come with me." He tugged her gently along.

Elaine basked in delicious warmth and comfort, knowing that in this moment, words were far from necessary.

"Elaine," Hank spoke her name softly. "What are you doing out here all by yourself?"

"I needed to think." She couldn't help sighing. This was where she belonged, close to Hank, inside a circle of light with the darkness and all the mean and cruel things of life shut out.

"Have you made a decision?" he asked.

"Yes."

"And?" He frowned now, knowing by her hesitation that it would not be in his favor.

"I...I'm going to sell the campground to Jim." She felt Hank's hurt and his withdrawal. "I'm sorry, but I think I can talk him into leaving a good portion of the wilderness alone."

"I thought you liked my ideas." Hank looked stunned, as if she'd slapped him.

"Your ideas are good, but I think Reva might have a different scheme--that industrial complex. It doesn't matter, anyway. I have to save what I can; you know I must take care of Granddad and help with Scotty's expenses when he moves. Jim's money can help me do that. It all means so much to me, it's overwhelming."

"Are you saying it doesn't matter to me?"

"Well, no, but it matters about keeping Reva happy and running your business the most efficiently you can." Tensing, she pulled slightly away from him.

"In other words, you think I'm a money-grubbing cad whose life is run by a woman," he said in bitter summary. "You've got yourself locked into the campground idea, and you can't see when somebody is trying to help fulfill your dreams and goals."

Refusal to answer would antagonize him further, but she didn't know what to say, so she remained silent.

"There you are," called Reva coming out the front door. "Isn't Jim clever? I'd like to get to know him better; I could learn a lot from him." She hooked her arm through Hank's then sobered. "What's the matter," she said, looking from one to the other. "Did somebody die or something?"

Elaine's composure was leaking away now that Reva had joined them. She didn't want to tell her anything. Hank would do it, she felt sure. They could talk it over together.

Reva tilted her head contemptuously at Elaine. "Are you worrying about those wild animals again? I can't see why you let that bother you so much. Most of them are rodents and vermin, anyway, aren't they?"

"All God's creatures have a right to live in a decent habitat." Elaine drew herself up to her full height and looked down at the other woman.

"Let's talk about all this some other time," Hank said. "Right now, we're supposed to be at Jean's party. Come on in and have some dessert." Both women ignored him.

"Surely you don't believe that sentimental pap about animal rights," Reva challenged, "and you can't possibly think Jim does."

Elaine opened her mouth to object. She was an environmental conservationist, not an animal-rights activist; but she knew explaining would be a waste of breath.

"Maybe I'll offer him a good price," Reva said. "After all, he's a businessman, and we could negotiate." She gave a slow, calculating grin and swung to Hank. "At any rate, you won't need to hang around out there any more as soon as you finish construction on the piece you're working on."

"Reva," he said, "be a good sport." He was subdued, quiet, and cool —the perfect gentleman. "Elaine has to do what's right for her. If we've missed the deal we were looking for, we have to forget it and move on. I'm going to tell Jean 'good night' and head back to the camper."

Reva stood on tiptoe to kiss him, but he turned his face away. Taking her by the shoulders, he gently set her back. "Good night, Reva," he said firmly. Hank gave Elaine an unreadable look and walked away.

"Good night," Elaine said, wondering if she'd ever see him again.

Elaine by-passed the dining room and headed for her assigned quarters. She found Scotty sitting on the floor, close to the T. V., watching the weather channel. She perched on the end of the bed with her elbows on her knees and her chin in her hands, and watched brindled clouds move in a circular pattern over Cuba.

Hank was gone, but she still had Scotty and Granddad, and the campground; a campground, at least. She'd never give up fighting for them. Never.

"Hi, where you been?" Scotty twisted around to look at her. "There's a hurricane coming." He announced it delightedly, ready for any kind of excitement.

"A tropical depression has taken a western curve and is gathering strength in the Atlantic," the announcer said. "It's too soon to predict the path it will take. Store extra food and water, and have alternate methods of light available. Tape your windows to prevent flying glass. Take in loose items so they won't become flying missiles."

"It probably won't amount to anything," Elaine told Scotty. "Tropical depressions happen every year; they usually dissipate before they get to land."

She got up and wandered into the living room where Jim, Jean, and Monica had gathered and sat sunken into soft couches.

"Come sit by me, darling," said her mother. "You missed a delicious dessert, worth breaking the rules for. Your knee is bleeding." Elaine looked down at her dress and saw bright red amongst the cool colors in the skirt. She hadn't even felt it.

~

For the rest of the week, Elaine and Monica visited Granddad in the hospital twice a day and in between went shopping in exclusive areas and out to lunch. For some reason, Elaine kept putting off telling anyone else of her decision. Monica tried to draw her out, but Elaine couldn't bear to talk about it.

Jim rented a car and took Scotty around the countryside looking at property. As they came and went, Elaine watched their attachment weave itself tighter. Everyone followed the progress of the tropical depression as it built daily into a hurricane. Elaine still didn't worry because she knew no major hurricane had hit their area in recorded history.

One evening, Scotty came into her room and joined her on the bed. "I have to talk to you," he said, and her heart sank.

"I think I know what it is," she answered.

"Then you aren't mad?" His innocent brown eyes gave him the look of a trusting, puppy.

"Go on, tell me about it." She touched the crown of his head where the cowlick grew and mourned with tender melancholy.

"Jim says I ought to come live with him. He wants to put me in a good school to learn the stuff I'll need to know, computers and all, so I can maybe be his partner some day, and take over the businesses when he retires."

Elaine's eyes stung, but for Scotty's sake, she had to swallow her tears. Why upset him when it might be right for him? It would be a while until her own affairs were settled; until then she didn't even know where she would be living. When she and Granddad knew, she could bring her brother home. In the meantime, he had a right to know and love his father; and Jim had an obligation to provide a father's attention and teaching.

"Maybe a few months in New York with your dad will be good for you. But there's one thing that bothers me."

"What?" He moved closer.

"What does he say about never coming to see you all the time you were growing up?"

"I had everything I needed. He was so busy making a living that he didn't have time to think about anything else. One morning, he saw some gray hair in the mirror--he says it showed up overnight--and he started wondering what he was working so hard for when he already had lots of money and someday he was going to die, and then what?

"All of a sudden, he remembered he had a son--me--and he thought; why not get to know me? I'm his only kid, as far as he knows, Laney. We have to give him a chance."

Elaine could see that Scotty wanted this more than he'd ever wanted anything. She hoped he'd be all right now that Jim had decided to recognize his own son.

"Besides," Scotty continued, "Granddad, says we have to forgive. I think my dad is sorry and lonely. If I go to New York, I can see Mother sometimes, too. I'll miss you and Granddad something awful, but Dad says I can take Rags if I'll walk her every day, and I have to take a little bag to pick up after her, or they'll throw me in jail.

"I'm going to get an aquarium and some hamsters. He'll get me my own cell phone, isn't that boss, Laney? I can call you any time I want to, and they both want you to come visit, and maybe even live there some day. Besides, I can come back here summers. What's a pent-house, Laney?"

"It's an apartment on the top story of a very tall building. You'll find New York a lot different from Sacred Spring. I hope you'll be happy there after running free in the woods most of your life," she said doubtfully. "Who will take care of you when you're not in school? Jim and Monica work a lot, you know."

"Jim's got a house-boy. Ha-Gee. He sounds cool. He'll teach me karate and he raises bonsai. What's 'bonsai?'" he asked, but didn't pause in his headlong account to get an answer. "I've got my mind made up."

As he slid under her arm, she thought of all the times they'd sat this way on her bed, on their porch swing, at the pool, in a booth at the Old Mill. "Is it really okay?" he asked.

"I don't want you to go." Her voice broke. "But do you remember how Granddad always told us if we loved somebody we had to let go of them and someday they would come back to us?"

"I know." He nodded sagely, and all at once, she could see the caring, sensitive man he would become. Jim could not change that no matter what he did. "My dad needs me." He brightened. "Maybe I'll learn how to make money so I can help you and Granddad."

"All right, remember, though, you will always have a home with me wherever I am. I love you." This encounter was the final blow to all her hopes and dreams, but she mustn't make him feel guilty about leaving her.

"I love you, too. I'm going to tell Jim you'll let me go." He jumped off the bed.

Elaine laughed ruefully. "As if I had any choice; there's no way I could keep you. I'll have to sign you back over to him."

CHAPTER 29

The three women and Scotty met at the hospital on the evening of Monica's last day in Orlando. A nurse interrupted their chatter. "Dr. Potter's looking for you. He said he'd meet you in Mr. Thompson's room." They sprang to their feet and hurried down the hall. Let it be good news, Elaine prayed.

"Come in, all of you!" He grabbed Elaine's arm and led them to Ira's bed.

"Ira, your family is here," said Dr. Potter. Ira slowly opened his eyes and looked directly at Elaine. She breathed a *thank-heaven* sigh. Next to her, Monica began to weep. Annie whispered, "Ira," in a voice of longing and hope. Dr. Potter held up his hand, and they waited, not daring to breathe.

Ira's gaze traveled from one to the other. "Monica, my little girl." His words came in small puffs. He reached a fragile, shaking hand toward Elaine and smiled weakly. His gaze found Annie's face. "And there's my Annie," he said, "all the women I love. And Scotty. Hey, son."

"Oh, Granddad, we've missed you so." Elaine sank onto the edge of the bed and held his hand while Annie and Monica stood by with their arms around each other.

"By golly! If this keeps up, we'll have him up and at 'em in no time," Dr. Potter briskly rubbed his hands together. I've got to go, but you three stay and visit." He laid his finger on his nose. "For a short time."

"When you get well, we'll take you to New York, Dad," Monica said.

"He can come live with me," Annie said, smiling dreamily. "I'll take care of him."

"Monica, princess, how's… life been treating you?"

"Good, Dad. I'm so glad you're awake and to know you're safe, because I really must leave now. I have a job in Europe that can't wait. I'll come back in a month or so."

"I'll be my old self by then, darlin', " he said. "Hurry back."

The next day, after Monica left for Europe, Jim and Scotty took off for New York City in Jim's new Lincoln Aviator SUV. Elaine and Jean took Missy out to the driveway to wave them off. It was one of the hardest things Elaine had ever done. The storm had stalled, but would soon start moving again. Scotty had a small carrier for Rags.

"I can't thank you, enough, Elaine, for letting the boy go." Before he got in the car, Jim pumped her hand. "I'll call in a few days, and maybe we'll draw up some papers for the campground. I'll take care of the guardianship legalities, too, and let you know if you need to do anything."

She nodded wordlessly, not sure why she couldn't make a final commitment to Jim's plan. At the last minute, Scotty threw his arms around her waist and clung like a stick-tight-seed. Holding him close, she choked back her emotions for his sake. "I'll come up to the city and see how you're doing," she promised, disengaging herself from his arms. "Jim's waiting; you've got to go now."

Jim picked up the dog-carrier, and Jean took her arm as they walked away, but Elaine stopped to glance back, through tears, at the small, wistful figure waving at them before he got in the car. She waved and threw him a kiss.

Later that day, Elaine went to the hospital to tell Ira about selling the campground to Jim. When she got to his room, she was glad to see their Annie sitting by his side.

"Jim, huh?" said Ira. "Yeah, your mother brought him up to see me. What happened to that Hank fellow we was thinking about selling to? I liked him."

"Elaine will explain all that later, Ira. Maybe it would be good to talk about what you'd like to do when they release you from here. Got any ideas?" Annie said.

"I saw myself going back to Sacred Spring and looking after the truck and the kids," he said.

"I'm sorry, darlin', but things have changed so drastically we're going to need to talk about some new plans." Annie patted his arm. "You'll need someone to look after you and to drive you back and forth to therapy," she said. "Elaine has a lot to deal with, right now. Why don't you come and stay with me? They have all kinds of home health care now to help us. I'd love to have you."

"Why sure, if it will help Laney," the old man said. His voice was barely audible, and a tear slid onto his cheek.

"There's only one thing." Annie stood to her full height of five feet as Elaine turned to look at her. "You can't live with me unless we're married. We'd look like a couple of old fools."

Elaine heard Ira chuckle, and gladness bathed her spirits. "Yes, ma'am, that's right. I guess you'd have to marry me so's not to ruin my reputation."

"If we're going to spend the rest of our old age together, it would be more seemly."

"Hmm," Granddad mused. "As soon as I get out of here, we'll just go and get hitched, then."

Elaine was happy for them; she certainly didn't want to be selfish. She wished them well, but because Scotty had gone to live with Jim, when Ira moved to Annie's, she would have no one left.

"You come with us, Elaine." Annie held out her hands to Elaine.

"You know how huge that house is, and you can work things out from there."

"Thank you, dear, dear friend," Elaine answered, "but I need time to think. As soon as I know what I'm going to do, I'll tell you."

"Anyway, I will take care of Ira." Annie smiled a glorious smile that lit up the room. Her fondest dreams, though long delayed, were now coming true.

"Are you sure you want to take on a sick old man like me?" Ira's voice rang with joy even though he was obviously tiring. "I ain't going to be able to do much work for a while."

"I want you if all you can do is keep me company while I knit," Annie said, "but I believe you'll soon get a lot better."

"We're moving into a private room today," the nurse said as she came in. "It will take some time. He'll have to rest afterwards. No more visits today."

"A private room? That costs…" Elaine was appalled.

"Don't worry, dear," the nurse said. "Medicaid and your mother took care of everything. You look like you need some rest, too. Go home."

"Missy has a new word," Jean said as Elaine got into the car.

"What is it?" Elaine asked listlessly, not much caring.

"Scotty." Jean laughed. "She adores him."

From the car seat in the back, Missy said, "Totty!"

"Would you mind driving me out to the campground? The Braithwaites are leaving and I need to see to things out there."

"They're predicting winds up to a hundred miles an hour by dark," Jean objected, eyes on the traffic. "Ethel is spinning off the coast like a top. It's not safe for you to be out there now, especially alone."

"They don't always know what's going to happen. Maybe they're wrong; hurricanes change direction all the time. Please, Jean. I don't care about all that. I've been at the campground during lots of bad storms. I can take care of myself. It means a lot to me."

As they drove away from the airport, Elaine saw the effects of Ethel's long black skirts brushing the tops of the queen palms. Navigating through town, Jean steered around downed branches and swerved to avoid garbage barrels rolling in the street.

At each intersection, rain-blurred traffic lights danced the tarantella on their cables, looking as if they might fall at any moment. Dry palm fronds skittered along the gutter and she watched as one of them took flight over the traffic. Jean turned onto the highway, commenting on the ominous signs, but Elaine headed off any attempt to keep her in town.

"I'll drive you out there since you insist. You're a big girl, but I want you to know I'll protest when Hank gets mad at me. I'll tell him I did it against my better judgment."

"Hank doesn't care any more."

"Why would you even think that?" Jean was shocked.

"I told him I was going to sell out to Jim...and it hurt him, and now he doesn't want me around anymore."

"That doesn't sound like Hank."

"It would never work; our goals are too different," Elaine said, closing the subject.

When they turned into the campground an hour later, Elaine's despair deepened. All was dark, rain shrouded, and depressing. Looking past swishing windshield wipers, Elaine was again painfully aware of the smallness of the old house, with its peeling paint and saggy porch.

"Thanks for everything." She opened the car door a crack, but before she could slip out, Jean grabbed her arm.

"Wait. You can't do anything here. Let me help check the Old Mill, and then you come on back with me. I have to take Missy home where it's safe, or I'd stay with you. I'm worried about this storm. I shouldn't have let you talk me into this."

"I'll be fine." Elaine sprang from the car, let the door swing closed, and made a dash for the house. By the time she got inside, she was wet through. She looked out the front window, saw the red lights of Jean's car pause, and then disappear into the storm.

She wanted to change her mind and go where it would be warm and safe, and where other people would be around her. The wind whapped repeatedly against the outside walls, making everything in the house rattle. The air was hot and charged with static electricity as pressure built inside, until Elaine thought the house might implode.

She opened the door, but it flew out of her hands and slammed up against the side of the house. She struggled to pull it closed again. Her nerves crawled and the hair on her arms stood up as she went into the kitchen. She flicked the light switch, but nothing happened.

Peering around the gloom, she saw that the room, the refrigerator, the table, and the stove had all grown smaller in her absence. She grabbed a dishcloth and wiped the dust-covered counter. The first thing I'll do, she vowed, is give this place a good cleaning, and then I'll get some paint.

In the bedroom, she looked at the faded cover on her bed, the rag rug, and the old dressing table and compared them with the elegant furnishings of the bedroom she had recently occupied. Nevertheless, this is my home, she reminded herself, angry at such disloyal thoughts.

She kicked off the shoes Hank and Jean had given her and removed the new jeans she had slipped away to buy at the discount store without her mother's knowledge. Her legs had turned blue from their dye. She picked up a pair of shorts from the closet floor, and plucked a tee shirt off a hanger.

"At least I have dry clothes," she muttered. "My own dry clothes, old clothes, comfortable clothes, my own dry, comfortable, old clothes," she recited in a litany that somehow comforted her.

As she started for the Old Mill in Granddad's heavy yellow slicker, she could barely hold on to the umbrella she had hoped would help protect her. Before she arrived, it turned inside out and escaped into the sky. She splashed through puddles up to her ankles.

The palm trees doubled over, their fronds sweeping the ground. The undeniably hurricane-force winds tore at the trees along the river. She hoped the eagles would be all right. At least their babies would have fledged by now.

To her relief, everything was as it should be at the Old Mill: the shutters fastened tight, and the chairs upside-down on the tables, which meant the Braithwaites had mopped before they left. The restaurant smelled clean, but stuffy from disuse.

She hung the dripping slicker on one chair and got down another one to sit on while she decided what to do next. Rain battered the windows like fistfuls of gravel kicking up from the parking lot. A drop of cold water dripped onto her head, then another and another.

She looked up. The water was coming in around the ceiling light fixture. We'll have to get that fixed, she thought. Something thudded onto the roof. She admitted finally that this storm was going to be the first to do damage to her area in recorded history.

It was growing cooler. She looked up and saw a huge crack in the ceiling, she watched it split open and the ceiling begin to open and break apart. That was her warning, but there was no time to move. She fell beneath the tumbling beams.

CHAPTER 30

*E*laine tasted blood in her mouth. She wiggled and felt that nothing was broken. She tried to get up, but discovered she was in a sort of fallen timber shelter. She squeezed her eyes shut and tried to figure out where she was and what had happened.

Oh yes, she thought, I should have let Hank prune that branch. She gathered her strength and tried again to shift the wreckage and maybe find a passage out of the detritus. Her strength wasn't enough--not nearly enough. A sense of hopelessness washed over her and she lay perfectly still, listening to the howling wind, the clatter of rain, and the dripping of water nearby.

She couldn't believe she had fallen asleep under these conditions, but when she woke, her mouth was dry and her heart was pounding.

"Help!" she called as loudly as she could. No voice but that of the storm's blowing and rattling answered her in the wild night.

After she had rested a few moments, she yelled some more. Once her voice was gone, she whimpered. Wind continued to assault the beams that lay half protecting, half threatening her. You'd better lie still, she told herself. If you don't, the rubble will shift, and you'll be crushed. Drawing a deep breath of musty-smelling air, she gave up and fell asleep again.

～

She jerked her face out of the chilly puddle that had collected under her cheek while she slept. If you don't stay awake you'll drown, dummy, she scolded herself. You might not see anything to live for, but you don't want to go this way.

For the rest of the night, she lay in the low, dark cave, protected by a single beam that kept the whole roof from collapsing. Alternately, she fell into a stupor and jolted herself back to reality. Her body felt numbed and she tried some isometric exercises. I never appreciated what a luxury, what a miracle, freedom and movement were, she thought.

The rooster crowed. Ah, the chickens got through the storm, then. Funny how that simple thought cheered her. She heard the high-pitched sound of thousands of frogs that sounds like a herd of calves bawling. The storm was over. The dripping slowed and eventually ceased.

Jasmine and wild thyme released their fragrances in a heady potpourri of scent as the sun barely began to peek into her night's home. When she tried to move again, she felt the pile of debris that rested above her shift and immediately stilled. It's too bad, she thought, that a quiet body did not necessarily mean a tranquil mind.

She thought about Hank and laughed a little at how much she had enjoyed smacking that mosquito on his arm the day they met. She knew more about him now. She knew that even mosquitoes respected him and that they would not sting him or drink his blood.

She saw him standing in the clearing, thumbs hooked in the pockets of his jeans, exuding the confidence of one who usually sees things go his way. She'd wanted to shock him out of his arrogance, but the sparkle of pure joy in the emerald eyes captured her attention. She had succumbed to the power of his strong body and mind as if she were a young girl with no worldly wisdom at all. Had she fallen in love with him that day?

My love for Hank, she marveled, is the best and truest emotion I've ever experienced. Before him, all I wanted was to live at Sacred Spring and work with nature. I still want that, but now, because of Hank, I know for sure, there is a God who loves me. If I can't have Hank, I will at least have that.

"*Come unto me all ye that labor and are heavy laden, and I will give you rest.*" She recalled the scripture near the painting in the church, I've never been more heavily laden, she thought. I'll just have to trust him.

"Well, Lord," she whispered, "I've lost the campground, my family--and Hank. I have nothing left but you. Do you still want me?"

Bubbling from the depths of her heart came a knowing, an intuition. "*Up to now, your dreams have not been big enough. Sacred Spring contains acres of prime wilderness, and you have a master's degree in biology; you know Florida wildlife inside out. Don't tell me you have nothing left.*"

Is this how he talked to people--quietly--in their own minds? If it was, he sounded highly optimistic. In spite of the close quarters, within her body and mind, her spirit soared. Wouldn't it be wonderful to find out she could actually talk things over with God, learning to trust him, to hear his voice as others seemed to do? "Oh, Lord, please help me," she cried.

For years, fear of losing control had closed her mind to new ideas about life and God. Now heart and head united, letting insight bloom, and she became more aware and insightful than she had ever been in her life.

"In the beginning," she muttered, praying now. "You told man to take care of the Earth. We haven't done too well, but perhaps there's still time."

A thrill of anticipation filled her as fingers of golden light poked through cracks in the rubble. She felt like leaping and dancing, if she could only move. For the first time in her life, she knew what the phrase "a new lease on life" meant. She began to understand that God didn't help those who helped themselves so much as he helped those who were confused, fearful, impoverished; those who couldn't help themselves and more importantly, those who asked.

Well, God, she thought, I suppose the first thing I need to ask you for is get me out of here...but I'll stay if that's what you want because I'm beginning to believe you know best, no matter how things look.

～

The sun rose and beat down on Elaine's prison, turning it into an oven. When a human-generated sound came, she didn't recognize it at first. Was It Hank's truck? Oh God, let it be Hank! A door slammed...footsteps on the gravel drive ... his deep voice calling her name.

"Are you in there?" A thrill ran through her at the desperation in his voice. Hank had arrived. She croaked like a bullfrog when she tried to answer. He couldn't have heard her anyhow because he kept up a patter of, "I'm coming, hold on, I'll be right there.".

"I'm over here under the rubble," she gasped, "where the kitchen used to be."

The rubble moved slightly, and she could hear pieces of wood thudding to the ground outside. Heavy boots crunched.

"Are you hurt?" he asked, sounding closer now.

"I don't think so; can you get me out?"

"I have to get my ax and a crowbar."

"I'll wait right here," she joked, feeling giddy.

After a few minutes, she heard him working and could imagine him swinging the ax, *thwack*, prying up boards, *creeak*, and pausing to throw debris off the pile.

"Be careful!" Elaine cried. "The whole thing could shift." He was in too much of a hurry to hear. He broke through and almost at once, she had more room to move in.

"Don't get up yet," he warned, jumping down into the hole with her. She laughed aloud, joyful in knowing he was there and today, after the night she'd been through, she was freer than she'd ever been in her life.

"I'm fine," she said, moving her arms and legs to make sure. "My shoulder hurts a little, that's all." He cleared a space for himself and maneuvered down beside her.

"I can't believe you survived the roof falling on you!" he said.

"From what I could tell," she answered, "the beams made a v-shaped space that protected me. Is it safe for me to get up now?"

"Turn over first." He helped her. Lying on her back, she flexed numb legs. Hank's eyes clouded with compassion and concern.

"I just need to stretch," she said. A moan mixed of pain and relief escaped as the nerves began to come alive again.

"Are my pupils the same size?" she asked.

"They're fantastic," he said gazing into her blue eyes. "I was so worried when we couldn't contact you." His voice broke slightly. "Are you truly all right?" A tear fell. In wonder, she touched his cheek.

"I'm sorry." His head bent as he looked away, embarrassed. He used the tips of his fingers to wipe his eyes, but he couldn't conceal the sobs coming from deep in his chest. A man weeps so differently from a woman, Elaine thought. They probably don't get enough practice.

He drew her closer, and as he held her, she felt her muscles and joints begin to heal.

"I'm so relieved that you're all right." He squeezed her even tighter.

"Why?" Elaine wanted to hear more of this kind of talk.

"Don't you know how much I love you?" Hank spoke softly.

"I only knew I loved you." Joy fluttered in her chest. "But then, so does everybody else. I thought I was just another one of your fans. Did you know how I felt?" She snuggled closer against him as a warm lethargy spread from head to toe.

"I thought maybe...when I held you at Jean's and you seemed so...so..."

"Willing? Did I shock you?" She could ask it now that she knew her feelings were safe with him. "Was it wicked of me?"

"No! You didn't shock me. I loved you and I wanted you so much, but I wanted to ask you to be my wife and a man doesn't treat his future wife that way. Did you think I didn't want you?"

"I was embarrassed that I got so carried away," she whispered. "That has never happened to me before. His mouth brushed hers tentatively; then the smoldering embers burst into flame, burning with the hunger and passion hovering between them since the day they met.

"Hadn't we better get out of this hole?" She fitted the tip of her little finger into the cleft in his chin, in no hurry to have him take her up on it.

"I guess so, but I don't want to turn you loose, even for a minute."

"Hank, a couple of things..."

"Anything!" The corners of his mouth curved in an even wider smile.

"About Reva..."

His smile vanished. "We'd better get you out of here, and then we'll discuss Reva."

"Are you avoiding my question?"

"I'll tell you anything you want to know, but right now we need to get out." He helped her climb out and stood her on her feet in the dazzling summer morning. It's beautiful," she said, "even if most of our mill is gone." She couldn't believe she was taking the destruction of her restaurant so calmly. Sure enough, the renegade branch as big as a tree lay smack in the middle of the mill roof.

"It can be rebuilt," he said. "What would the place be without it?"

"The house survived." He pointed at Elaine's home. "Let's see if we can get in so you can get some dry clothes.

"And a shower," she said.

Dead palm branches and some limbs blocked the front and back doors, so he boosted her through the window and left to start the clean up while she bathed.

"Now tell me about Reva," Elaine said as they sat on the front porch making crunching sounds as they chewed on limp granola bars she found in the kitchen cupboard.

"What do you want to know?" he asked, sipping at a glass of water.

"Would you let her build an industrial park on my property?"

"I'm usually the last to be told about Reva's plans for the business," Hank answered. "But I believe she would like to do that."

"That's not what Sacred Spring needs! It would be awful," Elaine said.

"You're right. I wasn't in on her plans and I don't approve of them."

He reached over and gently rubbed Elaine's shoulder. "How do you feel?" he inquired. "It's not every day you have a house fall on you." She thrilled to the intimacy in his soft, caring voice. She put her hand over his and a satisfied *umm* escaped.

"I couldn't sleep last night," Hank said. "I was at the trailer, and the wind made so much racket, I expected the camper to take off like lumbering blimp. I got in some serious thinking and praying." His eyes sparkled with happiness. "Got answers, though, so I was grateful. I drove home to see if you were at Casa Del Sol. I was upset when Jean said she brought you out here and left you in that storm."

"She knew you wouldn't like that, but I insisted," Elaine said.

"Somebody's coming." He cocked his head, listening.

They got up and stepped off the porch as the Mercedes pulled in. Elaine's heart fell when she saw Reva, more gorgeous than ever with her shining black hair brushing her shoulders. She wore a figure-revealing white dress with a low Grecian neckline, a gold belt, and shoes. Dressed to kill, Elaine thought, stroking down her own unruly locks.

Reva marched up to the porch, her face a mask of fury.

"Where have you been?" she demanded of Hank, craning her neck to look up at them.

"I needed to talk to Elaine." He shrugged and Elaine was surprised that he seemed neither angry at her tone, nor overcome by Reva's beauty. She looked at the other woman again and had to admit that her bad humor had a bad effect on her looks. The downturned mouth and furrowed brow definitely aged her.

"What's the matter with you? You're a mess." Reva's gaze shifted to Elaine. The spoiled-brat set of her face reminded Elaine of Annie's saying about beauty being only skin-deep. She determined to keep her dignity, no matter what provocation the other woman offered.

"It's me you're mad at, remember?" Hank reminded her, trying to draw her fire.

"Where were you last night? You were supposed to take me to the mayor's fund raiser."

"They didn't cancel?" he asked.

"Yes, but you didn't even try to call and check with me? You forgot all about it and me." Her voice rose an octave as she accused stridently, "You knew it was a chance to get in solid with some of the most important politicians in town. Two of our bankers were going to be there. You forgot because you don't care about the money we need to finance our projects. You forgot because you don't care about me."

Now she was pouting like a twelve-year-old who had been told to clean her room. Elaine could see how she got a lot of mileage out of that, but it didn't work this time. Hank was immune. You'll go when they schedule it again, I'll see to that."

"I don't think so," he said. "Even if you had discussed it with me, I wasn't ready to commit to any kind of industrial park." Hank pushed at her hand. "Besides, Elaine's going to sell to somebody else, and that's her prerogative."

"Fine! I'll buy from him, then." Reva stood scowling at both of them.

"I'm going to finance my next project myself, anyway," said Hank. "I'm tired of using other people's money. There's no point in owing." Hank was forcing her back with the sheer power of his personality.

"What's going on here, anyway?" Reva's eyes narrowed as she looked from him to Elaine.

"Hank and I are discussing business," Elaine said.

"Yeah, sure. Well, you needn't bother. We're buying the property, if not from you, then from Jim. I'm not going to let this one get away." Reva moved to Hank's side and snuggled against him, laying her head on his chest. Her tone became wheedling, but his arms remained at his sides. "We'll make a lot, Hank, sweetie, and you know it's better to use someone else's money."

"I'm not going to sell Sacred Spring," Elaine announced suddenly, squaring her shoulders, "to Jim, to you, to anybody."

"You think you have a choice?" Reva's rage flared again.

"I'm not selling," Elaine repeated in a flat voice. "So you can forget whatever plans you have for my property."

"You'll have to; you're nothing but a destitute Florida Cracker. "

"You're a Cracker yourself if you mean having been descended from the original settlers, but never mind. I've decided to find an investor of my own," Elaine answered primly.

"What a coincidence. I happen to be looking for a campground to invest in." Hank's eyes seemed to glow as he looked at her.

"That happens to be exactly what I want to talk to you about," Elaine said, ignoring Reva. "I was thinking you and I could start an environmental consulting firm--your money, my property."

"Right!" In growing excitement, he took hold of Elaine's arm. "The difference between that and an industrial park is...?"

"The difference between life and death," Elaine finished for him. Reva's face put the hurricane's fury to shame. "You were all ready for it." Elaine spoke to Hank as if there were no one else present. "How did you know?"

"I've got my sources." He slid his arm around Elaine. "We'll negotiate with government agencies and builders and figure out how to conserve as much land as possible," he said, giving her an exuberant squeeze. Maybe we'll even be able to give some to the Nature Conservancy, if they'll take it."

Elaine's heart danced. How could it be that they both had been thinking the same things? "...with a camp and a research facility," she added.

"We can teach how to build responsibly, and we'll make the campground an outdoor laboratory. We can run a camp for inner city kids. And no, Elaine, to answer your unasked question, I am not now, nor have I ever been engaged to Reva. She bought that ring herself."

"Jean told you what I thought," she said, glad it was all out in the open now.

"You would have bought it sooner or later; you weasel. I just got tired of waiting. You've always done everything I wanted." Reva said, her face flushing. Elaine leaned a bit into Hank to comfort him, but

Reva was so bent on hurting him that Elaine had to wonder whether someone else had hurt Reva. For the first time, she found pity in her heart for the woman.

"You're right." He spoke slowly, feeling his way. "I've always gone along with everything you wanted, but that was because you needed protection. However, I think we're grown up enough now to go our own ways. Don't you think that would be best?"

"You can't go in with those environmentalists. They're our worst enemies. They..." she sputtered. "You...you can't do anything without me, you're too soft on people. You don't want money badly enough. I'm your partner. We have to vote," Reva finished imperiously.

"You forget, the business was left to the three surviving children-- you, me, and Jean. I think Jean will go along with Elaine and me."

"You can't do it." Reva's voice dripped with malice. "I'm the one with my finger on the pulse of the business world. I'm the one who knows how to make things work. All you ever do is putter around with your old earth-moving machines and your dumb little houses, and you're always trying to stay within the law when you could fudge only a little and we'd make a lot more money."

"Reva," Hank explained, "our country is having a hard time balancing environmental laws with the rights and needs of people. We have to change the laws that aren't reasonable, but we still need some sort of system. People can't continue using land, water, and air as they did fifty years ago; it isn't healthy.

"We're responsible for the welfare of God's Earth. Elaine and I will do fine, don't worry about us. We might even invite you to the wedding if you're nice."

He looked at Elaine and she nodded with a big smile on her face as Hank went on talking to Reva. "You do what you want, but leave me out of it. With Elaine's knowledge of nature and my builder's background, we'll make things better. We can include you, if you want, but as far as the business end of things goes, Jean's style is different from yours, but will work just as well, no doubt about that."

"You bunch of goody-goodies make me sick," Reva said through clenched teeth. "Our business wouldn't be where we are now if it weren't for me. You don't have the killer instinct. How do you think we got a chance at buying this place?"

"You!" Elaine said. "You had them cancel my grant."

"That's business. I fixed it so you'd have to sell and we'd get it at a good price." She appealed once more to Hank. "You aren't going to let all my hard work go to waste, are you?"

"Hard work?" Hank echoed.

"I'm going to see my lawyers," Reva said, turning to leave. "We'll see who does what." She stomped away and got in her car.

Pulling Elaine into the house for a moment, he laughed and spun her around. They stood and watched Reva through the screen. No longer in control of herself or anybody else, she revved the engine. The motor roared. The wheels spun, throwing up sand, but the car didn't move.

"She's stuck." Hank took in a deep breath and let it out. "We'll have to help her."

"Okay, I'll show you where the boards are."

"You and I are going to make quite a team." Hank took her hand and they went back onto the porch where Elaine glanced up and saw two graceful forms soaring in the sky above Sacred Spring. "Oh, look," she cried. "The eagles survived."

The End